# COVERGIRL

**ALSO BY MAURA MOYNIHAN**

Yoga Hotel

# REGAN

*An Imprint of HarperCollinsPublishers*

# COVERGIRL
## CONFESSIONS OF A FLAWED HEDONIST
### REALITY FICTION

# MAURA MOYNIHAN

**Interior Photograph Credits:** pages xii, 114, 234: Peter Strongwater for *Interview*; pages 41, 112, 143, 159, 209: author's collection; page 72: (clockwise from top left) Ron Galella/Ron Galella, Ltd., author's collection, courtesy of Bill Cunningham/*The New York Times*, Nancy Jo Johnson; page 146: Lawson Knight; page 221: Mani Lama.

*Covergirl is a work of literary fiction, which I wrote over many years and through many drafts. I conceived of this novel as a contemporary rendering of the traditional roman à clef, popular in the nineteenth century, which incorporates portraits of the author's contemporaries, drawn from life and refined through the novelist's art. No real names are used. Some characters are composite creations, some are entirely imaginary. Every character, whether inspired by real persons and events or not, has been crafted by my own language and style to become a part of the book's narrative. This is in no way a biography, memoir, or historical account of my life or anyone else's life.*

—*Maura Moynihan*

HarperCollins books may be purchased for educational, business, or sales promotional use. For information please write: Special Markets Department, HarperCollins Publishers Inc., 10 East 53rd Street, New York, NY 10022.

FIRST EDITION

*Designed by Kris Tobiassen*

Library of Congress Cataloging-in-Publication Data has been applied for.

ISBN 10: 0-06-075657-8
ISBN 13: 978-0-06-075657-4

06 07 08 09 10 WBC/RRD 10 9 8 7 6 5 4 3 2 1

*To the Wandering Company, Ismail, Jim, Ruth, and Jhab*

GUIDES OF THE THREE CONTINENTS

*And in memory of John McCloskey Moynihan,*

WORLD TRAVELER, GREAT ARTIST,
DEAR BROTHER, AND PRECIOUS FRIEND

"Scandal is merely gossip made tedious by morality."

—OSCAR WILDE

"Beauty is a form of intelligence."

—ANDY WARHOL

"No man is a hypocrite in his pleasures."

—DR. JOHNSON

# ACKNOWLEDGMENTS

I am forever filled with love, gratitude, and admiration for my wonderful mother Liz Moynihan, who has always encouraged and supported my quest to be a writer. And my son Michael Avedon, who is also an excellent writer and storyteller, is my greatest inspiration and the joy of my life.

I wish to thank my brilliant publisher Judith Regan for her everlasting friendship and support. Katherine Mosby and Victoria Stevenson were fabulously talented readers and advisors who helped me immeasurably. I will always be indebted to Aliza Fogelson for her encouragement, her wisdom, and her dedicated belief in books and the power of words. And special thanks to Anna Bliss, for her invaluable insights, her steadfast discipline, and editorial guidance, which made this book come to life.

# CONTENTS

# PART I

# Welcome to Manhattan

# Happy Birthday, Winston

**VERONICA STEPPED INTO THE GOLDEN-PINK GLOW OF THE PARK** Legend lobby, walked past the cocktail terrace with the gigantic flowers, around the statues of Artemis and Athena, through the swarms of tourists and conventioneers and luggage trolleys, to the entrance of the Tower Apartments. She halted, ducked into the ladies' lounge, locked the door, and bent over the sink to splash cold water on her face and neck. She had miscalculated the strength of her morning hangover, blithely assuming that by now it would've politely taken its leave; but no, it wanted to go to the party too.

Veronica surveyed the information in the full-length mirror: her short skirt barely covering the rip in her left stocking, her right jacket lapel crumpled, her hair three days overdue for a shampoo. Helena, her mother, would notice, but there was no turning back now. She leaned closer for one last perusal, searching for her reliable escape hatch . . . ah yes, there it was, thanks be to God, her natural beauty, weirdly aglow, hangover notwithstanding. Neither anxiety, sleep deprivation, nor alcohol overdose could deplete it. She swallowed three aspirins, applied vermillion lipstick, repositioned the run in her left stocking, and marched resolutely toward the Towers.

The elevator ascended through the 20s, 30s, 40s, and into the 50s, where her new extended family residence was on proud display. Veronica's father, Winston Ferris, had recently been named something of note at UNICEF, the UN's last bastion of über-WASP patrician elders, and with the new job came an exclusive residence in the Park Legend Towers. As diplomats, the Ferris family had for years perpetually shuttled from city to hotel to VIP lounge, but the Park Legend was the Mona Lisa of transit shelters. It functioned as an independent city-state amid midtown's roaring chaos; it housed visiting heads of state and had the best security, ballrooms, state rooms, restaurants, cafes, shops—and probably hookers and smugglers—collected under one vast, video-monitored roof. And for its bright new citizens, Winston and Helena Ferris, lifelong ambitions were now fulfilled; Winston had UNICEF and Helena had the crown jewel of real estate with an attendant five-star hotel staff. And so Winston's birthday had become one of the most exorbitant of the season's power-mingling rituals.

The elevator opened; Veronica stepped into the cheerful thunder of talk and drink that spilled into the long, salmon-orange hallway. Veronica saw Winston's pink-and-white head bobbing above the crowd. Her own head was not cooperating, so she grabbed a gin and tonic and raised the glass to her lips, when she caught sight of Helena's new bronze power helmet, every hair lacquered firmly into place; the oversized sparkling earrings (her trademark accessory), the long neck emerging from between bony shoulders; the moon-white, wrinkle-free skin, and the rest of her expensively maintained body encased in a silver taffeta tube that was supposed to be a dress . . . yes, the vast, swarming apparition loomed and approached. Tonight Helena was declaring her sovereignty over the upper tiers of Manhattan as she whirled magisterially about her new apartment, and it was scary as hell. Veronica momentarily considered fleeing, but Helena's antennae instantly identified the presence of a child, late and improperly attired.

"Young lady, what have you done to your hair?"

Curiosity had recently prompted Veronica to dye her long, chestnut-red hair jet black. Bad timing. "Why Mom, does it look different?"

"It's like you poured shoe polish on it. It looks terrible."

A man sidled up to Helena, winding his arm around her waist, and suddenly she was all effervescent grace, bending and dipping to tap a cigarette over an ashtray and tilting her ear to his confidential whisper. Veronica planted herself between the curtains and the buffet table to study the crowd. So here paraded two hundred of the world's wealthiest and most successful people, whose self-worth and happiness hinged on whether or not they got invited to a birthday party. It was a definite coup for the New Helena, who deployed party invitations to avenge grudges, solidify alliances, and commandeer useful new talent.

The New Helena's parties were a reliable index of which professions were currently fashionable. Helena had grown very fond of CEOs of late, and politicians were back on her list after a long absence, as were writers. Veronica's gaze glided toward a famous anchorman who was making a camera-worthy entrance. She had recently nursed a hangover staring dumbly at his nightly newscast, so seeing him in three-dimensional kinesis was weirdly disorienting. Even in the flesh, he didn't appear mortal; it was as if a marketing analyst had mixed the iconographic needs of the average American television viewer to come up with a successful fusion of prototypes, such as an insurance salesman who got fan mail. His wife, petite, blonde, and pink, was thoroughly perfumed, sanitized, and hygienically sealed. She was obviously the type of female who had never gone a day without mouthwash, deodorant, and hairspray. Veronica's habits would have horrified her.

Veronica also noticed several literary party fixtures in the crowd, now that Helena was an author again, with a cookbook entitled *American Flavors Far From Home* that had recently scored an undeserved two-page spread in *Vogue*. There was the feared and admired Jock Krispy, the once-prolific novelist willingly corrupted by celebrity, whose eyebrows writhed and bobbed beneath a tortured contrivance that suggested hair. And there warbled Irvy Wall, the renowned journalist and elevator lech. Irvy, you see, sensibly seized opportunity when it presented itself. Irvy was busy chatting up ballet-spinster/publishing heiress Bitsy Whipplair, a favorite lunch partner of Helena's who was similarly encased in a creepy tube that was supposed to be a dress.

Irvy and Bitsy were joined by Dolly Seabrook, Helena's tennis partner, a terrifying riot of color—yellow hair, orange lips, turquoise blouse, magenta suit—who readily believed it when anyone told her she looked ravishing. Dolly began flirting with Arno Slipper, a Wall Streeter who did something inscrutable that made him obscenely rich. Arno held a drink under his chin and waved his free hand in the air, while Dolly played coyly with her pearls, made her best debutante grin, and made eyes at Jack Macomb, a newly famous CEO, and his consort-of-the-month, a wide-angled, smiling Miss Universe facsimile.

Exhausted, Veronica leaned her cheek against the cold window glass. She knew that she ought to go and mingle. Deference was her duty! She scanned the room once again, looking for a suitable place to penetrate, and saw her little brother Jamie talking to their older half-brother Grayson, one of Winston's four sons from his first marriage. Grayson was running for something in California and was therefore scouring the room for funds and surrogates. Youngest child Jamie looked wildly out of place in the midst of the furious power-hustling all about him; he still held fast to the cherished hippie ideals of yester-decade, which deemed having any professional ambitions and cutting one's hair crimes of equal stature. Veronica did not feel like talking to Jamie since he had recently become dogmatic about macrobiotics and expelled her from a taxi in the middle of the night for lighting a cigarette.

Veronica skillfully dodged Bitsy Whipplair when she saw the Hart-mans, Bill and Joan. Bill had served as Winston's Deputy Chief of Mission in Manila, Winston's most recent diplomatic posting. Joan—large, dowdy, earnest, your reliable all-American spouse—was wearing her party uniform, a full-length tartan skirt and a shiny white blouse with balloon-sized sleeves and a bow that was bigger than her head.

Veronica was now alert to the dreaded possibility of running into Bill and Joan's daughter Susan. Helena always showered Susan Hartman with fulsome praise, as she was obedient and dull, qualities Helena cherished in other people. Susan Hartman fiercely criticized Veronica's beauty as clear evidence that she was dangerous and unruly, which was, of course, true. Veronica agreed without protest that life would've been a hell of a lot easier if she had turned out like Susan Hartman, who was headed for law school and respectability, whereas she was headed for a nightclub rendezvous with Occo in about thirty-five minutes.

She noticed that Bill and Joan were about to turn around, but no, she couldn't play dutiful debutante right now, *help*. . . . A new congressman was diligently working the crowd under the stewardship of

Maxine Weller, rival party hostess and skillful appropriator of other women's husbands, and a retired governor who was one of Veronica's favorite adults.

"Hello, Governor," Veronica tapped his arm.

"Veronica, my gosh! How are ya sweetie?" The governor wrapped a bulky arm around Veronica's shoulders. *Thank God for some unconditional enthusiasm.*

Maxine, sensing intimacy, darted between Veronica and the governor. "So Veronica, now that you've finished college what are you up to these days?"

"I guess I'm up to no good." *Yikes, that came out too fast.*

"Did you hear that? She's up to no good! That's my gal!" The governor wheezed and howled with laughter. Maxine seemed not to appreciate the joke.

"What's that thing on your blouse? Oh, it's beads." Maxine's fingers pulled at Veronica's necklace. "That's very strange, what is it?"

"It's from Tibet."

"I was just invited to a Tibet benefit at Morgan's. It looks old. Is it old? It needs polishing."

"Veronica, your mother says you speak five languages! That must be awfully handy!" chirped the famous anchorman's pink-and-white wife. This was one of Helena's favorite exaggerations. She had to prop up the myth that Jamie and Veronica weren't free-loading layabouts, but, well, you know, creative types filled with dazzling esoteric talents that were too rare for the confinements of, say, business school.

Veronica sensed a man's attention bearing down on her. Sandy Graver, journalist, party fixture and reputed ladies man, was staring from a nearby cluster. She let her gaze mingle with his for a few extra seconds. *Oh, are we getting just a little flustered, Mr. Graver?* Noting that Sandy's cheeks did look a bit pink, she turned away with a tinge of satisfaction. If there was one thing Veronica knew how to handle it was the power of feminine beauty. She used it recklessly, carelessly, always with astonishing success. In Helena's world, she was usually careful to restrain it, but tonight it was rising in revolt. She slid her left hand down her hip, synchronized with Sandy's expectant line of vision—when suddenly she saw the silver taffeta column careening through the crowd. *Control yourself, Veronica, you are not among friends! You'll be in Occo's limo in half an hour where you can do what you like.* She gulped the remains of her drink and headed toward the back bar where she collided with Aaron Eastman, Winston's UN aide, erstwhile peace activist turned pro-war zealot, currently the professionally expedient move in Washington.

"Hello, Miss Ferris!" Aaron displayed his massively unattractive teeth in what was supposed to be a smile.

"Hi, Aaron."

"So, whither the princess of the Ferris dynasty?" Defying the probable, Aaron exhibited even more teeth. "Do tell, Veronica, are you going to join the ranks of commoners and go nine to five, or remain on extended vacation?"

"I haven't applied to law school, if that's what you're trying to find out." Not that she hadn't considered it, if only to shut up people like Aaron who asked those so-what-are-you-doing-with-yourself-these-days questions.

"Doesn't look like either of the Ferris children will be following in the family footsteps." Aaron nodded toward Jamie, who was wearing clean blue jeans and an embroidered Guatemalan shirt, his idea of formal wear. Aaron brimmed with pride that, unlike Jamie and Veronica, he knew how to work a room. When Aaron crashed a party, no power-dispensing hand was left unshaken and no obsequious, career-enhancing comment was left unspoken.

"Aaron, maybe you should drop the tiresome asshole routine and see how it fits." *Oh Christ, what did I just call him?*

"Excuse me?"

"I said, I'm tired." Veronica seized a champagne flute and crashed into Irvy Wall.

"Little Veronica, you've certainly grown since I last saw you, no longer the spacey freshman in the love beads. Isn't this exciting!"

"Oh Irvy, so glad you could come!" Veronica smiled sweetly and pumped his moist, unsanitary hand. When confronting large, drunken creeps, one's diplomatic party training definitely came in handy. She caught a glimpse of Asian hair near the dining room—maybe it was Shanta Rana, the ravenous, gorgeous, cynical Nepali princess, cursed and blessed in equal measure, who was always reliably filled with bizarre and effective survival advice. Veronica veered left and was suddenly pressed up close and personal with Dolly Seabrook, who pinned her tight against the buffet table with no hope of escape.

"Well, here's a little Ferris. Do you know Arno Slipper?"

"Delighted." Arno extended a crustacean palm.

"Veronica just graduated from college."

"Gee, that's terrific." Arno started chewing an ice cube.

"What did you major in, Veronica?"

"Oriental Philosophy."

Dolly appeared shocked and horrified. "Really? Did you graduate with honors?"

*Hey lady, this is supposed to be a party.* "A few." Never mind what kind.

Are you planning to take the foreign service exam?"

"Not this week." *Will someone tell this broad to lay off? From now on I'm gonna say "Law School" to shut people up.*

"If you're interested in finance give me a call." Arno wiped his glasses on his shirttail. Dolly would've been heartbroken to discover that Veronica was doing better than her own daughter, a humorless lacrosse champion who worked for the Young Republican Leadership Forum. Maybe the compassionate thing would be to tell Dolly that young Veronica was en route to a drunken liaison with a gang of dissolute European playboys.

"Veronica, look at you!" Oh no, it was Joan and Bill Hartman. *Why God, why . . .* Joan Hartman was oozing fake enthusiasm, true to form. "Tell us, Veronica, what are you up to these days?"

"I'm going to law school."

"Law school!" Joan tried, and failed, to control the shock waves that visibly crashed through her psyche.

"Well, well, this is exciting news . . ." exclaimed Bill. "Our Susan's taking her LSATS next month. She's been studying like a banshee!"

A sudden clinking of glasses summoned all present toward the living room. Helena ignited a large TV screen that played the birthday video of Winston Through the Ages. Among über-WASPS, Winston was a tribal chieftain, presiding over the Southampton summer cocktail hour in hot-pink and lime-green psychedelic frog-motif shorts as only an über-WASP could. There he stood, offering witty quips on Tai-wanese independence, emerging from limos, properly tuxedoed for diplomatic dinners, playing a little tennis, a little golf, and yes, playing with the kids. Moments of great significance, such as experimenting with ice skates and throwing Frisbees, had been dutifully recorded for future generations of Ferrises and Ferris biographers.

There was much embarrassing evidence of adolescence; Veronica in waist-length braids and braces, Jamie stuffed into a suit and tie for Win-ston's presentation of credentials to a Third World strongman. There were a few oblique references to Grayson, Skyler, Cliff, and Bradley—sons number one, two, three, and four, but nary a mention of Bettina, wife number one, a stern academic with a formidable bun of perma-nently graying hair. Bettina and Helena loathed each other and were in a death match for Winston's trust funds, which, apparently, were only to be bequeathed to wives, not offspring, though Grayson was clearly working on this.

The film kept on going. Veronica couldn't bear to be reminded of her magical childhood, which had so suddenly and painfully vanished when high school came to an end. She crept down the hall to Win-ston's study, which had always been a sanctuary. Helena had a supreme gift for re-creating the family hearth in every transitory domicile through which the Ferris family passed. How reassuring to discover Winston's new study, as ever decorated with the paraphernalia of offi-cialdom: plaques, citations, certificates, silver trays from the Dubai Golf Association, paperweights from the Korean Free Trade Association, cof-fee mugs from the Cricket Club of Karachi. The Golden Age of Glob-alization owed much to the Honorable Winston Ferris. He had a noble internationalist vision to which he was devoted. Born in Lennox Hill hospital and raised on Park Avenue, Winston loved New York in a spe-cial way. Veronica had also been born in New York City, twenty-two years ago, but Winston instantly moved the family to Hong Kong, and so New York had henceforth only served as transit shelter between for-eign postings.

Now here she was, on top of Manhattan, the voracious turbine that required vast daily feedings of oil and gas and human labor to retain its supremacy among First-World metropolises. Four months in New York

City and she'd become just like it—ravenous, greedy, and buying on credit! But it was the only slice of real estate on the North American continent where finding a Tibetan disco was a feasible option, which reminded her to keep an open mind.

From one angle she could see parts of her reflection in the window glass, her diamond-white skin and lavender-blue eyes with tiny green facets and black lashes. She traced her hand along her neck and cheek, feeling terribly alone. Manhattan seemed a cold, hectic place, where lines between insiders and outsiders were defiantly marked. Veronica knew how to be an outsider; she'd had a lifetime of practice. In the course of her magical childhood she had lived in Hong Kong, Manila, Tokyo, Bangkok, New Delhi, Jakarta, Kabul, and Kathmandu. In every Asian capital Winston rented a vast, intricate compound with gardens and pools and legions of bearers, cooks, gardeners, and artisans. Veronica was a star student at all of her international schools. In Tokyo her mentor was Miss Tanaka, in Hong Kong it was Mr. Math from Malaysia; and in Jakarta, where she began high school, it was Danny Watson, the longhaired, multilingual, counterculture English teacher from California who had come to Indonesia with the Peace Corps and taught her how to play the guitar. In the ninth grade Veronica fell in love with Damion, the dashing son of an English journalist, but the next year Damion's father was transferred to Colombo, and two years after that the Ferrises were transferred to Islamabad, which broke Veronica's heart.

In Veronica's final year of high school she and Jamie took correspondence classes, a Diplomatic Corps dodge for those busy years when Dad wasn't sure of his next posting. For six months the family trundled between New Delhi and Islamabad, trapped in UN provisional housing, until Winston took them to Kathmandu, the Buddha Valley, where he availed himself of all manner of high-speed transport, including a helicopter for a brief visit to Everest Base Camp.

But when it was time for college, the family's Nepal sojourn ended, and it was during this frantic juncture in Veronica's life that things fell apart. The Old Helena transmogrified into the New Helena, who repudiated all vestiges of the family's Asian life, acquired a new circle of America-centric friends, craved couture, and glorified the Hamptons.

Veronica went to a college in Connecticut, close to her beloved grandparents. Winston's mother and father, Harry and Lilly, were adorable,
eccentric East Coast aristocrats who dressed for dinner, were committed to charade, poker, and port, and indulged their grandchildren in
everything amusing and forbidden. Harry and Lilly's two-thousand-
acre farm was a sanctuary of love and forgiveness. Their home and their
love were the only things in the whole world that Veronica had believed were immortal.

Over the years Winston had given Veronica so many beautiful gifts,
and the only safe repository for this trove was Harry and Lilly's farm.
But during Veronica's freshman year of college, Harry and Lilly both
fell ill and died, suddenly and without warning. Minutes after their
death a horde of minor relatives invaded the farm and grabbed everything in sight. When Veronica went to collect her Balinese masks, Fil-
ipino rice baskets, saris, kimonos, all of her books and photographs and
diaries, everything had vanished with Harry and Lilly. She feared and
repressed the memory of standing in the doorway of the empty barn,
waiting to hear her grandfather's voice, whereupon came the awful re-
alization that he was gone. She knew that everyone, everywhere, had to
bury their grandparents, but her losses wounded her no less acutely. For
months she awoke in tears, as her mind torturously retraced the loss of
her magical childhood.

If there was one irrefutable truth Veronica learned in college that
she didn't know before, it was this: Men could not be trusted. She was
singularly unprepared for the brutality of American college dating. Her
high school romances had all been courteous and observant of protocol. Diplomatic corps boys asked for proper dates, brought flowers, met
you with an embassy car plus driver, bestowed a good-night kiss in the
vestibule within sight of ubiquitous security guards, then followed up
with thank-you notes. Was courtesy instinctual in a diplomat's son? Or
was it the presence of so many elegant, well-mannered Asians that held
visitors in check? Damion from Jakarta wooed her with poetry books
sent through the diplomatic pouch. Sven, the nephew of the Finnish
ambassador, presented her with a Burmese ruby on their first date and
never kissed anything but her hand. Aziz, the son of the Pakistani High
Commissioner in Hong Kong, actually went down on one knee to ask

if she would accompany him to the Rotary Club Christmas Ball in Kowloon.

Veronica had assumed that the preppy boys she met in college would adhere to a few basic standards of international conduct. Their parents were paying a lot of money to send them to an expensive, private East Coast college, a co-ed institution with a few feminist professors. But the boys were resolutely crude and clearly resentful of having to compete with women in classes. They exacted revenge by treating their fellow female students as if they were auditioning for porn videos. In her freshman year she saw so many girls insulted, exploited, date-raped, limping home from the abortion clinic, and weeping in their bunk beds, only to have to face the louts in anthropology class the next day. And of course, Veronica herself was prized quarry: beautiful, charming, multilingual, she was everything a college brute wanted to destroy and then brag about destroying. She felt perilously alone. Jamie was imprisoned in a distant boarding school and Winston was, for the first time in her whole life, far away. She was never able to explain the disaster of her college years to her father; he'd say, "Buck up, dear, why not talk it over with your guidance counselor?"

And so Veronica felt that she had earned the right to be lazy and cynical. She had just survived four years in a grim dormitory packed with boors and jealous women who flattered, envied, and ridiculed her. In undergraduate mythology she was instantly deemed an eccentric with an exotic family history, and nothing she said or did during the next three years could modify this verdict. It was impossible to explain her life to anyone, and useless to try. It was much safer to use and discard men quickly and efficiently, before they got the chance to use and discard her first. So she kept her inner life concealed and wore a brave face in public. She maintained a double life, never forgetting the ex-pat eleventh commandment: Thou Shalt Not Get Busted.

But now she was free of college, and presumably free of the stifling company of untravelled people. She was in New York, a global metropolis and promising field of study. Perhaps New York City would be the place where she could recover her luck. She had learned from her travels that there was nothing more frightening than losing one's luck—it was the only thing in life that was truly indispensable. Her Asian friends had a deeply practical view of luck as something you could manufacture and store in a kind of psychic bank account. After four years in university purgatory, Veronica had nearly forgotten those secrets, dictums, and mantras that were said to magnetize luck. Among the shards of her magical childhood lost at Jack and Lilly's farm was a special lacquer box that held all manner of amulets, talismans, coins, seeds, and beads, collected from many distant and obscure holy places, which had once tethered Veronica to the past, to the old world, and all the protection the past contained. But that box was gone, and she wasn't in Asia, she was in New York. New York had proven lucky for many world travelers, so why shouldn't she give it a try?

"Oh Veronica, am I disturbing anything?" Sandy Graver stood in the doorway.

"No, nothing." She noticed his eyes taking salacious inventory of her body parts as she sank into the sofa and crossed her arms above her head.

Sandy lowered himself into an adjacent armchair. "So Veronica, how's Manhattan treating you?"

"Like most strangers, I find it baffling and alluring."

"I thought this was your hometown."

"No, I grew up abroad."

"Oh yes, of course . . ." Sandy's lips and brow tightened, obviously struggling to recall Winston's various diplomatic postings. "So tell me, Veronica, what do you want to do, now that you're here in New York?"

This was a vexing question, since most of Veronica's college friends were applying to business school, proofreading law briefs, or writing plays about the farm crisis. Veronica considered a polite, false answer versus the naked truth, which usually shocked people. Seeking attention, adulation, and excruciatingly loud music; wearing outrageous clothes; going over the top and staying up all night—such were her immediate ambitions.

"Well Sandy, I'd like to be a rock star. Not a serious, earnest rock star, more of the sex symbol variety." She crossed her legs, letting her velvet skirt careen up her smooth, lovely thighs, and gazed at Sandy with a thoughtful smile.

"Why, um, uh, would you want to be a, a sex symbol?" Sandy turned orange while his eyes predictably flickered toward the new exposure of leg.

"Because men would admire me and women would envy me."

Silence. *What, he didn't get it?* "Sandy, it's a venerable tradition."

The truth had obviously confused and titillated the hell out of Mr. Graver. Squirming in his chair and toying with his empty wine glass, he mumbled, "Unusual career choice for a girl who has unlimited opportunity and privilege."

Veronica sighed. It wasn't easy making the case against unlimited opportunity and privilege. "Maybe I've come to the wrong place. New York's getting so sanitized. Like a gigantic vertical mall."

Here Sandy brimmed and smirked, now that they were onto something he could pontificate about with authority. "Well, it's not what it used to be, but there are still vestiges of hipness around. There are icons of the avant-garde, like John Penn."

Sandy Graver's pretentious, caption-sized summations of people's careers instantly gave away what he did for a living. And John Penn—artist-photographer-filmmaker-starmaker, otherwise known as JP or Penn Station—had for years been the topic of many a fierce argument around Helena and Winston's dinner table. In photographs he appeared wizened and utterly charmless. People debated whether he was a dangerous fraud, a bizarre visionary, a portentous genius or just a very weird guy.

"Have you ever interviewed John Penn, Sandy?"

"No, no. Culture's not my beat. I've tried talking to him at parties. I doubt his films or pictures will be worth much in a few years." Somehow Sandy had maneuvered himself onto the couch, close to Veronica's lithe, fishnetted legs.

A spotlight beamed upward from Times Square, stroking the night sky. "Hey Sandy, what's going on down there?"

"There's a new club opening tonight. I've got an invitation. Would you like to go?"

Veronica turned and studied Sandy Graver, sitting there with his drink and his cocksure grin. He had a multi-hued beard and a thick torso partially concealed by a well-cut suit. He also had a well-established reputation as a womanizer. He wasn't known for going after restaurant tarts and other easy marks; he liked friends' wives and the daughters of European aristocrats. Of course, men with bad reputations were perversely attractive. One wanted to know how they got their bad reputations. And he did have an invitation to a nightclub opening. But he belonged to Helena and Winston's world and Veronica had always been careful to protect her double life. Unlike her younger brother Jamie, who was expelled from boarding school for smoking pot and substituting contributions to an anarchist website for homework, Veronica had never caused the family official embarrassment, been suspected by teachers, accused by parents, or exposed by tabloids. But now Sandy was finishing off the last of his drink and trying to edge a little closer . . .

"This is very sweet of you Sandy. Where shall we meet later?"

"Where, uh, are you going to be?"

"Meet me at Entwhistle's in an hour." She shot down the hall, back in the living room, where the party was still swirling at fever pitch. Veronica pushed toward the bar and landed with gratitude beside Bill Straw, who was negotiating the best way to hold a cigarette, appetizers, and a martini all at once. Bill was an amusingly caustic drunk and vital party ally who never asked invasive personal questions.

"Happy Winston's birthday, Bill."

"Jesus, how are you surviving this burlesque show?"

"I've had a lot of practice."

"Yeah I know, but this is a new one. Looks like your mom wants to corner the New York Benefit Ladies. And what the hell is Irvy Wall doing here?"

"He's a writer. Helena likes writers this year."

"Oh yeah, that was a helluva book he wrote. Please don't go to dinner with him if he asks you, which he will."

Veronica watched Irvy working on Bitsy Whiplair and felt reasonably sure that it wouldn't be a problem.

Suddenly Winston seized Veronica with a hug and clapped Bill on the back. The presence of her wonderful father soothed Veronica's heart and mind. She was about to wish him Happy Birthday, in as many languages as she could summon, when the dreaded Joan Hartman shoved her way into the circle.

"Winston, we've heard the big news!" cried Joan. "Veronica tells us she's going to law school! Someone else will be paying the bills for a change!"

Winston produced a glowing, standard-issue professional smile. "We-ell! That's a nice birthday surprise! Veronica has a unique gift for adaptation." Winston winked at Veronica. Bill Straw coughed and spilled his drink on Joan Hartman's bow. Piano chords thundered from the drawing room, heralding the arrival of the birthday cake. This was the time to escape, when Helena was leading the toasts. Veronica raced down the hall, through the master bedroom, into the bathroom. She removed her jacket, deftly knotted her pink scarf around her breasts, applied lipstick, shook her head vigorously to ensure that her jet-black mane was properly tousled, and then slipped her jacket back on. Pausing before the mirror, she took in her reflection with rich satisfaction. Onward to Occo! She darted through the outer hall toward the service entrance and the elevator when Helena hurled through the front door, holding a piece of birthday cake.

"Oh, hi, Mom . . ." *God help me, if she sees the pink scarf she'll know I've been going through the attic in Southampton . . .*

"What is this I hear about your going to law school?"

Veronica's senses scrambled wildly in an alibi shift. "Oh, uh, I was just sort of, um, thinking about it . . ."

"Since when have you, who squandered her undergraduate education on something as impractical as Oriental philosophy, ever considered going to law school?"

Veronica crossed her arms to keep her jacket closed over the pink scarf. "Mom, can we, like, talk about this later?"

"Young lady, you cannot come to your father's birthday party and announce to the world that you are going to law school and expect me to respond casually! I'll have to tell my press officer!"

"Mom, I wasn't being serious."

"Well, yes, this we know, that you cannot be serious about anything, especially a career!"

Before Helena could say another word, the swinging doors flew open and knocked her into the wall, allowing Veronica to escape.

# Disco Therapy

**THE PERUVIAN ELEVATOR OPERATOR LEERED AND BOWED AS**
Veronica stepped inside. He was full of peppy questions about the party,
which Veronica duly obliged all the way to the ground floor, whereupon she collected her wits to navigate the lobby. The front entrance
was too dangerous. The back entrance was also high-risk thoroughfare.
Upon deciding to go through one of the restaurants, she sailed into
Shingo, winked at the maître d', and stepped out onto Lexington Avenue. No taxis. She tried to recall the Japanese chant that Jamie used to
procure beneficial material conditions, hoping it might work for taxis,
too, when a yellow cab suddenly appeared and hurtled her past the drug
stores, furniture boutiques, Chinese laundries, and the French, Thai,
Italian, Indian, Japanese, and Greek restaurants of the Upper East Side
toward Occo and party refuge.

The cab pulled up to Entwhistle's. Veronica smoothed her long
black hair, stepped out of the cab, and strode into the familiar, dark,
clangorous room. The walls were Christmas-card green adorned with
hunting tableaux, and the doorways were framed by beagle sculptures
which doubled as umbrella stands. Entwhistle's, again! If there were so
many good restaurants in New York, why did everyone come to this
dump? Why, for that matter, did she? Because this was where the men
paid for pretty girls. Every pretty girl in New York was a food prosti-
tute. Meal whores, every one. Unfortunately, pretty girls had to manage
taxis on their own, to say nothing of rent.

Veronica spied a table of *Women's Wear* regulars, friendly rivals of Helena's with that concave look certain people get when they're worth over $100 million. They were gossiping so vigorously that they didn't notice Veronica as she squeezed past their table. She arrived safely in the back room where Occo and his guests were lined up at a long, drink-littered table.

"What, ho! This must be the delicious Ronnie!" A drunken Englishman to Occo's left waved a glass in the air. He was rotund and florid in body and raiment. He leaned across the table, proferring a hand. "I am the inscrutable and immoral Dickie Drake! And you must be one of Occo's favorite things!"

"Veronica, you keep us waiting so long we become too drunk!" Occo kissed Veronica twice on both cheeks and handed her a glass of champagne and a cigarette. Occo was an extravagant and excessively loaded Roman who proudly described himself as Manhattan's leading European decadent, tops in a highly competitive field. Ever since their chance meeting in the Park Legend lobby he had been pursuing Veronica wildly as he claimed. It was his ambition to sleep with as many Mayflower descendants as possible before his visa expired.

"Ronnie, sit next to our guest of honor, Mr. Wilhelm Streicher." Veronica eased herself into the chair beside Wilhelm, German tennis champion, star of the night club and the grass court. He had a state-of-the-art physique, a nimbus of white-gold hair, wanton fluorescent blue eyes, and a thoroughly fatuous grin. *What the fuck, he had to be more fun than Sandy Graver.*

"I want some disco," Wilhelm said squarely.

"Travesty is opening tonight. Someone has a ticket, no?" Wilhelm grinned foolishly at Veronica. What a relief to be around these European males, who, despite being perpetually drunk, had genuine admiration for Professional Beautiful Girls. If Veronica's pathetic college had given out grades for her kind of practical talent, she would definitely have graduated summa cum laude.

A badly dressed, counterfeit blonde pulled a chair between Veronica and Wilhelm and threaded her arm proprietarily though his.

"Where the hell you been?" Wilhelm grunted as he tried to dislodge the blonde's arm.

"In the ladies' room." The woman glared at Veronica, though she had yet committed no crime greater than shaking Wilhelm's hand.

"Hello, I'm Veronica."

"I'm Sondra." Sondra extended a stiff handshake without depreciating her glare, the telltale sign of a girlfriend who senses she's on the outs. What fun. Occo passed around a bottle of champagne and attempted to rescue a joke that had no apparent punch line. Veronica's headache was finally easing its grip. She shook out her hair and peered about the room. Apart from the clothes and the location of their summer houses, this crowd was no different from the crowd at the Park Legend. So the stimulants were a little different. There it was alcohol and prescription pills; here it was alcohol and nonprescription pills. There the women wore a lot of jewelry; here the men as well as the women wore a lot of jewelry. Everywhere everyone was screwing around. Women were powerless if they weren't beautiful or rich. Nobody liked to see anyone else succeed. And getting into the right party was the most important thing in life.

In this world, being beautiful was the equivalent of having a high IQ. It was beauty that commanded universal respect and secured passing grades. If you were lucky enough to be born with it, why not exploit it fully? With an unnecessarily broad range of motion calculated to call attention to her precariously knotted pink scarf, Veronica removed her jacket and stretched out her arms in a fake yawn. She could feel all male eyes in the room settling on her white shoulders and slender three-quarters exposed torso. Wilhelm pressed his leg against Veronica's thigh. *Ah yes, victory is mine. Let's be honest, it's enormously satisfying to be an object of lust. Why don't we maximize the effect here, pretend to yawn again and raise arms heavenwards.* Things were looking up, when suddenly she felt a cold hand on her bare shoulder.

"Hey there." There stood Sandy Graver, with cologne and without tie. Veronica gulped. It was all very well to flirt with Sandy at a dull grown-ups' party, but now she was rattling with booze and practically topless and Sandy did not fit in with the picture.

"Oh, uh, hi, Sandy, how did you get here?"

"In a taxi, how else?"

"Hello, who's this?"

"Sandy, this is Occo. Occo, Sandy."

"Hey."

"What's that? Hey!" Occo nearly wept with laughter. "I love Americans, they're so casual!"

"Travesty is having first open night, we go for dancing!" said Wilhelm.

"Sandy has a ticket, right Sandy?" Veronica smiled at him, remembering he was good for something.

"It's just for two . . ."

"One is all they need. When they see Wilhelm we all go, yes?" Occo steered guests into waiting limos and onward to the club. A frenzied, mink-coated, perfumed mob pushed against the velvet ropes like refugees trying to jump on the last train to the border. Women screamed at the sight of Wilhelm's platinum halo darting toward the entrance to safety. Inside, the place was loaded with silver balloons and a few nearly naked go-go girls writhed gamely on mini-columns. Everyone pretended not to study which celebrity was sitting where, and how they looked, raw and plain, and without professional lighting.

Veronica took a large swallow of champagne and lit a cigarette. Ah, chaos. Now she could relax. What was it about a noisy club that she found so soothing? Was it a physical manifestation of her inner mind— turbulent, lurid, and dancing? She felt marvelously dizzy. She leaned against a pillar, when a pair of hands seized her waist. She whirled around to discover Wilhelm, drunk and grinning.

"You look excellent tonight, baby." A fringe of white-gold hair covered his eyes, his breath stank of whiskey.

"Well thanks, Wilhelm, and you're looking a little tipsy."

His grin got bigger and dumber. Where was his girlfriend? Hopefully furthering her acquaintance with Occo's drugs and thus missing this little scene. She looked like the type who'd start a hairbrush fight.

"Hey baby, you turn me on . . ." Wilhelm sputtered and nuzzled into her neck, his hands sliding under her scarf. There was no need to employ the finer arts of seduction, as Wilhelm seemed most eager to be friends. He was awfully handsome, he wasn't American, and he'd won the U.S. Open at least once. She ran her fingers over his arms and shoulders—Oh Christ, Sandy Graver was watching, glaring.

"Veronica, I was wondering where you went." Sandy looked irritated. Veronica slipped free, and Wilhelm started writhing against a pillar. Sandy was acting like she owed him something. An exit strategy was imperative, as was another twelve-dollar cocktail.

"Let's go get drunk, we're not at Helena's party anymore." Veronica took Sandy's hand and steered him toward the bar. They stood in what appeared to be a line. Emboldened by proximity, Sandy put a hand on Veronica's back and started inching impatiently under the pink scarf. Behold the Graver Treatment! And how original it is, copping a feel in the dark. She had to dispense with him, fast.

"Sandy, should we get out of here? It's kind of crowded."

"I've got some terrific new records at home." His face flushed, triumphant.

Veronica steered him toward the door. "Oh wait, I forgot my jacket. Meet me outside." He smiled dumbly as she pushed him through the door. Sandy had conveniently forgotten that, once outside, he'd never get back in because the bouncer retained all invitations and Sandy wasn't a tennis player or a movie star or even midcareer Eurotrash. Amazing that he fell for it.

"Ronnie, we've been hunting for you. Come and dance!" Suddenly she was between Occo and Wilhelm on the dance floor. The music was good, terribly good. Wilhelm seized her waist and sunk his teeth into her neck. The masking tape holding her skirt together started to rip. *Goodness, there goes a leg.* She wrapped an arm around Wilhelm's hip in a mock tango. Even drunk, he wasn't bad on the dance floor. Strobe lights and camera bulbs exploded and she felt a surge of giddy delight as music poured through her. Yes, the dance floor was globalization's greatest instrument, the melting pot of the five continents. *Wilhelm, you rake . . .*

WHAT TIME IS IT? WHERE AM I? WHO IS THIS—OCCO? NO, IT'S *what's-his-name, William, no, Wilhelm . . . Oh no, too much wine . . . Oh shit . . . I must get out of here before he wakes up . . . These sheets are strangling me . . .* Wilhelm was so dead asleep he hardly appeared to be breathing. How did she get here? She had been carrying on as usual, at a party with Helena and Occo—together? *Oh God, no, two parties, same night . . .*

Wilhelm began to snore, a reassuring sign of life. Veronica slipped into the bathroom. The monogrammed towels informed her that she was in the Mayfair Regent. Her stockings were completely exhausted and her skirt was ripped straight to the waist. Lovely. She looked into the mirror. Her eyes were red and swollen, rimmed with debris of old mascara.

Crisp, brilliant colors assaulted her as she stepped out into the hallway and moved toward the elevator. The door opened, revealing a cargo of tall, clean, healthy, elegant people. She edged in, acutely aware of the many clear, penetrating eyes bearing down on her rumpled coat and disheveled hair. They knew exactly where she'd been and what she'd been doing. The ride was excruciatingly slow. At last the elevator door creaked open to reveal more well-rested, well-groomed people. The light was hurting her eyes. A row of taxis hummed outside, willing and ready to deliver her from the scrutiny of daylight. She dug her hands into her pockets in search of cash. Nothing, not even change! The sun was mercilessly cheerful. She was nauseous. She rushed through the revolving door, fleeing before she was caught by a member of Helena's lunch coven. A bus was out of the question. She'd have to jump the subway. Where was it? Ah, small blessing, it was just on the corner. She pulled her velvet jacket tight around her body and plunged into the filthy hole that led downtown.

Veronica opened the door to Meryl's flat, ran into the bathroom, tore off her clothes, turned on the faucet. She collapsed against the cold porcelain as hot water rose slowly over her body, turned her face into the filthy wall of the tub and sobbed. *Purify me, please . . .*

# Downtown Downtime

VERONICA LAY ON MERYL'S SOFA, WRAPPED IN TOWELS, STARING dumbly at the television screen as it flashed football scores, campaign profiles, military history, celebrity diet strategies, tips on baking a better orange pound cake, and the weather in Zimbabwe. She yawned and stretched out her pale, slender, undeniably magnificent legs. She reached for her jewelry box where she stored valiums under a tangle of chains and stones. Her fingers touched a piece of paper. It was an illustrated map of the pilgrimage route around the Kathmandu Valley. The paper was frayed at the edges and losing its color, yet it remained a link to the final episode of her magic childhood. She remembered rising at dawn with the cook and driver for collective immersion in the Bagmati River, the thick scent of sour milk and rosewater, the intense clarity of mind that she felt at every moment.

Helena loathed Kathmandu on sight; there were no department stores, not a single decent beauty salon, no Ladies of the Diplomatic Corps Book Clubs. Electricity came and went without notice, water was a poisonous substance, and the air pollution was such that twenty-four hours of breathing in Nepal was the equivalent to smoking seventy-five cigarettes. And so Helena brokered a deal whereby she could stay in Hong Kong, presumably to work on her new cookbook.

Without Helena's persistent fear of not having a proper dinner service, Winston threw regular dance parties with a live band, the Yakety Yaks, borrowed from the Canadian Club.

The three things Winston insisted upon for his children were reading, volunteer service, and language lessons. "You must always try to learn something of the local language or you'll never have any real fun," he would say. "And if you don't do some volunteer work, you're just a tourist—not that there's anything wrong with being a tourist, unless you pretend otherwise."

Winston was never without access to all manner of high-speed transport; in Nepal that meant Land Rovers and helicopters. Winston's favored companions for his trips were Captain Kumar, a Nepali royal, and Alo Tempa, a Khampa chieftain of legend. They spent hours around campfires, drinking and trading war stories of every variety. It was there that she met the old Tibetan Freedom Fighters, a small band of refugee soldiers who still pitched camps near the Tibetan border, waiting for the day they could return to their captured homeland.

But this was too painful for Veronica. Memory and nostalgia inevitably curdled into poisons. She had to live in the present, and the only things memorable about the present were the rock-and-roll clubs in the East Village, one of which was holding auditions next week. Veronica restored the map to its place in the jewelry box and reached for a stack of magazines on the table. There were lots of new pictures of downtown bands. The singer from the Motorboats was the new cute guy, though the bass player of the Sex Ventures was really cute, too. She saw that the band Penatgon was playing at Head Case. She could talk her way backstage, as ever, but what to wear? The red suede boots, perhaps. There'd be no danger of running into Aaron Eastman or Sandy Graver at Head Case.

She opened *Page*, John Penn's magazine. The *Page* Coverboy of the month was none other than Davey Name, the penultimate rock star—lithe, mean, ruthless, utter perfection. And a brilliant song writer. For years she had carefully cultivated a fantasy of being his girlfriend. Helena doubtless hoped her children nurtured other ambitions, such as being appointed undersecretary of interdevelopmental affairs for Southeast Asia or marrying a member of the Maidstone Club. But Veronica had

always envisioned herself as the kind of girl who could confuse someone as attractive and inaccessible as Davey Name. She envisioned them
racing away in taxis, causing stirs at restaurants. But Davey Name lived
in a remote celebrity galaxy, very far away. What did one have to do to
get a visa? Write a song? Well, she could do that. But then someone
would have to hear her song, and like it, and invite her to a backstage
after party . . .

Of all the American dreams on sale, she liked Rock Star best of all.
Rock stars had been her private saviors, her psychic intercessors. Veronica and Jamie were always the new kids in a new country, so they had to
do something to fit in, and they had to do it quickly. Singing, dancing,
and party-throwing were survival skills. And in the Golden Age of
Globalization, rock 'n' roll was the lingua franca of the five continents.
Winston had tentacles reaching into every commissary and diplomatic
pouch in Eurasia, so Jamie and Veronica always had the newest records,
the highest fidelity stereos, the tallest bottles of Jack Daniels, and the
widest cartons of Marlboros—all of which could be offered as tribute
to one's new hosts, whoever they were. Veronica was a genius at intercontinental karaoke, as she spoke many levels of many languages. Winston had taught her early in life the key language tricks: practice
whenever you can and don't be afraid to be bad.

She opened her notebook to a page of song lyrics. She had a new
one called "Disco Darshan":

> *I'm in my Ginza boots, specs and suits in regulation black*
> *If I don't get on a dance floor soon I swear I'll have a panic attack*
> *Yes I might be your typical intercontinental frequent traveler girl*
> *Looking for the longest wildest party in the world*
> *I like living on airplanes and saltines and out of suitcases*
> *Pursuing the groove always on the move to all kinds of places*
> *Book me in business I'm spending the night on a 747*
> *And when I hit the PRC I'll be in my disco heaven.*
> *You are my disco darshan . . .*

*Darshan,* Sanskrit for sacred vision, might be too obscure a reference
for the First-World crowd. Better consult a thesaurus. She went into

Meryl's bedroom where she found some of her own books stacked against the wall. She pulled *Tantric Yoga Secrets*, which had been background reading for a Buddhist philosophy seminar, and opened to a chapter entitled "Tantra in Action." It began, "The tantric adept must undertake study of utilization of the Five Powerful Enjoyments, through the awakening of the dormant sexual energy, the locus of which is Muldhara Chakra at the base of the spine where the Kundalini energy languishes in repose. The Five Powerful Enjoyments are drinking of alcohol, smoking of tobacco, meat and fish eating, imbibing of opium, hashish and other intoxicants and the employment of unorthodox sexual practices." *Just what I wanted to hear. It's okay Mom, it's religious, see?*

She continued reading: "None of these activities waylay the seeker on his quest if pursued under the tutelage of a self-realized guru who can transform what is potentially a tamasic (destructive) activity into a sattvic (purifying) activity . . ." *Oh boy, if Winston and Helena ever found out how their tuition dollars were spent . . .* "The three Gunas, or qualities, are sattva, rajas and tamas, meaning purity, energy and darkness." Veronica was pretty sure that drinking coffee and alcohol and smoking cigarettes was tamasic, but was disco dancing rajasic or tamasic? Hard to say. It was certainly good exercise. She'd never go to one of those ridiculous health clubs to be harangued by someone hardly qualified to pass judgment on her altogether superior body . . . "Nonetheless, success in pursuit requires engagement of Five Powerful Enjoyments with pure ritual devotion." Well, communal dancing is ritual, so dancing at Travesty could in fact chalk up enlightenment points, correct?

The doorbell screeched. Veronica rolled off the couch, as the door swung open and Meryl filled the room like a great, angry stampede: "Goddamn this fucking weather! I feel like I just took a shower in the Hudson River! I'm moving to LA, you can have the apartment."

Meryl's scarf and coat sank into a sodden heap on the floor as she plundered the refrigerator for beer. Meryl and Veronica had been roommates at college. Veronica had been sleeping on Meryl's couch ever since discovering that Helena didn't want her despoiling the pristine interiors of the Park Legend pad. Meryl permitted Veronica to cohabitate rent free in exchange for occasional gossip column items, gleaned from Veronica's full-time nightlife research project. Meryl's supreme ambition was to be a well-paid Hollywood screenwriter, and she was building her resume by working as an assistant gossip columnist.

"So Meryl, how was work?"

"We broke a big story today. Candy Acker gained weight and got axed from the Castillo account." Meryl sprawled over the couch and thumbed through a weathered issue of *TV Guide*. "How was your mom's party?"

"Big. And loud." Veronica hastily washed her breakfast dishes.

"See anything good?"

"Irvy Wall brought a new wife, and Jack Macomb was with a quasi–Miss Universe." Veronica joined Meryl in the living room.

"Jack Macomb married Miss Universe?"

"No, a *quasi*–Miss Universe."

"Damn." Meryl gazed thoughtfully at her beer bottle. "That would've made a great picture item. Beauty Queen Bites Cracker King."

"Who's the Cracker King?"

Meryl rolled her eyes. "Jack Macomb. He's Mr. Triscuit. That's how he got so rich. Didn't your parents teach you anything?" Meryl took a fulsome swallow of beer and wiped her mouth with her sleeve. "Who else was there?"

"That newscaster from Channel 5, the guy with the sponge hair."

"Wow. What's he like?"

"I didn't talk to him."

"Man, for someone who gets A-listed on a regular basis, you really do not know the basics of working a room." Meryl yawned and stretched her thick arms over her head. Meryl was always hunting down men, though she didn't put much effort into her own visual presentation. She refused to rethink her shag haircut and wore tight, pale jeans, which did not add grace or elegance to her ample hips. "Veronica, you made a mistake sticking with artsy types in college. You should've dated some football players. It would've equipped you for New York nightlife a lot better. You don't know how to handle macho."

"The only thing approximating macho in my ex-boyfriend collection is a self-important editor on the school paper who wore Lennon glasses, had a Che Guevara poster in the bathroom, and wouldn't shut up about Deconstructivism."

"You thought a newspaper editor was macho?"

"What, they aren't?"

"Maybe it's a question of perspective. But these disco Euros have a jock mentality. Trust me. I'm a reporter. Nightlife is my beat."

Veronica had heard Occo and his friends talk in that cold, hard way about women they'd seduced, dissecting every phase of conquest, laughing about the fake endearments that worked every time.

"Meryl, I might have done something stupid."

"What?" Meryl's eyes darted upwards from the *TV Guide*.

"I, I sort of slept with one of Occo's friends."

"So, who?"

"A German."

"Wilhelm Streicher?"

Veronica froze. "Who told you?"

"I just guessed 'cause he's in town. By the way, how can you 'sort of' sleep with someone? You lie in bed and doze?"

"Meryl, you can't put *any* of this in your column!"

"I won't, I promise." Meryl was now perched against the edge of the couch, tapping her oversized trek boots against her chair, determined to pursue the Wilhelm case. "So how did you leave it with Mr. U.S. Open? Did he have any column-worthy scoops?"

"We didn't do a lot of talking."

"Here's what you should do. Don't take their calls. It'll restore some of your value if the guy talked. And trust me, guys talk. You should hear the anonymous tipsters who call us at the paper. Talk about sex education." Meryl unwrapped a fresh pack of Lucky Strikes. "You should go public with someone else right now. What about Dirk, your ex-part-time boyfriend? He's heavy on the integrity bit, right?" Dirk was Veronica's holdover date reservist, a humorless artist whose PC rigidity was redeemed only by extreme handsomeness.

"Dirk and I aren't talking these days. He's become one of those secondhand smoke alarmists."

"Oh, yeah. Fuck that." Meryl strode into the kitchen to retrieve another beer. Veronica skimmed the headlines, advertisements, and fundraising appeals. There were so many things to care about—global warming, tax reform, radon gas, adult illiteracy, grants for the ballet, all kinds of cancers, and police states that were arresting painters and novelists. If there was so much to worry about, why didn't she care about any of it? Helena's new set, the Benefit Ladies, had made her deeply cynical about the Good Cause business. During her first round on the charity circuit, Helena had committed to some early childhood education programs, but the field was crowded and the big money and the top names were all into diseases, so Helena started hosting lunches for bone marrow research—or was it skin cancer? Veronica couldn't remember.

"Hey, Veronica, I have a work thing and I need you to come with me. I'm gonna take a shower then we'll split."

"I'm kind of tired, do we have to?"

"Yes, we have to. It's work. Okay?" Meryl slammed the bathroom door shut. Veronica got the message that if she didn't make a showing she wouldn't be sleeping on Meryl's couch much longer. *Please smile on me, Lord of Gossip . . .*

# Disco Karma

**MERYL'S WORK ASSIGNMENT WAS A FASHION PARTY AT LUNA**
Ticks. The usual hordes of publicists, reporters, production assistants, and gate crashers clogged the doorway in the primordial quest for free food and drink. Meryl and Veronica pushed forward to the front table where guests were being cleared for admittance. Veronica often used a fake name, such as Princess Dimitria or Contessa Silverino, while assuming a bogus regal bearing, a technique that never failed. Once more the velvet rope parted and they were thrust into a cavernous party room clogged with frantic guests, craning necks, and straining vocal chords.

Meryl scanned the room, eyes narrowed. "There's beaucoup item potential."

"What's item potential?"

"Items for the column. This is what I do. Just watch how I work the room, you'll learn something." Meryl spotted an enormous man in cowboy regalia at the center table. "Veronica, look, see that guy?" She pointed to the giant in the fringed shirt. "That's Rory Racker. Olympic Swimmer. Two golds. A definite picture item."

"Why?"

" 'Cause he's not from New York, he's underexposed and hot. In-towners have to do something to get a picture item, but all I need from Racker is a quote." Meryl pushed her way to the giant's side and unfurled her reporter pad. "Mr. Racker, how did you enjoy the show?"

Rory turned his head from the crush of starlets parading before him and settled a dilatory gaze upon Meryl, eagerly poised with pen and pad. "Gee, Ah lahked it viry much. Ah always have fun when Ah come to New Yahk." He then stared at Veronica with an idiotic smile. "How'd y'all lahk the show, little lady?"

"We missed it."

"Gosh, that is a true pity."

Christ, the man was boring. Veronica yawned and leaned against a chair. Meryl was pushing all the right buttons with Rory, who was now generously imparting his philosophy of success to a sitcom star whose orange hair flew off her temples in a hysterical tangle. Maybe adulthood wasn't what it was cracked up to be. As a child, Veronica gazed in wonder at adults standing, talking, drinking, uttering portentous statements that were exclusive to the unknowable adult world. It all seemed so important, so meaningful, until she became a grown-up and realized that this is what she'd be doing *for the rest of her life*!

A man and woman edged past Veronica and floated down a flight of stairs. They slipped off their coats, flashed a sparkling gown and glossy hair, whispered and laughed into each others' shoulders, then disappeared behind a red door into some kind of private party. Veronica went down the stairs, expecting to find a bouncer ready to eject the uninvited, but the door opened upon a gold-and-purple room, filled with cheerful delirium.

"Veronica! Mio cara!" It was Occo proffering pink champagne in icicle-shaped glasses. "We holiday tonight, tutti in casa! I just buy a new painting! You come to look!" Occo pointed to a vast, turgid swirl at the far end of the room. "My new prize. Come, you must see it up close."

They approached the canvas and gazed with due reverence for a moment before Occo launched into an explanation of the painting's symbolism. His discourse was interrupted by the clamorous arrival of two of the season's reigning models, in identical red-and-silver leather dresses. The music got louder, the lights redder. Veronica withdrew a pair of pink sunglasses from her purse and put them on. One of the models was trying, and failing, to climb onto the mantle piece.

"You're the beauty from last night!" Three bursts of light exploded in her face, followed by oscillating black spots and an apparition in black and white, a small, pale man in dark glasses. Her vision captured him in fragments—ragged white hair, black turtleneck shirt, shabby black jacket, delicate hands clutching a camera and a tape recorder—the sum of which identified him as John Penn, the artist. She felt his eyes probing her intensely through the black lenses. He raised the camera and the lights burst again. Veronica felt strangely titillated.

"Who are you?" Veronica asked, knowing full well who he was.

"Oh, I'm John Penn. Who are you?"

"Veronica Ferris."

"Oh wow, Ferris like a wheel? Do you work in a circus?"

"No."

"You'd look great on a trapeze."

"You're a filmmaker, correct?"

"Oh, yeah." His body tightened as a wave of pink flushed through his tiny round cheeks. Standing before her, three dimensional and human, he was hardly the inanimate, bleached, phantasmal creature of photograph and legend. She could see his eyes sparkling with an excited, needy glint, like that of a child. "Why don't you come have lunch with us?"

"Who is us?"

"Oh, just the office—" He left the sentence, and the thought, dangling.

"Where is it?"

"The address is in here." He handed her a large magazine of colored newsprint. "I'll take your picture again if you come."

A large, spangled woman seized John by the arm and squired him away. It would be much too dangerous to go visit him in his office. If Helena found out, it would jeopardize her double life.

# Double Life Insurance

**AFTER A FORTY-FIVE-MINUTE SHOWER, THREE CUPS OF COFFEE,** four pieces of toast, a handful of vitamins, and a headstand, Veronica felt partially prepared for a visit to the Park Legend. Winston had promised to give her a check, and she had just enough money in her jewelry box for three subway rides, so a journey to the home front was imperative.

The corridors of the Park Legend hummed with a busy traffic of chic females, preoccupied businessmen, and porters in quasi-feudal uniforms. It would be pleasantly convenient to live amid such luxury, courtesy, and artistry, ordering room service and fresh towels all day long. You could have your shirts pressed, shoes shined, back massaged, and hair done without ever taking a step onto Lexington Avenue. Nevertheless, Helena managed to find plenty to complain about; she thought the vegetables overdone, the laundry insensitive, the vacuuming inadequate.

Once Veronica arrived at the Towers elevator she couldn't bring herself to go straight to the family apartment. Instead, she lowered herself onto a blue velvet couch, lit a cigarette, and flirted shamelessly with a Japanese conventioneer who squinted and blushed and dropped his wallet in a wastebasket. Playing the disco tart consistently delivered high returns with minimal investment. She ought to be a stock option. But then a blue-suited Wall Streeter sat on the couch and sneered at Veronica's distressed raiment, before withdrawing into a fresh copy of *Crain's New York Business*. Why didn't educated men evince any respect for women? Veronica had read Sandy Graver's eyes as he tried to get his hand on her leg. Hypocritical bastard, he deserved to be locked out of that nightclub. People loved to see children of privilege slipping up, just as men loved to be reassured that beautiful women were stupid.

Veronica stared at the art deco murals, gazed up toward the marble lilies that sprouted from the mirrored wall above the tea room, and studied the bronze clock above the crimson settee, on which several sullen, package-laden women stared into the carpet. The shopping arcade was filled with vitrines displaying enamel vases, glossy suits, useless knickknacks, big necklaces, ersatz oriental dragons and fairies—a sorry waste of good lapis lazuli and malachite. Veronica gazed upon the display with wonder. Who bought this stuff? No self-respecting New Yorker would permit this junk near the service elevator.

At the end of the arcade, beside the inadequate bookstore, was the Modern Antique Showroom, an Asian art gallery that belonged to the Jarewallas, a family of Gujaratis who famously supplied their business with icons pillaged from temple homes. The showroom smelled of incense, cigarettes, and curry, and it brimmed with the queer allure of something you wanted because you knew it wasn't good for you. The display cases were filled with miniatures depicting the amorous exploits of Krishna. In one painting Krishna stood in a streambed while being caressed by a horde of naked women. Awfully similar to a famous album cover of Davey Name, rock star extraordinaire and plenipotentiary, lying on a bed caressed by twelve girls.

One of the several Mr. Jarewallas shot Veronica a glare as she entered, and upon deciding that she was inconsequential, looked away. She stood near a miniature painting, surreptitiously eyeing Mr. Jarewalla as he sat on the floor, eating his lunch. He ate with his hands, Indian style, and made a good deal of noise when he chewed. He had long hair and wore thick diamond and ruby rings on both hands. His suit was expensive and appropriate, but his high-heeled footwear, neatly lined against the counter, would've seemed excessive on a 60s pop star. He looked up and caught her watching him.

"May I help you, Madame?"

"Just admiring your things." She peered curiously at his lunch tiffin. "May I try some of your khanna?"

"Oh ho! You are fond of Hindi language! You have visited our India?"

"Yes, and I used to live in Nepal. A long time ago."

"My goodness. Please to sit." Mr. Jarewalla stared quizzically at Veronica as she lowered herself to the floor. His eyes were soft and effeminate, unlike the rest of him, nevertheless it was unsettling to be the object of their scrutiny. Veronica saw a thread of smoke rising from a shrine in the back of the showroom. The deities were freshly anointed with red powder and the flowers at their feet had not yet begun to wilt, which meant that Mr. Jarewalla had just completed his prayers. She was curious to see if he kept the usual businessman's shrine with Laxmi, Sarasawti, and Ganesh, or if he was worshipping anything peculiar back there. As she reached down to take the paratha, Mr. Jarewalla caught sight of the bangle on her wrist.

"From where did you obtain this piece? It is of Nepali origin, yes?" Indeed, it was a massive hunk of Nepali gold inlaid with jewels, borrowed from Helena without permission. She slipped it off her wrist at once.

"Allow me to examine." Mr. Jarewalla snatched the bangle and rolled it between plump fingers. "You are interesting to sell? I make friend price."

"No thanks." Veronica grabbed the bangle and slipped it into her purse. Mr. Jarewalla's eyes scanned her body for other items of value, until Veronica regained consciousness of their physical proximity and the odor of Mr. Jarewalla's hair oil mixed with his curried lunch. She coughed, the moment's weird profundity evaporated, and she felt mildly embarrassed to be sitting on the floor of an art gallery, eating parathas out of a tiffin.

She wiped her hands on a weathered napkin and stood up. "Thanks for the paratha. I have to go."

"No mention. If you care to be selling some item, please to consider myself first. Have a card."

"I know where you are." Veronica reached into the basket of calling cards. Hocking the odd trinket might soothe those frequent and distracting cab fare crises and accessory cravings. She stopped before the mirror. How reassuring, she looked significantly less depleted than she felt. She leaned into the glass to practice a new blink/pout combination when she saw a man standing in the doorway, staring at her. She blushed, buttoned her jacket. Getting caught preening before the mirror was worse than being caught drunk or naked. Exposing one's vanity was true nakedness. She faced the man abruptly, which in ordinary circumstances would induce a gasp of admiration. But this man stared back, unfazed. He had shining black hair, combed and oiled, and curling below his ears. He wore a dark green jacket, jeweled rings gleamed on his long fingers, and a dzi bead, just like hers, dangled from his neck. The unique copper glow of his skin could only have belonged to a Tibetan.

"From where did you get this?" His hand reached forward to touch Veronica's dzi bead.

"Kathmandu. You're from Tibet, aren't you?"

He smiled, strangely. "How did you know?"

"You have a dzi bead too." Yes, it was that distinctive jewel, and the copper glow in his skin, and something about his stare. "What part of Tibet are you from?"

"Me? I am from Lithang."

"So that means you are a Khampa."

"Yes, I am a Khampa." Suddenly they were instantly locked into that peculiar intimacy which occurs when two strangers discover that they share an esoteric knowledge or experience. She knew all about the Khampas; they were Winston's favorites. The Khampas were the legendary warriors who bore the young Dalai Lama to safety in India, outpacing the Maoist hordes under cover of night, on horseback no less. Fiercely loyal, these Buddhists always carried at least one knife, killed for pleasure and honor, and were reputed to be unforgettable lovers.

Winston had frequently invited them over for long dinners in Kathmandu and Hong Kong. Veronica had studied these gatherings from the hallway or the staircase; sometimes strange things came in and out of briefcases, as voices lowered and heads nodded in hushed accord. And now a real live Khampa was standing in front of her, narrowing his eyes at her . . . Ah, here it came, the Khampa X-ray, that maddening, uncanny power to undress, seduce, and ravage with eyeballs alone. It was fast-acting poison, rendering the victim completely helpless to escape or complain, because technically speaking, it involved no physical contact. What did the Hippie Elders say about Khampas, imagine a Buddhist Apache Indian? Something like that.

"Nice to meet you," Veronica said nervously, pulling away as soon as the man had slipped his card into her hand. She rushed to the elevator without looking back, waited for the doors to close and peered at the card, a florid red-and-gold text engraved onto rice paper, which read:

## MR. NORBU

TANTRIC TREASURE GALLERIES

*Antiquities and Specialties of Arts of the Himalayas*

NEW YORK-PARIS-KATHMANDU-HONG KONG-TOKYO

*Gemstone Consultations Available*

The elevator doors opened upon Helena's apartment and Veronica stumbled into a churning sea of drop cloths, ladders, paint cans, and fabric samples. Helena had heard that pale and floral was all the rage in Knightsbridge drawing rooms, and was therefore determined to beat her Park Avenue neighbors to a profile in *W* magazine, so pale and floral it would be.

Wu, Winston's ancient and faithful Chinese butler, scowled and muttered as he ambled into the vestibule carrying four pairs of Winston's wooden shoe trees. Veronica deposited her coat on an empty chair as Wu fussed with the mail.

"Hi, Wu."

"Yes, yes, Miss Lonya." He'd never get her name right, even if another twenty-two years went by. Neither would he strive to improve his English, which he kept deliberately broken, perhaps a clever way to play dumb when Helena had one of her tantrums.

"Is Mother in?"

"She not happy. Look mad." He made a pained grimace. "She see paper."

Veronica shuddered. That party at Travesty. With all those VIPS. That meant a lot of paparazzi must have been stalking the place. Oh no—when she was dancing with Wilhelm. And the pink scarf. Now

Helena would know she'd been through the attic in the Hampton house.

"Where are the papers?"

"She got. No like a lot." Wu could be counted on to let you know when hell was preparing to break loose. Veronica heard Helena raising her voice above the anxious murmur of her decorator. *Maybe I should split now, while I'm ahead. No, I need the goddamn check. Better get this over with.* She took a deep breath and walked into the study. Helena was poised on the loveseat, wearing a crisp, ochre suit, with fabric samples, date book, and three daily papers arranged on the coffee table, like troops marshaled for combat. The hapless decorator stood in the corner appearing timid and annoyed while Helena wailed about the bathroom wallpaper. Veronica reconsidered fleeing, just as Helena whirled around and sent her date book flying.

"Ah, Randy, this is my famous daughter, or shall I say my infamous daughter, Veronica Ferris."

"Oh, wow, it's just great to meet you! I saw your picture in the paper!" Randy the interior decorator seemed supremely relieved that the conversation had switched course from bathroom wallpaper to tabloid gossip.

"I have to buy the papers myself to find out where she is and what she's been doing." Helena's jaw was beginning to grate. Something pretty bad must have made the papers. "She never comes to see her parents because apparently she's out dancing every night."

"Gosh, if you ever need a dancing partner, give me a call!" Randy winked. Veronica wished she and the decorator could go have a nice long coffee, suspecting that he shared the sentiment.

"Well, you two certainly have a lot to talk about, don't you!" Helena was getting wise to their scheme.

Randy turned professional. "Mrs. Ferris, I'll order the orange wallpaper right away. I'm sorry about this misunderstanding." He reeled backward in a swift exit.

"Well, young lady, if your ambition in life is to embarrass your family, you're making tremendous progress." Helena thrust the *Star* at Veronica. Prominently featured was a large photograph of Veronica caught in a wildly calisthenic pose with a leering Wilhelm. The caption read:

"Lucious party girl Veronica Ferris, daughter of high society's swelle-gant scribe Helena, gets down and dirty with the Boppin' Berliner, playboy tennis ace Wilhelm Streicher, at the opening of Travesty, Gotham's newest hotspot. The pair wowed onlookers with their un-inhibited dance moves while a gaggle of glitterati, including Venice Beach and John Penn, boogied the night away."

This was pretty bad. At least it was a flattering picture.

Helena was perched on the loveseat, brow and jaw steeled for com-bat. "Miss Ferris, is this the way the daughter of a prominent and shall I say important New York family should behave in public? Your grand-father Jack would simply die if he were alive to see this."

"Correction, Jack would have congratulated me on the fabulous picture."

"What was that, young lady?"

"Come on Mom, no one's breaking the law here. It's just, you know, kids, having fun." Never mind that Occo was pushing fifty.

"Who is this Wilhelm Striecher?"

"He's a very successful tennis player. He's admired by millions." Veronica hoped that would calm her down, as the New Helena was deeply respectful of fame.

"You're having an affair with him, aren't you?"

"No, I'm not." A one-night stand was not an affair. "We were just dancing."

"I don't know what your father and I ever did except give you ab-solutely everything we thought was good for you—"

Veronica stormed out of the study and paced back and forth in the cluttered hallway. The Old Helena wouldn't have been so out of whack about a tabloid photo. The Old Helena had been too busy fretting end-lessly over youngest child Jamie, who would often pull stunts like disap-pearing into Sumatra with a Swedish bicycle team, or going diving, fully clothed, in Causeway Bay.

"*Veronica!*"

There was no way to get Winston's check and avoid a confronta-tion. Veronica slunk back to the study. Wu, inured to family quarrels, stood absently in the corner.

"I understand you were very rude to Aaron at your father's party and his feelings were hurt. Aaron is extremely fond of you and you would do well to cultivate him. He is a remarkable young man."

"Yes, remarkably obnoxious."

"What did you say?"

"I agree, he's remarkable."

"Have you been cavorting with that John Penn character? According to the papers you 'boogied the night away' with him."

"Well, that was a coincidence."

"John Penn is a very dangerous man. Do you know what he does to young girls?"

"What, he takes them to parties?" Was partying soon to be outlawed in public?

"He lures them into acts of exhibitionism."

"What about your new friend Peppy Uptone? He's got the same reputation but your lunch friends seem to love him." Conjuring Peppy Uptone, a raucous, overweight society fixture and perpetual favorite of the Lunch Coven due to his gift for obsequiousness and his presumed asexuality, shattered Helena for an instant.

"Veronica, you—you don't understand what it's like, with your father's new job. It's a different set of people and expectations." Helena's punctiliously manicured nails were now digging into her leather date book.

"So? I'm listening." Veronica was deeply curious to hear the New Helena's mission statement.

"I'm in discussions with some investors about starting my own design firm."

"You were always brilliant at that, Mom." This was one of Helena's unique talents: she could create the infrastructure of home in the most unlikely places. Whether is was the Park Legend Hotel or the Marine House in Dacca, Helena set up camp with Jack and Lilly's needlepoint pillows, Winston's favorite cocktail tumblers, and, in season, Christmas ornaments and stockings, even in the Gulf of Siam or the Khyber Pass.

"I never thought of it as something that could become a business, but I am very concerned about your half-brother Grayson. He wants your father's money to fund his political ambitions. Your father just won't focus on it. He has a blind spot for his sons, for all his children! So I'm trying to build something here. I worry about your brother Jamie, and—"

Veronica suppressed a yawn. This was Helena's familiar lament about the MacDouglas millions. Helena's parents did not establish trusts for their progeny, so her great fear was that they'd die and lawyers would get everything, not an unreasonable concern. Since relocating to Manhattan, Helena had flown down to her parents' Palm Beach estate twice a month to beg them to give her control of their estate, whereupon hands flew in the air and Mrs. MacDouglas would cry, "How would we live? And who'd take care of the garden?" Garden, hell, they never used the thing. Veronica detected urgency in Helena's voice. Now she was competing with Dolly Seabrook and Bitsy Whipplair, the Benefit Ladies! She had to refurbish the flat, replenish her wardrobe, and be a player at the Skin Cancer Benefit and the Winter Bone Marrow Fund Drive.

Wu, angel of mercy, appeared at the door. "Meesis Ferns, you gotta visitor."

Helena's hands instinctively flew to her coiffure. "Who is it?"

"Doby Seelook."

"What?"

"I think he means Dolly Seabrook," Veronica piped in helpfully.

"Helena, dear, so sorry to be late. My eldest is just back from a semester in England and we've been going through her clothes. Oh hello, Veronica." Dolly came striding into the room, all fur and cashmere. She was a tall, bony blonde who was fiercely competitive about things like tennis and children's achievements. Dolly turned her full, inquisitorial gaze upon Veronica, who slouched in a chair, calmly skimming through the newspapers. "So Veronica, you're creating quite a sensation about town these days."

"Am I? How nice." Veronica offered Dolly a smile of innocent warmth.

"You seem to be having a lot of fun." Dolly's tone turned aggressive. For the Benefit Ladies, having fun meant you didn't take your parties seriously.

"I'm delighted to be out of school."

"We understand that you cut quite a figure on campus!" Dolly's mouth settled into a smug, coral-colored bow. Every family had a problem child. Dolly's eldest son had been kicked out of numerous New England boarding schools before eventually settling into the ignominious vocation of year-round handyman on Martha's Vineyard. Veronica suspected that the Benefit Ladies felt Helena had enjoyed altogether too much success, with a fabulous new apartment in the Park Legend and a flattering spread in *Vogue*, so she deserved a little failure. The Lunch Coven would be only too pleased to take full measure of Veronica's turbulent double life.

Helena whisked Dolly out the door, allowing Veronica the opportunity to sneak off to the new master bedroom in search of missing letters, books, and of course, jewelry. The bedroom was a solemn, ostentatious space filled with canopies, curtains, and bookshelves. There was a pile of books on Winston's bedside table, a World Bank symposium on the future, biographies of Pompei and Disraeli, and an OXFAM report on world hunger. Veronica touched the small brass alarm clock that had awakened Winston every day for forty years.

She stared at Winston's nail clippers, tortoise shell comb, clothes brush, a malachite dish filled with collar stubs, a small photograph of Helena, Jamie, and Veronica. Winston had notoriously high standards. Embassy staffs bristled with trepidation when his appointments were announced. The envoy who had preceded him in Manila was an easygoing drunk who lived on the golf course and let the staff wear bush shirts and loafers, whereas Winston insisted on suits in the office, even when the heat exceeded one hundred degrees Fahrenheit.

Veronica feared that her failure to cope with life in America made her a hideous embarrassment, even a liability, to her father. She prayed that Winston would grant her the Only Daughter Exemption, an unwritten bylaw that would absolve her if she simply married someone respectable. That seemed infinitely more difficult than managing a career, but it was always an escape clause, and a viable career option for the ambitious and well-prepared Beautiful Girl. Some of Veronica's dorm mates had managed to graduate from college with a diploma plus a husband, whereas she'd barely escaped with four sacks of clothes, half of her Bollywood disco underground tapes, and one box of her Asian-language books, because everything had vanished from Jack and Lilly's farm. All the talismans of her magical childhood—gone in an instant.

The corner table displayed a fulsome family shrine with a token portrait of Winston and his elder sons, a collage of Helena and Winston's wedding, an old photograph of an audience with the pope, a shot of Helena dancing with a French movie star, one of Winston golfing with the king of Nepal, one of Helena cutting the ribbon at a hydroelectric project in Thailand, and one of pre-teen Jamie and Veronica receiving lollipops from Imelda Marcos. There were several recent, quasi-official portraits of Helena in evening dress. Her smile and hair were getting harder every year. Veronica saw a photo of the Old Helena tucked behind the others, which for years had been hidden away and was for some reason back on the altar. It was Helena in Jakarta, looking decidedly bohemian with long hair wrapped in a scarf, long neck rising from a striped shirt, a cigarette in one hand, chin resting on the other, eyes dreamy and marvelous.

"Veronica my dear!" Winston seized his daughter in an adoring hug. "I hardly saw you at my birthday party, and you ran away so quickly!"

"It was so crowded and I didn't know half the guests."

"Your mother's got some new friends who keep telling her she should run a salon of some sort. I thought that was exactly what we'd been doing for twenty-five years, but some would say that outside of Manhattan it doesn't count." Veronica had observed Winston moving among Helena's new pack of vain, extravagant lunch partners, appearing as detached from the scene as Wu with the drinks tray. She wondered if he missed Asia.

"Good afternoon, Veronica!" There stood Aaron Eastman, manicured, Brooks Brothered, and ready for the General Assembly. "That was quite the photo of you in the *Star*."

"A photo of Veronica! How nice." Winston smiled innocently.

"If you'll excuse us, Aaron, I need to talk to Dad for a minute?"

"Certainly. Ambassador Ferris, I'll be in the drawing room."

"Thank you, kind sir!" Aaron made a gratuitous, throat-clearing sound as his face eased into his characteristically pious don't-you-understand-I'm-gonna-be-an-ambassador-one-day grin. Veronica wondered if Aaron knew that Winston called everybody "kind sir," including Wu.

Once Aaron was out of sight, Winston opened his wallet and

handed Veronica a folded check, then coughed into his fist and polished his glasses on a napkin. "Dear, do you mind if I ask how old you are?"

"Twenty-two."

"I'm not good with family numbers, as you know, and your mother's never forgiven me for it. My four older boys taught me that it's futile to tell children what they should or shouldn't do until they're at least twenty-eight. The only way they'll ever avoid mistakes is to make a few when they are still young enough to recover. But I do worry about you, my dear girl, how are you surviving?"

"Dad—" She didn't know how to say it, that sometimes she wished she were Susan Hartman, heading straight for law school and respectability, in a kilt and penny loafers.

"Dad, I know you wish I was more like—Susan Hartman!"

"Susan Hartman? Oh, you mean Bill's daughter. But, Veronica, why would I want you to be anything else but my darling girl?" Winston looked at her in such pained confusion, it both touched and wounded her. Those awful years in college had left her with an imprint of life mismanaged and misused, when she had failed to be graceful, tough, and cunning, that rare combination Winston possessed in great measure. She wanted to cry, it seemed so much easier than explaining.

"My dear girl, you mustn't be so unhappy. You're only twenty-two and what a life you've already had—"

"I know Dad, I know, but our magical life—mine and Jamie's—now it's just a dream . . ." This was the curse of a magical childhood, that one would only know how to live in a dream, had never known that life was unfair and frequently cruel, and that most people thought manners were for cowards. All the grace and wisdom that Winston had bequeathed to her was unwanted, sometimes ridiculed.

"Veronica, think of New York as just another new city. You've done this so many times before. You didn't want to move to Jakarta, and remember how you loved it?"

"But Jakarta was in Asia." And in Jakarta she had a house with a swimming pool, a tropical garden, a driver, cook, butler, security guard, diplomatic immunity, and an abundant weekly allowance.

"I know that you and Jamie feel Asia is your continent, but this city is unique. I love it in a special way, because I was born here and so were

you. It is a miracle that it functions at all. New York has a unique quality. Its many and varied citizens have figured out how to get along with
each other. It is a supremely tolerant city, with a sense of humor." Winston then repositioned his glasses on the bridge of his elegant nose and
opened his briefcase. He had moved on to a new thought, a new problem. Ever the instinctive diplomat, Winston did not like to belabor issues, he sought to resolve them. Family politics included.

"Look at this my dear, there's a new linguistic trend emerging from
the UN communications department. They are now asking us to—let
me read this to you—"define what's in a diplomat's tool kit." I thought
tool kits were for electricians. Am I missing something here?"

"It's the new jargon, 'skill set,' 'tool kit,' everyone's using it."

"I see. So let's look in my briefcase and see what we've got here.
Well, first and foremost, a current passport. If possible, always have a
second passport. As you know, I have three. Cash, and a credit card.
Other forms of ID are always useful. Carrying a valid plane ticket to
anywhere should be a priority. You never know when your luck will
run out and sometimes you've got to make a run for it. I've had to do
it on a number of occasions. Nothing too spectacular, like the Saigon
airlift."

"Excuse me, Ambassador Ferris, we have lunch with the Danish
delegation." There stood Aaron Eastman, wielding his briefcase like a
pistol.

"Yes, yes Aaron, off we go." Winston kissed Veronica on the forehead. "Veronica dear, I want you to enjoy this city while you can. Remember how you took Tokyo by storm when you were eleven!"

Winston and Aaron headed toward the elevator, with Wu shuffling
behind. Was Winston giving her permission to pursue her double life?
There was one way to find out, and that was to accept John Penn's
luncheon invitation.

# Meeting Mr. Penn

THE BUILDING WHERE JOHN WORKED WAS SOMEWHERE IN A cavernous midtown intersection. Veronica saw John standing outside in blue jeans, a black jacket, and cowboy boots, holding a large, nylon knapsack, the kind a college student might use as a book bag. He smiled when he saw her.

"Hi!"

"Hi."

"You're coming to lunch today!" His face was curious, glowing.

"I can't find the elevator," Veronica said with mild embarrassment.

"It's here." He walked to the far corner of the lobby and opened a steel door. They rode up in silence. Under the harsh elevator light Veronica could see him better. He was a delicate assemblage of ligament, bone, and flesh, all of the same dull, white hue, except for his blue eyes and brows and lashes, which had been dyed black, as a fine line of white at the root of the hairs indicated.

The elevator opened on the sixth floor. A security guard buzzed open the glass doors of the studio. Veronica followed as John marched through a vast maze of rooms and corridors. In the office, John's gestures were brisk and his voice was firm as he assumed command. The staff gazed at him in silent, reverential awe as he passed. The place had an unfinished quality, as if someone had been packing and unpacking for several years without coming to any decisions about where to put everything. Plastic sculptures loomed over antique chests; beautifully crafted tables were piled with crystal bowls, cheap toys, brass ornaments, polished stones, and art supplies; shelves were crammed with tee shirts, ties, books, hairbrushes, granola bars, tea cartons; boxes overflowed with records, newspapers, letters, and magazines. Veronica had never seen anything quite like it. But the arrangements were not random; John had selected and assembled everything into dense chaos according to his own inscrutable plan. The inflatable Oreo cookie footstool belonged on top of the Mayan funeral urn; the television was of course nestled into the huge Edwardian rocker; the paint cans needed to be stored under the Chinese armoire.

A polished blond man in a pale blue suit stepped forward with a date book.

"John, the people from Vivant are coming over at 1:45. Should we keep lunch for them?"

"Oh—yeah—hey, look at the new girl I found!" John whirled around and presented Veronica. A crowd materialized, mute and fascinated. They were all young and pretty and dressed in expensive sweaters from downtown boutiques.

"She just graduated from college and she's going out with a tennis player!"

"I'm not going out with him!" Veronica blushed.

"You're not?"

"No, I merely danced with him—"

"So what do you like better? Movie stars? Rock stars?"

"Oh, well, rock stars, of course. I fall in line with most American teenagers." *Though technically I'm not supposed to be a teenager anymore . . .*

"Rock stars are the best! That's why you have to be a model! Rock stars always need a new one. It's like buying a car." John held a frail, white hand to his lips and fixed his gaze upon Veronica. His eyes were brilliant and blue, gleaming and intent. He summoned a tiny Asian man who brought him a large Polaroid camera.

"Stand here." He pointed to a blank wall. She obeyed. He held the camera close to her face and began to snap.

"What should I do?"

"Nothing."

She stared into the black lens. John clicked the shutter and pulled the film from the camera several times, then walked over to a table and placed the photographs in a neat line. Her face slowly emerged from the white paper squares. Each image was identical, beautiful, remote. With a mere Polaroid he'd transformed her into one of his icons.

"So Veronica, what's your favorite place for dancing?"

"Oh, definitely Bangkok. And Kathmandu."

"Bangkok is better than Travesty?"

"Much better. Those countries have better disco archetypes."

"Disco archetypes! Like, what?"

"God Krishna is the ultimate rock star."

"Krishna is a rock star?"

"Of course. Krishna plays a flute, like Davey Name plays a guitar. It drives all the women crazy. It's just like worshipping the power embodied by a rock star. And if God really is omnipotent, he must be at the disco, too, right?"

"That's so great—having a crush on God!" John rocked back and forth, laughing. His enthusiasm was touching.

Veronica curled her legs over the arm of her chair. She noticed a collection of plastic icons on the sideboard, Madonna and Child, Jesus of the Sacred Heart.

"Are you a Catholic, John?"

"Oh yeah. I go to church every Sunday. Hey, look at my new miniature Mercury." He pointed to a plasticine replica of Grand Central Station. "I also love skyscrapers."

"New York is a city of illuminated lingams."

"Illuminated whats?"

"This whole city is one big electrified Shiva temple. Look at it, it's packed with these huge steel, concrete, neon lingams. It's one big fluorescent Shiva temple."

John was now laughing so hard he had to remove his glasses and wipe his dyed eyelashes on his coat sleeve. Veronica followed John into the lunch room. They sat alone at the head of the huge oval table while the Asian man displayed food in tinfoil trays. John clasped his hands under his chin and stared at Veronica. She was accustomed to arousing attention. As a child she had charmed everyone from diplomats to school teachers. Later, she elicited passionate sentiments in the friends of her older half brothers Grayson and Bradley. And in college, she had no difficulty convincing the male teaching assistants to grant her any number of extensions on term papers.

"I saw your mom and dad on the eleven o'clock news."

"What were they doing?"

"Red carpet. In front of the Met, I think. Does your Dad like his new job at UNICEF?"

"He's kind of confused because the communications department asked him to describe what's in a diplomat's tool kit. I mean, who cares? Wouldn't you rather know what's in an intercontinental party girl's tool kit?"

"What? So tell us!" How odd that he referred to himself in the plural, not singular, when they were alone, just the two of them in the lunch room.

"Those women's magazines never give you the real information on the things you really need to know."

"Like what?"

"Like, let's see . . ." Veronica opened her diary and began to read. "New tips on how to get upgraded to first class without paying for it. How to play dumb at customs. Effective strategies for hogging the limelight. How to break up with a guy and make him feel guilty. How to go native without looking ridiculous. To pierce or not to pierce. Test your international IQ. Some thoughts on borrowing your friend's clothes. Disco Feng Shui Updates. And last but not least, Hangover Management Round Table. I mean, this is the stuff girls really need to know."

Veronica saw a tape recorder humming quietly in John's lap.

"Why do you have that machine on?" Good God, had she said anything compromising or stupid? Probably.

"Oh, 'cause everything's so interesting, that's all." He slipped the machine furtively under his jacket. So was it too late for editing, for retractions—*for God's sake, protect your double life!*

"John, if you're going to print any of this, can I use a pen name?"

"A Penn Name!"

"Yes, like—a John Penn name!"

"So what is your Penn Name?"

"How about . . . Maya Smith?"

"What's the Maya for?"

"Maya is illusion in Sanskrit. We have coppersmiths, silversmiths, leathersmiths, so how about a Maya Smith?"

"Maya Smith, can we put a picture of you in the magazine?"

"Why would you want to put me in the magazine?"

"Because you're so pretty!" More pink waves rippled through John's cheeks. She knew the stories of girls being chosen, anointed, and then hastily abandoned. This odd little man with fake hair and dyed eyelashes, with his strangely graceful body and his fierce eyes riveted on her, had woven a legend. But she felt no reason to resist him. Why not give in and see what happens?

A security guard charged through the door leading a pack of disoriented Frenchmen. The blond man in the blue suit rushed to John's side.

"John, I'm sorry, they came early."

"Who are they?"

"The Vivant people."

"Oh right, we just signed a contract. Veronica, don't go away! I haven't asked you everything." John led the French delegation into the studio. Veronica stared at her Polaroid portraits and finished eating the dandelion salad.

# Take My Picture Please

VERONICA AWOKE AT THE ABYSMAL HOUR OF NINE, TOOK A FEE-
ble shower, downed some coffee. Little brother Jamie frequently as-
sailed her with obscure data about the evils of caffeine. Okay, so she
shouldn't drink coffee. She shouldn't spend every night dancing at
Galaxy either! But getting photographed at discos with German tennis
players and other assorted glitterati, well, the millions of patriotic
Americans who dutifully read their weekly celebrity magazines considered this the pinnacle of achievement. What a fabulous hoax! Who
knew life could be so simple?

John had arranged for Veronica to have a photo session with Willy
Westwood, the celebrity/fashion photographer who'd made his mark by
"pushing the envelope" with a series of erotic handbag ads. Veronica arrived at Westwood's monolithic granite SoHo lobby a respectable seven-
teen minutes late. The faint timbre of disco music emanated from the
end of the hall. Veronica pressed the buzzer and it swung open, revealing
a blank, immaculate room, entirely white, except for people and cameras.

"So you're today's girl. Veronica, right?" Willy Westwood flashed a
huge, professional smile as he looked her up and down. He was tall,
sleek, tan, in expertly faded jeans, red shirt, and white tennis sneakers.
"Welcome to our little den." Sauntering over to the kitchenette, he of-

fered, "What kind of medicine can we give you? Are we talking a caffeine morning or a vitamin C morning or both?"

"Caffeine, please."

Willy tipped a pitcher of steaming black liquid into a vermillion mug. "Veronica, this is Ted, he'll be doing your makeup. Jeff, he's hair. And Holiday is our stylist this morning. Tad here works with John, as I'm sure you know." Ah yes, he was the shiny one in the pale blue suit, carrying the date book. A flurry of eyes, hands, and murmurs enveloped her. Willy handed her the mug of coffee just in time. Jeff ran his fingers expertly over her cheeks and forehead.

"I'm not wearing any makeup," Veronica confessed.

"Thank God! Girls come in with eight hours of work on their face. It's like I'm an archeologist, scraping layers. Hmm, nice eyebrows . . ."

"Honey, I've got to be straight with you," declared Jeff, touching her ragged bangs. "This stuff in the front is a disaster. You have to go short. You've got the face for it. And can we go back to your natural color, which is trying to peek through this disaster? I mean, why would anyone dye naturally red hair?"

Veronica shrugged. What the hell, it was time for a change anyway. "Do what you can."

Ted withdrew long scissors from his supply case and went to work. Black shreds fell over her arms and onto the floor. Jeff and Holiday shared diet strategies. Willy and Tad huddled in the corner, flipping through fashion magazines and skewering the models.

"Oof, when she was in here last week she was so fat we couldn't even get the clothes on. Or off."

"Kitten's looking fabulous!"

"Thanks to chemicals."

"She wants to be the next Tiger Street."

"Tiger Street knows how to get booked."

"Only by Condé Nast. Tiger says she wants a big rock star boyfriend, and she's trying to reel in Davey Name, who likes to keep his evenings free."

"Take a look, kids. It's a real work of art." Jeff beamed proudly as he handed Veronica a mirror. With some kind of chemical he'd stripped away the black dye and restored her chestnut-burgundy locks.

On one side, her hair was cropped over her ear, and on the other it swooped below her chin. Actually, it looked fantastic.

"Veronica, any special music to get you in the mood?"

"Old funk would do fine."

"Suffering from disco overkill?" Willy clucked smugly. Was he at Galaxy last night? Forty minutes later James came over to supervise their progress as Ted was finishing with the eyelash curler.

"Oh, Ted! That's much too much mauve on the brow bone!"

"I thought today's girl was supposed to be too much!"

"Look at her eyes—purple! This girl is a specimen. You don't get purple eyes every day. I think you shouldn't go any further than rose. That's what the sponsor color chart says."

Ted rolled his eyes and tossed the eyelash curler on the table.

"Ted, you've done excellent work so far but mauve's going overboard!"

Veronica couldn't turn to a mirror to see what the fuss was about. What the hell was going to happen when they got to lipstick? Trying very hard to keep her face perfectly still, per Ted's instructions, she reached for her coffee mug and nearly upset his color box. She contemplated modeling as a career. Just sit still and listen to music for three hours and then briefly show off for a man with a camera. It was the most up-front statement of purpose for a Beautiful Girl. Asians often said that beauty was the reward for having been patient or generous in a past life. What a peculiar reward, when it seemed more like a karmic test. Professional Beautiful Girls had to be careful that their special gift didn't make them insecure, lazy, or cruel. Veronica felt fortunate that her kind of beauty erupted spontaneously, didn't need extensive care. She could turn it on and off at will. Being the center of attention all the time would become tiresome. And how would she find time to write songs?

As Jeff worked the hot curler through her hair, Veronica leafed through a pile of fashion magazines. Tiger Street, a large, pouty, camera-wise blonde, was part of a lengthy feature on "The World's Most Beautiful Women." The accompanying text read:

Being one of the world's most beautiful women may stir envy in the hearts of many, but mega-model Tiger Street says even in her super-perfect world things aren't always worry-free: "Being beautiful can sometimes be a great burden, people really treat you differently, they don't always see the real you behind the glamour." Oh yeah, it's really hard having all kinds of attractive men hitting on you day and night, and getting free clothes from designers. Those are problems the rest of us could learn to live with . . . But Tiger's meowing about her new role, lady love of one of rock 'n' roll's baddest boys, Davey Name!

Tiger Street had a visa to that rock 'n' roll galaxy where one could have chance encounters with people like Davey Name. Veronica wondered how she could get one without risking extradition to Helena's sitting room. She'd have to find a visa sponsor letter.

"So what did you do to John that makes him think you're special?" Jeff asked.

"I wouldn't know. Call him up and ask him." John's interest was something scores of pretty girls and boys, eccentrics, artists, aspiring stars, and even established stars desperately coveted. They paraded before him at dinner parties and nightclubs at their most exotic and outlandish, hoping for a nod of recognition, a part in a film, a place in his celebrity pantheon. If you were christened Face of the Moment you could eat out on it for months. A New Girl in Town could get into any club and on every guest list for a full year. But to make Covergirl or Coverboy lasted for life.

"Time for clothes!" Holiday wheeled a large clothes rack into the center of the room, plucked out a black-and-gold striped tunic and handed it to Veronica. "I think it's very Veronica."

Veronica slipped on the tunic and peered into the mirror. Willy Westwood's coworkers had tamed and refined her unkempt, downwardly mobile chic, and made her glamorous. Something about the new, short haircut accented the diamond-whiteness of her skin and her lavender-blue eyes with gold-green facets and black lashes. The tunic showed off her marvelously sleek torso and her exceptionally well-contoured legs. Dolly Seabrook and Susan Hartman, and all the Benefit Ladies, would croak. How nice of John to give her the chance to play her trump card. Didn't glamour plus beauty make you eligible for a visa to the Rock God Realm?

"Okay, come over here under the cellophane," Willy instructed.

Veronica entered a circle of gold at the far end of the room and sat on a stool.

"What should I do?" asked Veronica.

"Just be yourself. If you can. That's how most girls blow it."

"In front of the camera or off duty?"

"Both, sometimes." Willy stared hard at her. There was something unnerving about the scrutiny of a photographer. It was severe, penetrating, impossible to cheat. He clasped the camera like a race car driver.

"Crank up the music for you honey?" Funky President exploded over the stereo. Veronica's legs started to vibrate as Willy crouched over the camera. She had never done this before. She often disguised herself as a scruffy hippie, and she didn't have much practice wearing couture. But she knew how to channel jouissance. Her eighth-grade Balinese dance teacher had taught her how to radiate inner heat, how to sit still and glow like a jewel. She extended a long, slender leg around the stool, pulled her shoulder toward the back ceiling, eased her mouth into a classic Bangkok smile, then stared, cool and undaunted, into Willy Westwood's camera.

"Okay, turn it to the left, yeah, terrific, now a little smile, just a little one, nice, yeah, very, very nice . . . Oh yeah, man, you got some talent yikes . . ." Veronica was now lying on the floor with her legs in the air. Willy Westwood looked up and smiled admiringly.

*Gee, if this is work, who needs Occo?*

# How Things Change

SEVERAL REPETITIVE AND UNINSPIRING WEEKS PASSED. OCCO was somewhere in South America. Willy Westwood didn't call or extend any party invitations. And, conspicuously, no calls came from John Penn. When Veronica finally phoned his office a curt secretarial voice said he was in Japan and hung up.

Veronica slipped on a pair of perilously high heels and roamed about Meryl's living room, imagining all of the extraordinarily creative ways she would spend her trust fund, if she had one. She had absolutely no fear that she would become a trust fund victim. If she had tons of money she'd have tons of motivation! You inherited a mixed bag of skills from a globalized upbringing. You knew all about airports, climates, religion, how to penetrate a room full of strangers and become the center of attention within an hour. You did not, however, learn to make beds, cook breakfast, or anticipate the future. You did know many languages, codes, and dialects. Veronica spoke fluent international small talk about what kind of visas were best for long visits to India or China, comparisons of the commissaries in Timbuktu and Bangkok, housing in Bogota, and of course, tales of disease and illness, always the big party favorites, along with accounts of professional begging in Calcutta and Bombay. It wasn't vastly different from New York party talk. You had only to switch the nouns: "I heard that (Tibet/the Mudd Club) is really hard to get into." Or "Actually, (Bhutan/Soho House) is more fun if you can obtain (a visa/membership card)." Or "When we went to

(Thailand/Orso's) Wendy and I got (malaria/pesto)." To which the response might be, "Oh, really? We got (typhoid/clams on the half shell) which probably wasn't as heavy." And so on and so forth.

The phone rang and it was Meryl, sounding more aggressive than usual: "Hey, you better get your hands on a copy of the late edition."

"What's in it for me?"

"There's a story about your friend Wilhelm, the tennis player. He's started up with Candy Acker, that panty hose model. There's a big story about his other conquests and you made the list."

"What?" Veronica bolted upright and fumbled for a cigarette amid the wreckage of the coffee table. "Why didn't you keep my name out, for God's sake?"

"Hey, like if you'd been a little more helpful in the past I might have been able to convince my editor not to hurt a valued source. But frankly, you haven't been such a terrific fount of info, and this story is news."

"Please correct me if I'm mistaken, but I thought my private, unfamous life was off the record."

"Granted, but I also have a professional responsibility to my column. Look, I'll call you in an hour. And get some cigarettes. You smoked my backup supply."

"Fuck you." Veronica slammed down the phone, heaved herself off the couch, searched for and found a pack of matches, which enabled her to smoke, with great satisfaction, the last of Meryl's cigarettes. *I shouldn't be living here. This is absolutely the last time I will ever smoke anything that belongs to Meryl. I cannot trust her. She's a journalist. I will never, ever again sleep on a journalist's couch. Nor will I flirt with, kiss, or dance with a journalist, or a tennis player.* She rummaged through tangles of satin and polyester on the closet floor for something clean and modest. *Can't dress like a disco slut, not today. Must face the truth, must go out and read Meryl's column, then find another place to hide. Fuck. No normal clothes. Must borrow something from Meryl.* This was problematic, as Meryl's clothes were very large and excruciatingly preppy, but she was able to find a plain black sweater and some old jeans that were manageable with a belt and some Swiss sandals.

Assaulted by daylight and traffic noise, Veronica headed toward the delicatessen. *Lord, give me night, give me darkness, give me illusion and surcease. Give me a trust fund while you're at it.* The deli manager, Mr. Siddiqi, was a cheerful, toothless Pakistani with whom Veronica had made the supreme error of revealing a knowledge of his native language, which made it impossible to get the paper without joining him in mirthful singing of a favorite film song or a meticulous analysis of favorite Punjabi foods. Today, fortunately, he was explaining the rules of the lottery to a coworker and took no notice as she entered. There, in a towering gray pile, was the *Star.* The front page had a fuzzy picture of a movie star stepping out of a car beside the headline: MOVIE BIG: COKE NO JOKE.

Veronica flipped forward to the gossip section. There was Wilhelm, grinning as usual, in the possessive embrace of a sturdy brunette. The long caption read:

> Back from tennis triumphs in Europe, the ever-hot Wilhelm Streicher and his newest galpal Candy Acker flutter like lovebirds at Luna Ticks last night. It seems that Candy has aced out her competitors to win a romantic Grand Slam. Among the beauties who've rallied with "Blue Boy" Wilhelm, so named for his famous eye color, are songstress Sondra Silver, model Gina Glisser, in-demand deejay Ina Gruve, and luscious party girl Veronica Ferris, stunning daughter of high society's scribe missus, Helena Ferris. While Gina has moved to the arm of a rival tennis pro, Veronica Ferris is said to be "distraught and in hiding" after the breakup.

*Breakup? What fucking breakup?* Veronica stared at the text uncomprehendingly. She'd just have to go to every newsstand in town and buy up all the *Stars,* starting here. But she only had two pennies and a dime on her. She'd have to prevail upon Mr. Siddiqi for some credit . . . *what was that picture, over there . . .* she'd seen it somewhere . . . didn't she see it at Willy Westwood's? Yeah, it was that, that. . . . *oh . . . oh my God . . . no . . . yes . . . oh no, it's . . . it's me, on the cover of* Page . . . *what the hell am I doing there, oh no, oh yes . . .*

From that moment on everything was different.

# Fifteen Minutes and Counting

**THE PHONE RANG LIKE CRAZY. INVITATIONS TO PARTIES AND** galas poured in. Minor acquaintances were suddenly best friends. Designers offered to make clothes. Journalists begged for interviews. Strangers begged for dates. Occo begged for a date. Wilhelm pleaded for a reconciliation. Dickie Drake offered a job at his gallery. Helena was livid. Winston, thank God, was wrapping up the Conference of the Future at the Millennial Choices Summit in Johannesburg and thus far removed from the hysteria.

Veronica hadn't realized how far-reaching and ubiquitous the influence of John Penn and his *Page* magazine was. Covergirl and Coverboy fame was coveted by movie stars, rock stars, and professional athletes. You had to be going somewhere very, very fast; you had to have a movie in the works or a hot new band or hit a lot of home runs. There were Girls of the Moment who'd been servile to John for years hoping to make Covergirl, accompanying him to hundreds of parties, posing for piles of Polaroids, praying, scheming, and begging to be on the cover. So naturally everyone was wondering and asking what it was about Veronica Ferris that had caused this upset, this insurrection, this coup.

Meryl phoned hourly to report on how Veronica's face and story worked their way through the media.

"Hey, it's your moment, okay? Everyone thinks you're hot. Some of the stuff you said is a little way out, but the pictures really score. You better get an agent."

"Why do I need an agent? Venice Beach just gave me a Travesty Life Time After Party Pass."

"You don't get it! Candy Acker wanted Covergirl so bad she went broke buying John's paintings and he still wouldn't do it. Valerie Vale is really pissed 'cause she has a comeback TV role in the works and she wanted the cover bad. It's gonna be in the column tomorrow. Hold it, I've got to take this call."

"Bye." Veronica hung up and turned on the radio. She needed loud music to drown out all the commotion. She had to figure out what the hell to do. She opened *Page* to her six-photo display. The pictures were good, extremely good, but the text was excruciating. All that meandering blather about rock 'n' roll, plus the pretentious inanity about religion. But to her relief, the Intercontinental Party Girl Survival Guide was attributed to Maya Smith, not Veronica Ferris, without a photo. So John was protecting her double life. He understood. The phone rang again.

"Well hello, Veronica, how nice that you'll still exchange words with the lesser mortals such as we who toil in the unglamorous world of international affairs!"

"Hi, Aaron." Oh, hell, Aaron Eastman. This was really, really unfair. She fumbled with the stereo dial to get the volume at a manageable level. "So Aaron, what can I do for you today?"

"Oh quite a bit, actually . . ." She heard a loud rustle of papers, which heralded serious business. "It seems that your, ah, shall we say, highly original theories about the Hindu faith have disturbed some of your father's colleagues. It appears that the Indian delegation considers your interpretations to be, shall we say, somewhat irregular."

"I see."

"Veronica?"

"Yes, Aaron?"

"Perhaps we should discuss this further."

"Sure, sure. What the fuck do you mean by 'somewhat irregular?'" Veronica heard an awkward clearing of the throat. Funny how the most basic and widely circulated curse words freaked Aaron out.

"Uh, well, the ambassador feels that your view departs from orthodox opinion and has caused offense to the some one billion Hindus. Let us say that a highly combustible situation now exists with respect to UNICEF's relations with the Indian delegation."

"Please elaborate, Aaron, I know so little about the law, being a humanities major."

"Yes, yes of course . . ." Aaron, a poli-econ snob, chuckled loudly and in earnest. "But the Indian ambassador is an orthodox Vaishnavite who has threatened a fast unto death unless you repudiate your statements comparing the rock musician Davey Name to Lord Krishna. Other UN employees from India, and there are many, have threatened to stage a demonstration at the General Assembly this week. We suggest that—"

"Aaron, what was printed in *Page* was not a 'statement' that was 'released.' I was not speaking on behalf of UNICEF."

"But under the circumstances your utterances reflect on official U.S. policy and we now have to contend with a situation that is highly volatile, considering our present negotiations with Pakistan." Aaron prattled away while Veronica sank into the tangle of clothes and newspapers upon which she slept. Ah, she could only imagine the memos Aaron was going to write about this. Aaron, a master stylist among major blowhards, didn't know that Veronica had made him famous by stealing several of his memos and reading them aloud at dinner parties. They proved highly durable entertainment. But this was different, because her double life was getting dangerously overexposed.

"Aaron, I'll go talk to the fasting ambassador if you like. I'm usually a hit with those sorts of Indians."

"Oh, no, please don't, I will brief you further."

"Fine, fine, if that's what you prefer."

"And perhaps you should, shall we say, keep a low profile."

# Double Damage Control

THE INDIAN AMBASSADOR ISSUED SEVERAL STATEMENTS AND gave a great many interviews during the preparations for his fast until death to protest Veronica's comparison of Davey Name with Lord Krishna. However, he abandoned the fast after his doctor warned him that it might put undue pressure on his kidneys if undertaken for a prolonged period of time.

Veronica induced Meryl to run a story which she hoped would fully express her dismay over causing any offense to the Indian delegation. Below a photograph of Veronica looking sultry and vacant read the following:

> Newest Penngirl Veronica Ferris says she's sorry about any misreading of her remarks in this month's *Page* in which she says rock legend Davey Name is like a Hindu God, which has the Indian Delegation at the UN stirring up a monsoon of trouble. What she meant to say is that Ravi Shankar's okay, but Dave's her fave, that's all.

"Hey, thanks for making me look like an idiot," said Veronica, sitting on the bed with Meryl's column open on her lap.

"What are you whining about? It's a cute picture. We've received a lot of calls for you today. Everyone wants to go to your party."

"What party?"

"The party John's giving for you."

"John's giving me a party?"

"Come on, Veronica, everyone's talking about it. Why don't you borrow a dress from one of those designer guys? They'll give you anything you want. Talk to Mr. Mentor and call me later."

When Veronica phoned John at his office her call went through immediately.

"John, what did you do to me?"

"You're a Covergirl now, better get used to it."

"But I haven't seen you since—did you go Japan?"

"Oh yeah, Japan. Who will you bring to the party we're giving for you Friday night at Kitsch?"

"I don't have any legitimate boyfriends." She hardly knew this man but they were talking like college roommates. Why did she automatically trust him?

"Don't bring Dickie Drake, he's really nutty."

"Dickie says you're really good friends."

"Everybody says that, but we aren't. So what are you going to wear?"

Veronica positioned the phone against her shoulder, peered into the mirror and pondered what was happening to her.

# Party Planners of the World Unite

**WITH THE PARTY HOUR LOOMING, VERONICA HAD TO FIND A** dress, some stockings, and some money. The evening sky burned crimson, the streets were swollen with people released from offices, on their way to theaters, restaurants, bars, and parties. She was lured into a thrift shop by a psychedelic Pucci bodysuit hanging perfunctorily near the cashier, crying out for a loving home. A death on the Upper East Side had brought a donation of some incredible couture outfits, all size six. Veronica bought eight, which left $4.80 from Winston's recent gift of $80, not enough for stockings. She'd just have to say holes were the next big thing. John would back her up.

Meryl had a friend who was promoting a young designer who was allegedly the "Next Halston" and was "dying to dress Veronica," and now that Veronica was a Covergirl she needed someone to be "her" designer. But tonight everyone would be watching, and she neither wanted to be outfitted in some eyesore from the Next Halston nor crammed into some hideous velvet cast-off of her mother's. Resolving to be true to herself, she laid out her new purchases back at Meryl's place and chose the raincoat dress, circa 1967, a tube of red-and-orange vinyl squares stitched together with pink plastic string. Veronica cleaned it with Windex. With the cheap white go-go boots it was perfect. The left boot had a loose heel, but she figured with some Elmer's glue it might hold up through the after party.

The doorbell rang. Veronica slid open the locks, and there, of all visitors, was little brother Jamie, with two suitcases.

"Hey, sis! Can I hang here tonight? Mom wigged out and I can't deal."

"What happened?" Jamie was Helena's favorite by virtue of being the *boy*, so the offense must have been extreme.

"I had some people over and we were having a jam session in the living room when Dad walked in with some reporters. Mom went nuts and said I was a security risk. Got any food?" Jamie plundered Meryl's fridge and sat cross-legged on the couch and attempted to coax life out of a dead pizza. "So what's up with you and this Penn dude?"

"He's actually a really nice person."

"He's really negative and weird and his stuff is all about rich people and death. It's completely fucked up." Coming of age in Asia had made Jamie a bona fide hippie, with all that was good and bad about the creed. He professed a doctrine of brotherhood and nonviolence as he condemned people who had jobs and wore suits; his speech was clogged with slogans about the virtues of the proletariat, even though he would never survive without the hefty financial support of his capitalist parents. But she loved Jamie's stubborn, impractical idealism, his refusal to Go Native when that meant Be American.

Giving up on the cold pizza, Jamie turned on the TV and unfurled a bag of pot. "Mind if I roll up?"

"Go ahead."

"All these Bond movies follow the basic mythic structure of the superhero overcoming extraordinary obstacles and performing superhuman feats of physical strength and willpower," Jamie declared, staring at the TV screen.

Hey, where'd you get this stuff?" asked Veronica.

"From this guy who's doing a Ph.D. in plant biology. He goes to Colombia four times a year and brings it back for research. Oh wow, the movie's over." Jamie observed.

"Try Channel 4," Veronica said, leaning over to twist the TV dial.

"Stop right there." An imperiled female was being rescued from danger by Mighty Mouse. "Mighty Mouse also acts as a divine inter-cessor."

"He kind of functions like the Holy Spirit," Veronica added.

"Yeah, like Batman, except Batman doesn't have natural aerody-namics. He's mortal, like Bond. What I don't understand is why Mar-vel Comics uses flying rodents as hero-liberators. The other day I got a really good idea about the parallels of unity resolution as a comedic norm in contemporary and Elizabethan drama 'cause I'd just been watch-ing a Love Boat episode . . ." Jamie turned the dial again. A large white head was commenting authoritatively on the culinary traditions of the Pacific Rim, then segued into a close-up of a bronze coiffure framing huge spangled earrings. A caption at the bottom flashed "Mrs. Winston Ferris, food analyst and author of *American Flavors Far From Home.*"

"Hey, change it, will you?" Veronica told her brother, trying to pre-serve the sanctity of this Helena-free zone that was Meryl's apartment. When Jamie didn't change the channel, Veronica lunged for the TV, tripped over a tangle of clothes, and crashed into the coffee table.

Meryl opened the door, clutching a stack of magazines.

"Isn't John coming to pick you up in fifteen minutes?"

"Oh, yes, my Covergirl party, I forgot . . ."

"Come on, get dressed! By the way, who's this?"

"This is my brother, Jamie."

"Oh. I see. Hi, I'm Meryl. And this is my place."

"Cool, so like, can I stay here tonight?"

"Yeah, but give me a hit."

The buzzer rang. When Veronica heard John's voice on the inter-com, she slipped into the raincoat dress and ran downstairs, leaving Jamie and Meryl to get acquainted. John's mouth flew open as she climbed into the back of his taxi and pulled the door shut.

"That's a great dress!"

"Hope it's not too loud."

"Noooooo! Everyone's talking about you! And everyone wants to meet Maya Smith. So who's coming?" John's fingers were tightly curled around an active tape recorder. She noticed that his nails were neatly manicured and coated with clear polish.

"I asked Bennett."

"Bennett! Who's Bennett?"

"We went to college together. We never dated but he's very cute."

John laughed and his eyes rolled back into his head. The taxi pulled up in front of Kitsch, the brand-new downtown restaurant. The room was jammed. Pink lights illuminated ten enormous photos of Veronica from the Westwood shoot. The crowd gasped and pointed when Veronica and John entered.

"Penn Station's here with his new caboose!"

"Oh, it's JP and his new girl!"

"Check out the dress. Too weird!"

People swelled and swarmed as John and Veronica became the center of gravity. Eyes, hands, mouths, everywhere. What was she supposed to do? Just stand still and be beautiful, as if posing for one of John's Polaroids?

"John, tell us all about your new discovery!" It was Jerry Dollar, the movie producer, short, wide, and exorbitantly cheerful.

"She went to all the best schools and she speaks Thai and she's got eight boyfriends!"

"John, I don't have eight boyfriends!"

"Marvelous, marvelous! Loved the pictures in the magazine, too. Come have lunch with me next week," Jerry beamed, his eyes suddenly gazing past her shoulder.

"Ronnie baby, you're looking great!"

Veronica whirled around toward the familiar voice. Wilhelm! Who the hell invited him? "Oh, hello, Wilhelm."

"It's the tennis star!" John snapped pictures furiously.

"Veronica! Thanks so much for inviting me!" Bennett suddenly appeared out of nowhere.

"Bennett! I'm thrilled you could make it!" She threw her arms around his shoulders and gave him a hugely enthusiastic kiss. How propitious that he'd appeared just when she wanted to snub Wilhelm.

"Bennett, you must meet Mr. John Penn."

"Mr. Penn, it's a pleasure." Bennett was tall and strong and born to wear tee shirts. Tonight he was looking especially good. "Veronica, those pictures are just so glamorous. I couldn't believe it was the same girl who used to carouse about in a plastic catsuit!"

"You used to what?" John thrust the tape recorder between Bennett and Veronica.

"I just wore an old bathing suit to a costume party once. Nothing extraordinary."

"She's being altogether too modest, Mr. Penn. No one ever forgot it!"

"Why don't you go home and get it?" The tape recorder was now six inches from her mouth. More eyes and mouths and sleek, bangled limbs were closing in around her.

"Pennsylvania! How's tricks?" An enormous creature in white fur and of dubious sexuality pushed Bennett aside. John's face went blank as he pulled close to Veronica.

"So you're the new girl. I'm Susie Genius. Star of many old Penn films." The eyelids were weighted down with thick blue glitter, the cheeks rouged, the voice loud and husky. John shrank with fear in the creature's presence.

"Penn, I'm doing a show at The Crypt next week. You should film it. We want to have a retrospective—"

"Johnnie, what a super time as usual!" A luscious Asian woman in pink-and-gold silk displaced Susie Genius.

"Oh, Uma, this is Veronica."

"You're the one on the cover! How super! John's always promised—"

The music suddenly got louder. Balloons were floating up toward the ceiling. Amid all the heat and noise and spectacle, Veronica had to wonder whether she'd taken any drugs.

"Ooh, cake time!" Body builders in black ties and satin shorts pranced through the crowd bearing pink cakes festooned with sparklers. More balloons went up in the air. More lights flashed on Veronica's pictures.

John leaned into Veronica's ear. "Hey, Jerry Dollar wants to take us to dinner at this other place." It was, quite suddenly, 10:30. "Grab your friend." He motioned toward Bennett. Veronica clutched the edge of Bennett's shirt and followed John and Jerry through the crowd, out the door and into a car which delivered them to Nitrogen, an important-looking SoHo restaurant that served fusion food. The owner bowed obsequiously and marched the group into a private room in the back where a crowded table of dazzlingly handsome young men welcomed them with a cheer. Jerry Dollar barked commands at the waiters while the head waiter seated John and Veronica at the head of the table. Bennett looked confused.

Champagne was flowing, cigarettes were burning. So this was real-life *Disco Darshan*. She was the icon and John was the high priest. All the men around the table stared at Veronica as John interrogated her with his tape recorder rolling.

"Wow, Bennett's really cute."

"You don't think he's too preppy?" Bennett was bouncing one knee up and down while discussing exercise with one of the beautiful young men.

"Johnnie, eat something, you're wasting away!" Jerry Dollar was wolfing down a steak. John turned off the tape recorder and picked at his salad. The raincoat dress was getting a little uncomfortable. Vinyl didn't exactly breathe. She wished she had those Pucci pants on hand.

"I want to go home and put on my new pants."

John turned on the tape recorder. "Say that line again."

"I—want to go home and put on my new pants." He clicked off the machine and returned to his salad.

"Ronnie! Quel surprise!" A flocculent hand grasped Veronica's upper arm. It belonged to Venice Beach, nightclub entrepreneur and professional decadent, tuxedoed and smoking. "Veronica, you look outrageous. Who's doing your dosage?" Venice squinted at Veronica's torso. "Tell me, lovely, if you're serious about modeling because Jane Summerfield at *Bazaar* is an ancient family friend and I'd be tickled to send you over there."

Veronica checked an impulse to accept the favor. To be indebted to Venice Beach, what a headache. He'd charge interest, five lunches a week. "That's so sweet of you, but maybe I should wait until I have a real portfolio together."

Several of the young men began singing. Jerry was standing on his chair, playing conductor. A hand touched John's shoulder.

"Penn, what are you doing with all these crazy boys?"

Veronica looked up and couldn't believe her eyes.

*...alace at Luchow's in Union Square.* *...e left); Maura Moynihan, club owner...* *...right)*

The New York Times/Bill Cunningh...

**T**UESDAY night was birthday ... for two young women about to ... Maura Moynihan and Victoria. ... Moynihan, a rock singer who is ... only daughter of United States S... tor Daniel Patrick Moynihan, tu... 26 at a party thrown by Andy Wa... at Studio 54.

Mr. Warhol said he had agreed ... host for the party "because Mau... going to be a big rock star, s...

# Maura Moynihan at he...
## birthday party.

"Oh, Davey, this is our new Covergirl, Veronica. We just had a party for her."

Davey Name reached for Veronica's hand. "I always like to meet beautiful Covergirls." A dark green jacket over skintight trousers, black hair curling round an angular face, that deadly smile and legendary sex appeal—delicious, hard to get, and highly toxic, like a good drug.

"Pleased to meet you, Mr. Name." *He is smiling at me. He is touching my hand.*

"She grew up in Tokyo and Hong Kong and her father works at UNICEF!"

Davey shoved his hands into his hip pockets. His eyes were examining every part of her body . . .

"Her mother lives in the Park Legend and won't let her into the house!"

. . . caressing her breasts, kissing her neck . . .

"But she's got eight boys in love with her!"

. . . ravishing her thighs . . .

"And she only wears thrift shop clothes!"

. . . searing every ounce of her flesh . . .

"She really loves rock stars." Now addressing Veronica, he remarked, "Davey's got a new album coming out."

"Actually we're still in the studio. I'm heading over there now. Come by if you like."

"I've never been to a studio before . . ." *For God's sake, if you can't sound calm and intelligent and unimpressed just shut the fuck up!*

"Gee, why don't you take Veronica? She wants to be a rock star!"

What was he suggesting? "No John, I . . ." Veronica glanced helplessly at John. She had never seen his dimples so pronounced.

"Don't worry, Veronica, I'll take care of Bennett." Bennett, Jerry Dollar and the beautiful young men were uncorking more wine and bellowing "The Impossible Dream."

Davey smiled craftily. "Hey, JP, give a ring next week. We've got friends in town."

Veronica rose to her feet in a daze. Davey placed his hand on the small of her back as he led her out of the room. She felt her left heel giving way and she crossed the pavement and stepped into his huge black limo. They sat in the back, legs outstretched, holding drinks and watching the miniature television.

Davey described being a judge on a British television dance contest when he was starting out in the music business, but Veronica had trouble focusing on what he was saying. "Christ, these chicks in little dancing uniforms would come up to us and ask if we'd do these ridiculous bloody show numbers with them . . ." *I am alone in the back of a limo with Davey Name. This is really happening.*

The car pulled up to a grim, silent building. Davey pressed the buzzer and waited for the door to open. Veronica followed him down the corridor, trying not to slip on her fragile heel. Apart from the disinterested security guard there didn't seem to be anyone around. They were, in fact, alone, when Davey closed and locked the studio door.

"Here's where we do the work." He stood before the vast control board and toyed with the switches, one sleek hip thrust forward, the other joining the curve of his torso. Veronica recognized the green boots from his last album cover. The real, actual boots from the album cover.

He looked over to Veronica, smiling. "Listen to this." He pushed a button and summoned a rhythm track. "Now try this." Keyboards. "And put this on top." Guitar. "And there's a tune for you." It was a slow song. Not by any means a dance number. Veronica felt an exhilarating terror coursing through her veins. He picked up a guitar and began to strum along. *Look at him playing that thing. How he summons such incredible noise from those pieces of string and wood. Look how he holds it . . .* They listened for a while as he rearranged the tracks. "I rather fancy this reggae sound tonight. Don't know why. What about you?" His hands dropped away from the control board and slid into his jacket pockets as his head fell forward. How did the *Times* rock critic describe his last tour? Ah yes, "the furious intensity of his being gives off a feral, dangerous heat." A tad maudlin perhaps, but accurate. Davey leaned into his left hip and drew the tip of his right boot in a semicircle on the carpet. *He is thinking about the music, he is writing a song, right now, in his head . . .*

Then he shifted his weight onto his outstretched heel and turned to Veronica. His eyes grabbed her face and held it, tight. He started com-

ing toward her. Now he was standing in front of her. There was nothing she could do. She simply couldn't resist or escape. To do so would
be a violation of every natural law. All women were Davey Name's by
birthright. He lifted his hands and placed them on her neck, leaned forward and placed his mouth on hers. *What is he doing . . . is he? . . . he's
kissing me.* His hands began to slide down her neck and across her
shoulders. He pulled her closer. She felt the "intensity of his being, the
feral, dangerous heat" or whatever the fuck it was the *Times* critic
wrote, and their mouths merged into one single, perfect unit. She raised
her hands and touched the leather belt snaked though his trousers, the
world-famous skintight trousers. A cool draft caressed her back. The
vinyl seemed less oppressive, somehow . . . *wait, he's unzipped the back of
my dress, he's taking it off* . . . His mouth was now on her neck, his green
jacket was on the floor, suddenly the go-go boots were on the floor, and
then they were on the floor, and their arms and legs had merged into
one, single perfect unit. The music kept playing and did not stop . . .

# English Rock Stars and Tibetan Smugglers Think Alike

**"SO WHAT HAPPENED?"**

"I think he likes me."

"How do you know he likes you?"

"Because he . . . uh . . . tried to kiss me at the studio."

"Did you let him?"

"Well, I sort of had to."

"Then what happened?"

"We listened to music and he asked for my phone number."

"Then what happened?"

"He pleaded with me to stay at his place but I said no." John dropped the phone. Veronica heard howls and scuffles.

John picked up the phone again. "You've hit it big. You've hit it really big." *What does that mean?* "No turning back now."

"But he has that girlfriend. Tiger Street, right?"

"Steal him."

"Won't she go after me?"

"We'll protect you. We'll find him tonight. I'll pick you up at 7:30. There's a party tonight at Suki Dean's gallery. He's going alone. Tiger Street's working in Paris." John really did know everything about everybody.

"What should I wear?"

"Something old again."

"You'll come here at 7:30?"

"Yeah, I'll have a car."

"Oh, okay, thanks, bye."

"Bye."

Veronica put down the receiver and sat for a moment, dazed and incredulous. The clock on the radio read 4:23. Three hours and seven minutes until John arrived. He was always meticulously punctual. She went into Meryl's bedroom, lit some incense, sat very still, and listened to the hum of the air conditioner, the groan of traffic. She considered the dust accumulating on the table, the food decomposing in the fridge. *Now, hold on a minute. Did I, in fact, spend last evening with Davey Name? Yes, you did, and you kissed him, too. Oh Lord, no one will ever believe me.* But how did it happen? It was John, something about John, some weird contagion. There were hundreds, thousands of beautiful girls in New York with innumerable lucrative industries created to service them and market them. But the girls John anointed had a status beyond those who won ordinary beauty contests. Whatever it was, it worked on rock stars.

Veronica took John's advice and selected a short, spotted 60s party dress that had once been a full-length muumuu. The fabric was stiff and flammable and streaked with neon pink and frog-skin green. She put on pale pink lipstick, thick eyeliner only on top, as John preferred, and enormous dangling earrings culled from a rummage sale. She looked about fourteen. John was onto something with his wear-something-old theme.

Fifteen minutes later Veronica stepped into John's taxi.

"You look great again!"

"It's not too weird?"

"Noooooo! I love it. Look who's coming with us!"

"Bennett!" The taxi pulled up to a corner and Bennett hopped in.

"Gosh, that was so much fun last night! Veronica, you were too sweet to invite me." Veronica noticed Bennett and John holding hands underneath John's book bag. Well then, no need to worry about Bennett's prospects, he'd found a new patron of his arts.

It was strange and titillating, entering Suki Dean's gallery party with Bennett pressing into her arm and John clutching her hand. People stared with a peculiar mix of jealousy and awe. John maintained a cool, disciplined silence. As promised, there stood Davey Name, smoking in the corner, in white pants and a pink-and-blue checkered shirt with an orange hat. Everyone in the room attempted to appear blasé while straining to keep an eye on Davey and John. A woman in a green suit pounced on Davey with an attack of histrionic kisses, doubtless meant to inform all present that they were acquainted.

Davey deftly unwound himself and sidled over to the bar. He was clearly enjoying himself. Yes, life must be easy when you know you're universally acknowledged as the most attractive man in the world. Veronica had long ago trained herself never to put faith in the attentions of extremely attractive men; from keen self-observation she knew that opportunity corrupted. She had never been sufficiently enamored of any man to think his fidelity was either necessary or appealing. She reached for another drink, turned around, and saw Davey whispering in John's ear. A few flashbulbs exploded. The murmur level rose perceptibly. Should she construe the fact that he hadn't spoken to her as a good thing or an irrelevant thing?

A girl with pink hair and a short skirt was trying to levy her way into the celebrity nook and predictably resurfaced near Davey's left elbow. She started a vigorous flirtation, and Davey started flirting back. For the first time in her life, Veronica felt the unpleasant sting of sexual jealousy. She had to get Davey to fall in love with her, so she'd be the girl he craves but can't control—the secret subject of a future hit song.

"Hey, Veronica, let's go eat," John said, clutching his many copies of *Page* and his army fatigue green nylon knapsack.

They filed into cabs and drove to Kitsch. As they were about to step into the club, Davey pulled Veronica into a closet, slammed the door shut and kissed her. *Some men just have more charm than other men, it's really true isn't it . . .*

# Inside the Rock-God Realm

**SHE AWOKE AT 3:00 A.M. IN A LARGE, WARM BED IN AN UNFAMILIAR** room. It wasn't a hotel, and it certainly wasn't Meryl's couch. It was Davey Name's bedroom. The place was as sloppy as a college dorm, albeit an expensive one filled with antiques and million-dollar paintings. The clothes, strewn about the chairs and spilling from the closet floor out to the hallway, were also expensive and hand-tailored. Tables, chests, and shelves were loaded with art books, history books, novels, road maps, and auction catalogs.

Veronica went into the bathroom to hunt for anything approximating a sleeping pill. As she tapped a light switch, a dozen mirrors illuminated the most elaborate bathing facility she had ever seen. She then opened the mirrored chest and found prima facie evidence of a girlfriend—a gleaming horde of lipsticks, mascaras, eyeshadows, perfumes. So what if he had another girlfriend? Wasn't that to be expected? Maybe the makeup was leftover junk from a tour, a promotion, or—she willed herself to stop thinking about it.

In the living room the television was on, probably had been for days. She settled on the couch, pulled a blanket over her legs and flicked the remote control to an old movie.

"Where did you go?" Davey stood in the doorway, wearing only a pair of boxer shorts, yawning and scratching his head. He looked gaunt and worn, constrained by ordinary human needs, such as sleep, food, and affection. This was reassuring, because in restaurants and taxi cabs he was even more attractive than in photographs, which propagated the myth that rock stars were a separate species.

"I can't sleep if I'm left alone," he confided, joining her on the couch. He took her hand and pressed it against his cheek. "I hope John won't mind if I steal you. He's very possessive."

"He is?"

"John likes to live through his girls. You watch. He'll always talk about doing some musical or film project or God knows what. He'll talk about it forever and keep you waiting for the money. He's bloody cheap."

"But John's so generous to me." People always said that John was cheap, but when they were together John paid for everything. He never left her alone for a minute and always drove her back to Meryl's and made sure she was safely inside the apartment before driving off. Was Davey Name actually jealous of John Penn?

"He needs someone like you around." Davey began to stroke her hair, then took her face in his hands and began to kiss her. *God, he's such a good kisser. Maybe I really should consider falling in love with him . . .*

# Hello Tiger

**"DAVEY DARLING, DON'T YOU WANT TO COME SEE ME IN THE** show?" Tiger moaned as she examined her lips in her Estée Lauder pocket mirror. Her lustrous hair, which had inspired millions of women to purchase her preferred brand of hair care products, hung in twin blonde sheaths around her supremely photogenic face, the market value of which had recently been estimated at about two million dollars. Tiger scrutinized the surface of her sparkling white complexion (which the *Times of London* had recently hailed as "a radiant and luminous alabaster"), touched her lips with a tissue, restored the mirror to its place in her handbag, slid her left leg over her right thigh and heaved a tremulous, world-weary sigh.

"Davey, why don't you ever come see me when I'm working? I always come to your shows. It's not fair, and Angelo's giving me the evening dress in the finale this time." Tiger held her indigo nails against her magenta blouse sleeve to see if the colors harmonized.

"I told you I've got a mixing session and I can't get away. A lot of players are flying in for it. That costs money," Davey replied, opening a newspaper.

Tiger rolled down the car window, placed her chin on her fist, and pushed her lips into her famous pout.

John wasn't sure what had happened to Davey. Meryl heard that Davey was out of town, which would explain why Veronica hadn't heard from him for the past four days. But Veronica suspected the real reason he hadn't called: a reunion with Tiger, that peculiar oversized English model girlfriend whom Dickie Drake always said was "just so super."

Veronica's only recourse was to go out every night with John. In one week they'd been to two Broadway openings, four gallery openings, a club crawl with Venice Beach, a pub crawl with two English painters, and a dance marathon at Travesty and Galaxy. For John, all of this was work; he recorded and photographed and analyzed every party, large and small, and he needed Veronica to flirt, dance, charm people, and keep him company.

Jerry Dollar invited John and Veronica to his new uptown Pacific Rim–themed restaurant, which he described as "beyond sushi." After several hours of drinking saki and eating soba, Jerry bench-pressed everyone into a late-night visit to Dickie Drake's townhouse. Dickie Drake, in a red-gold kimono, led his guests into a room that was only somewhat less pretentious, colonial, and stuffy than Entwhistle's.

Veronica slid beside John on a couch clogged with batik throw pillows. John was perched on the edge, camera in hand, tape recorder uncharacteristically disabled. Veronica glanced up—Good God, it was Davey Name, her secret boyfriend! Was he alone? Oh no, not alone, he was with Tiger Street, and Tiger's best model friend, part-time Wilhelm Streicher squeeze Candy Acker. Another eight-foot blonde in an ersatz bondage costume. Okay, her legs were considerably longer than most, but they did look a little peculiar, kind of rectilinear, like the rest of her. The match Veronica was holding, which was about to light a cigarette, had burned down to her fingers and caused her to shriek and leap to her feet.

"Ronnie dearest, has a mouse got hold of your back side?" inquired the solicitous English voice of Dickie Drake. Davey, meanwhile, was engaged in nuzzling Tiger's neck. Veronica sank back into the couch next to John.

"Oh my God, it's *him*!" John whispered.

"Yes, John, I can see that."

"But he's with *her*!"

"Yes, I can see that, too."

"You've just got to get him away from her! Get him alone!"

"I somehow doubt that this really is the right time or place . . ." Veronica lurched to her feet but John clutched her skirt and pulled her back onto the couch.

"You can't leave now, he's coming over!"

"My goodness, it's Penny! Long time, no hear!" Davey was standing right in front of them, smiling at John.

"Oh gee, hi, hey, Veronica's here!" John's head swerved from Davey to Veronica and back to Davey.

"Why Veronica, hello!" In one smooth motion, Davey bent down and gave Veronica two perfectly polite kisses on each cheek.

"Hello, who's this?" Davey quickly pulled himself upright. There stood Tiger, in all her well-maintained glory, peering down at Veronica with steely eyes.

"Tiger, this is Veronica, John's new girlfriend." Davey grinned and winked at John.

"Oh right, you're the one on the cover, shot by Willy Westwood." Tiger's jaw tightened. "Hmmm, not terribly tall, are you?" she remarked, pulling her blonde hair over her left shoulder.

"But she looks great in pictures, don't you think so, Davey?" John elbowed Davey's ribcage.

"Veronica, have you got an agent?" Tiger was keen to continue the model conversation.

"No."

"You might have better luck in Europe. They like the sort of, you know, different look over there."

"Europe, that's where you got started, right?" Veronica could see John's fingers manipulating the tape recorder.

"Heavens no, mum was a great pal of all sorts of photographers so I was doing test shots from the time I was twelve. I've always been super lucky . . ." Man, this chick was tedious. John was attentively nodding and murmuring yeah at every one of Tiger's remarks while the tape recorder spun away. Tiger kept rearranging her gilded mane about her shoulders and toying with her gold earrings.

Davey caught Veronica's eye and held it. *Pretend, if you possibly can, that you don't know who he is even though he's one of the most famous people in the world and you just spent the night with him last week.*

Tiger continued, "I'm so desperately bored with France I didn't know what to say when Angelique invited me to Provence, but frankly, I'm rather inclined to just say to hell with it and ground myself in Majorca—Oh hell, my molars!"

Veronica felt her jaw muscles ready to switch into high gear and eclipse Tiger's inane stream of consciousness. Tiger was highly competitive, hated other women, and was devoid of scruples. Evidently, she could only talk about herself and had a severely limited vocabulary. All Veronica would have to do is employ her intelligent-new-girl-on-the-scene advantage against Tiger's been-around-the-block status, and deploy her superior legs as often as possible.

Candy Acker's conversation with an Argentinean banker had turned serious.

"I was just, like, reading about Vietnam, you know? I mean, it's amazing like, what we did there was really fucked up!" Candy sat erect, fists clenched. "It's like, do you have any idea what was going on over there?"

"What's everyone chatting about?" Tiger pulled up a chair.

"I've been thinking about Vietnam, like, a lot!" said Candy, with passion.

"You Americans started bombing when the first Beatles record came out. I remember 1963!" exclaimed the Argentinean banker, gulping his scotch and edging closer to Candy.

"Actually, the major U.S. military buildup occurred between 1965 and 1968 when military personnel increased from about twenty-nine thousand to half a million. The first American bombing of the North occurred in 1966," Veronica casually corrected.

"Tell us more!" insisted Candy. Everyone turned their attention to Veronica, as she spewed out facts about the Vietnam War to a dumb, pliable audience.

"The most controversial campaign was the bombing of Cambodia . . ."

"Davey dearest, do come here. Johnnie's new girlfriend is treating us to a little history lesson!" Tiger beckoned to Davey, who sauntered across the room and leaned against the settee. Veronica suddenly got flustered and lost her train of thought.

"How many guys were actually drafted?" asked Candy.

"Oh well, uh, fifty thousand American servicemen died . . ."

"Yes, but we want to know how many actually got sent over there," said Tiger, determined to usurp attention from Veronica now that Davey was watching.

"What I find so absurd were the efforts to keep the boys on good all-American diets!" Davey laughed. "Hot steak for dinner and ice cream delivered to bush patrolmen by helicopter!"

"Veronica still hasn't told us how many Americans got fed ice cream in the jungle!" cried Tiger.

"Well, the draft officially began in, in . . ." Veronica's mind went blank. Everyone was looking at her expectantly. "The anti-war protests escalated in 1968 . . ."

"We know all about that business. I want to know more about being rounded up, dramatic stories, not statistics. Davey knows lots about it," Tiger said, leaning back and dangling a shoe from the edge of her humungous foot.

"After the Americans evacuated Hanoi in the spring of 1975—"

"Don't you mean Saigon?" someone interjected.

"Oh, yes, of course. Historians have likened the Vietnam experience to Britain's Crimean War . . ." Veronica blurted, mortified that she was sounding pretentious.

Tiger blinked lazily at her and then wound her arms around Davey's bony torso. Someone popped open a champagne bottle. Veronica made her escape down the hall. She had to grab her coat from the bedroom and get the hell out. She pushed open a door and crashed into Dickie Drake, evidently naked beneath a purple dressing gown. Suddenly she felt his hand on her thigh and his putrid breath in her face. "Darling, you know, don't you, God meant for us to be naked together!" A hand found its way under her shirt and was crawling up her back.

"Uh, when you say 'us' do you mean 'us' you and me, or 'us' the human race?"

Taking this as a sign of encouragement, Dickie pressed his vast belly up against her, murmuring in her ear, "You must not disobey nature's mandate, you willful, willful girl!"

Veronica delivered a hearty kick which sent Dickie howling and crashing to the floor, toppling the table with the magazines, ashtrays, and wine glasses. "You're making a dreadful mistake! You've no idea how dreadful a mistake! You must stay and consummate God's will!" he roared drunkenly.

As Dickie rolled about in cigarette butts and his wine-soaked dressing gown, Veronica found her coat and ran down the stairs to the street, sliced by wind, her mind racing. With a few murmurs Tiger had devastated Veronica's intelligent-new-girl-on-the-scene advantage. Apparently, stupid and ruthless women knew how to thwart competition, doing whatever was required to stay gorgeous and outlast their rivals. Veronica wasn't prepared for this. What the hell was the point of a college education if you couldn't triumph over inferior people?

# Winston for Lunch

**THE NEXT DAY VERONICA AWOKE IN AN ESPECIALLY FOUL** mood, which was excellent preparation for the unwelcome news that Winston, under orders from Helena, had arranged a visit to John Penn's studio.

Veronica pushed open the door to the studio and saw John and Tad crouched on the floor, painting. Inspired by Maya Smith's idea of an intercontinental tool kit survival guide, John was working on a series of paintings of various tools, from hammers to buzz saws.

"John, my father's coming to lunch today. He'll be here at any moment."

"Your father? Today? Wow, that's great! I've always wanted to take his picture. He's so handsome!" John got up and started loading his Polaroid. Tad grabbed a fistful of brushes and tripped on a can of white paint.

John summoned the interns into the lunch room just as Winston sailed through the glass doors with two gray-suited, briefcase-wielding aides at his heels. Winston peered round the place with a look of mild concern, holding any outright disapproval in check until he got the facts straight. Veronica joined John and Tad as they came forward in greeting.

"Dad, this is John Penn and Tad Ward."

"How do you do, Mr. Penn. May I say that this is a remarkable place you've got here. And allow me to introduce my aides from UNICEF, Bill Wigglesworth and Kermit Taylor."

Winston perused the garbage sculpture and the styrofoam Statue of Liberty, the catatonic receptionist who sat knitting at her desk, the Tunisian side tables and the miniature Mercury. Clearing his throat and straightening his tie—signals that the discussion was about to get serious—Winston said, "So Mr. Penn, my wife and I are of course curious to know exactly what Veronica is doing for you."

"She's helping me with my magazine. She's got so many great ideas."

"Ambassador Ferris, we'd love to have you on the TV show," said Tad, pen and date book poised. "Maybe Veronica can interview you! Veronica has so many great ideas, she—"

"Isn't lunch ready?" Veronica interrupted.

"Absolutely, right this way." Tad led Winston and entourage into the lunch room. Tad handed Winston a plate and described the various macrobiotic offerings. Together, Winston and John made quite a pair—the former in his gold tie and blue suit, which bellowed über-WASP, and the latter in his green turtleneck and black jacket speckled with red-and-orange spots, fresh from his morning painting session.

Winston took a seat between John and Tad, while Veronica sat between Bill and Kermit. Interns hopped about, pouring wine. Veronica wondered if she ought to get Winston going with his august-statesman-with-tales-of-diplomatic-triumphs thing, in order to preclude what-exactly-are-you-doing-with-my-kid queries. Winston's senior aide was a generic United Nations lackey from whom all personal flair had been extinguished in service to bureaucratic ambition. The junior aide was technically very cute, one of those gov-poli-sci types who wore beat-up tweed jackets and wrinkled Brooks Brothers shirts in college and read a lot but wasn't afraid to dance at parties. Veronica felt that Winston's presence only further highlighted the inappropriateness of her romantic and professional choices. She couldn't imagine ever introducing Winston to Davey, or Davey to Helena—it was out of the question!

Winston peered around the lunch room, taking in the Mayan funeral urns, carousel horses, stacks of old *Page* magazines, the gigantic TV. "Mr. Penn, I would imagine that this is a Vincent building, correct?"

"Actually, it's a Fisher building," John replied.

"Is it really? There aren't many of them left, you know."

"I've bought another one uptown."

"My goodness, Penn, you've got a good eye." When Winston started using last names, it was a good sign. He gave John his full attention while John talked about architecture, design, and real estate. Before long, they had both delved deep into lively discussion. Winston's aides and John's interns discovered shared passions for cross-country skiing and Greer Garson movies.

After coffee John gave Winston a tour of the painting studios. Winston concluded that John's artistic fiefdom was unique, and in the course of his many tours of duty he had seen a great many. When John mentioned that he was going to Japan, Winston described Shinto temple rituals in detail. John took notes. Winston instructed his senior aide to make sure that Mr. Penn got the necessary letters of introduction in Japan, where Winston had so many friends and colleagues. "Not that any letters of introduction are required for a personage such as yourself!" Winston laughed, making John blush. Winston cheerfully obliged John's request that he pose for a Polaroid. John even got out his old Nikon for some color transparencies. After the photo session, Winston thanked John for the delicious lunch and wished him luck on all his ventures. Winston and his aides waved good-bye and Veronica wondered whether it was safe to relax.

# Helena for Dinner

**THREE DAYS AFTER THE LUNCH WITH WINSTON AN ENVELOPE** arrived at John's office with an invitation for John and Veronica to dinner with the Ferris family at the Park Legend. It was, of course, the last thing on the island of Manhattan that Veronica wanted to do. But Meryl said it would be "platinum A-list" and Veronica had to pay John back for all the free food, drinks, and parties he so generously and consistently provided.

The elevator opened upon Helena's new ochre hallway. There stood Wu, dressed in white.

"Oh wow, this place is huge!" John's tuxedo was frayed at the edges, and his white wig was tilting to the left. "Why don't you just move in here?"

"Ask my mother. I've been denied boarding rights."

"If the Chinese butler can stay here why can't you?"

"Wu knows how to behave at a party."

Wu bowed, took John and Veronica's coats and steered them down the hallway. Helena came forward smiling gloriously, arms outstretched, charm turned up full blast. Two bulbous ornaments swung from her earlobes. Her hair had been given its biannual overhaul to go with the "softer" makeup she was trying out.

"Veronica, John, how lovely to have you both. John, you've been so kind to look after Veronica. Being a diplomatic family, well, we were always traveling. I'm afraid we didn't prepare our children for America, so what a glorious surprise that someone's taken such an interest in her." Veronica was stunned. Helena really was a genius at condescension. In one deft stroke she'd reduced Veronica to a wayward kid and reincarnated John as a kindly guardian who'd agreed to look after her, as a family favor.

Helena slipped her arm through John's and escorted him to the freshly painted gold-and-green, sponge-patterned, semigloss, lavender-scented living room. Veronica trailed behind. She saw the dreaded Dolly Seabrook, but mercifully no Joan and Bill Hartman or Aaron Eastman. Bill Straw, her one trustworthy ally, was chatting with Suki Dean. Veronica felt a sharp pang of jealousy as she studied Suki Dean's bland composure, her shiny gold hair, her luxurious jewelry, her dermatologist-supervised complexion. Suki Dean's singular talent was looking great in restaurants, and with the honing of this skill she had secured an art gallery, a millionaire husband, peer jealousy, and approval from society columnists—all the things a Professional Beautiful Girl needed to be happy. All the things Veronica wasn't sure she needed or wanted, except for the millions.

"John, this is my friend Irene Haverford, one of my oldest and dearest."

"Hello, dear." Irene gave John a kiss. "I was one of his very first portraits, years ago. Isn't that right, John?" Helena didn't like hearing this; she wanted to be the first one of her group to have discovered John Penn.

"John, here's another mutual friend of ours, Dickie Drake!"

Veronica gulped. Dickie Drake! There he was, wearing a crisp tuxedo and twirling a martini glass in Helena's living room, appearing partially sober. So was it just money that secured Double-Life Insurance?

Dickie pumped John's hand. "Johnnie, old sport, I've made a reference to your religion series in my latest article. Helena, that outfit is a triumph."

"Dickie, you're too sweet. Jack, have you ever met John Penn?"

"We've moved past one another like rowboats through the cocktail hour. Greetings!" Jack Macomb shook John's hand with such speed and vigor that Veronica feared John's tiny phalanges might crumble. "My daughter wears your tee shirts."

"Did I make tee shirts?"

"It's a pink Mona Lisa. Is it still 'now'?"

"I don't know. What's she wearing now?"

"Penn, how good to have your company!" Winston greeted John warmly and summoned Wu to take his drink order. On Helena's arm the establishment exemplars who might otherwise have shunned John Penn or recoiled in fear now approached him with curiosity and wonder.

"Hey, Veronica, terrific to see you!" Oh Christ, Susan Hartman. "We've been following your adventures. You certainly got the mission in a fix with that interview! The Indian ambassador is still bothering us about it." Ah yes, Susan the parent-pleaser had beaten the odds and actually grown more obnoxious with age. But Susan's LSAT scores had done nothing for her weight problem or her lousy perm.

"So are you going to introduce me to Mr. Penn?"

"Oh, I thought you'd already met." Veronica bathed Susan in a sleek, fake smile. "So Susan, are you seeing anyone special?"

"I'm so busy with law school, I really don't have time." Susan fussed with her pearl necklace. *Correction, you're too fat and boring to get laid, let's be realistic here.*

"I have the perfect guy for you. Aaron Eastman. Dad just loves him."

"Aaron? Is he single?"

"I'll find out."

"Dinner is served!" Helena summoned all present to her gold-and-blue dining room, where the staff wore white gloves and jackets and the centerpieces coordinated with the official ivory-gold china that bore the U.S. seal.

John was seated center stage while Veronica was exiled to a stable in the far corner with Bill Straw and some of the second-tier diplomats.

"Who the hell gets impressed by that little eagle? It's on the Kleenex, for Chrissakes," Bill observed absentmindedly, finishing off his bourbon and starting in on the wine.

At the head of the table Helena tossed back her golden hair and laughed her gay, theatrical laugh to vanquish the insult to her prized china while John blushed with pride. Dinner was served, wine was poured, jokes were proffered, telephone numbers exchanged. After dessert, Helena summoned the guests into the living room for coffee.

Winston passed out cigars as the guests clustered around John, who was enthroned on the love seat.

"Mr. Penn, do you think realism is making a comeback?"

"No, everything's just as real now as it was last year."

"What do you think the Modernists are up to these days?"

"They're doing great. Robert just got married."

"The movement appears to have lost much of its vitality."

"But everyone takes so many vitamins now."

"It appears that the abstractionists are losing ground, correct?"

"Yeah, I know, Gerald had to sell his house 'cause his rent went up."

Helena poised herself on the sofa. She'd been conniving to outscore Irene Haverford on the portrait issue and had finally come up with a potential home run. "John, I've been asked to sit for an official portrait. Dickie thinks I should use an American Master, which of course means you!"

"Helena, I've always seen you as a grand Juno Lucetia, goddess of light, robed and garlanded!" exclaimed Dickie, twirling his cigar in the air.

"Helena's so beautifully adventurous. I'd be just too squeamish to get painted by Penn!" offered the British high commissioner's wife.

"So what do you think, Penn?" asked Winston.

"I'll do her as Lady Liberty."

"Oh gosh, I want one too!" cried Bitsy.

"Can I take Helena's picture?" John asked Winston, smiling like a little boy who wanted to try out the diving board.

"Of course you can. You two will have to begin your sitting schedule."

Helena posed by the Steinway, chin and eyebrows raised. John pulled his camera out from a pocket of his tuxedo and snapped furiously. Winston smiled and laughed. John seemed transcendently happy. Irene and Bitsy were maneuvering to get nearer to him, as Dickie Drake looked on in a state of inebriated amusement.

Veronica considered the possibility that success and old age had made John into another New York millionaire. But she had to admire him for it. After all, he was a businessman who needed clients, and the Benefit Lady circuit was thematically suited to his line of work. Veron-

ica curled her fingers around her wine glass, inhaled the mixed perfumes of coffee and cigars, which told her that Winston was near, ever
present and loving. He would reassure her that this wasn't the only
party in the world. This wasn't the only city in the world. *Remember, my
dear, maintain a double life.*

# Trespassing Alert

The following day, Meryl's column reported:

> At UN Ambassador Winston Ferris's nifty penthouse digs artist John Penn promised to produce a portrait of Helena as Lady Liberty for one of the walls. Wasting no time, Mr. Penn whipped out a camera and took his first test roll right then and there. Madame Helena, who was snapped by Beaton when but a mere tyke, will be the first Ambassadress to be Penned. Other new Penn pals Suki Dean and Bitsy Whittle have lined up appointments. Will Mrs. Ferris get a commission? "I'm flattered to be portrayed as Lady Liberty. I need no other compensation," quoth she.

"Oh, Veronica, we have a surprise for you!" Tad was straightening placemats and organizing silverware on the table. "Your mom's coming for lunch!"

"Lunch? Today?"

"Yes—and look, she's here!"

Veronica heard Helena's distinctive voice and the rustle of her coat. Then there she was, striding into the lunch room with Dolly Seabrook. Dinner at the Park Legend was one thing. This was trespassing.

"Hello, Veronica, we were hoping you'd join us." Helena was decked out in blue leather, a racier look than her dutiful State Department Spouse couture. Dolly Seabrook had on a bulbous jacket with a polka dot bow, as if there weren't enough bad clothes in the world.

"Here's the new *Page*." John passed a copy to Dolly and Helena.

"Oh, isn't that marvelous." Helena flipped through the magazine. "We were so surprised, a few months back, when you put Veronica on the cover. After all, she hadn't done anything."

"We knew she'd be big someday so now we can say we had her first." John explained, smiling gallantly, much to Veronica's relief.

"John, this magazine is just so original," Helena continued. "You have a truly remarkable eye." Veronica suppressed the desire to remind Helena that until very recently she'd referred to *Page* as "a tabloid for deviants."

"Now that Helena's a bestselling cookbook author I'll bet you have big plans for her with your magazine, Mr. Penn!" Dolly gushed, flashing John her of-course-I'm-in-the-Social-Register smile. John blinked quizzically and turned to Helena.

"Why don't you profile all the visiting heads of state for us?" John suggested. "They stay at the Park Legend. You can just have them over for breakfast."

"Well, yes, I could indeed," Helena replied. "Oh, what a lovely picture of Carol. I didn't know she was on the dinner committee for the Cancer Ball."

"You just missed Judy Stone and Valerie Vale. They're doing a big Leukemia Benefit," said John.

"Those Leukemia people are just adorable!" Dolly piped in. "I love that new doctor at the uptown blood center. Helena, are you going to the Skin Cancer Party at the Pierre on Tuesday?"

"No, that's Nancy Driscoll's benefit and she and I aren't speaking." Helena replied.

"You aren't? Why not?" Dolly asked.

Veronica saw John's pale fingers creeping toward the tape recorder.

"Nancy would repress a cure for AIDS if it helped fill the tables. And she stole my list."

"Your list?"

"My fundraising list! It had home numbers, not just offices. Nancy used it for the melanoma research she's promoting at Mount Sinai, which isn't pure science. The doctor gives her free face work in exchange for that annual dinner."

"What's wrong with that? Face work is expensive," said Tad, reasonably.

"But Nancy looks great! I saw her last week at the ballet party," said John.

"Don't tell me she's now on the dinner committee for the ballet!" cried Dolly. "That's my charity!"

Suddenly, John, Tad, Dolly, and Helena had formed a harmonious quartet, smiling and pointing to pictures in the magazine, talking about people they knew and restaurants they liked. Helena was sparkling and merry, John was eager and amused. Veronica flipped through her notebook in order to avoid eye contact with them. She wanted everyone to think she was fine with the new alliance forged over lunch; to show her dismay would grant victory to Helena.

But Veronica wasn't finished with her Penn Girl life. She just had to get into a different venue, where Maya Smith could do the talking.

# Free Tibet and
# Free Martinis

**IT WAS SATURDAY NIGHT, IT WAS BENEFIT SEASON, AND JOHN** had donated a painting to a Tibet benefit at Luna Ticks. Inside the club Tibetan monks in maroon cotton robes were crammed between models and actresses with contoured calves and plunging cleavage.

John pulled Veronica's coat sleeve. "Who's that woman in the purple pants? I think I'm supposed to know her." John pointed to a mid-career hipster chick in purple harem pants, spangled boots, piles of antique silver jewelry, and out-of-date, henna-soaked hair, who darted from monk to model and back to monk. Within twenty-five seconds she appeared at John's side.

"Well, hello, John! It's me! Jet Lag Janey!"

"Oh yeah, Janey, hey, this is Veronica. She's Covergirl and she grew up in Asia."

"So you made Covergirl, no less. Then you really should meet Namgyal Rinpoche!" Janey pointed to an elegant, seasoned Tibetan gentleman who was heartily enjoying himself as several glamorous Benefit Ladies fussed over who would get to host his next event.

"Who's Namgyal Rinpoche?" Veronica asked.

Janey rolled her eyes and replied, "Only *the* most important Dzogchen teacher in North America. Christ, that movie slut's got him, I don't believe it!"

Rinpoche was now graciously explaining an obscure feature of Buddhist doctrine to the awed starlet in a faux snakeskin mini-dress.

"Oh fuck it, let's get a drink." Janey steered John and Veronica into a velvet banquette with two women. One was Flemish, cute and cheerful, swathed in beige spandex, the other Slavic and humorless, in nomad jewelry and a maroon beret.

"You know what's wrong with this party?" said Jet Lag Janey, as she wedged herself between John and Veronica. "No good Khampa hunting."

"What's a Khampa?" asked the Flemish girl.

"What's a Khampa!" Janey howled. "Check the round table in the back corner." The Slavic woman pointed to the back. All eyes turned toward three outrageously handsome Tibetan men with black ponytails, hooded eyes, and, on closer inspection, knives dangling from studded leather belts. Veronica wondered why Davey Name wasn't here tonight, sitting at the Khampa table, instead of recording somewhere in the Caribbean.

"Imagine an Apache Indian plus Buddhism."

"Gamblers, thieves, fabulous horsemen, incredible lovers . . ."

"Saved the life of the Dalai Lama."

"Killed a lot of Chi-Coms."

"Buddhists who kill."

"A real one always carries a knife," said Janey.

"I thought everyone wanted a Pathan these days," said John, innocently.

"Pathans are so over!" Jet Lag Janey laughed. "Ever met a Khampa, Veronica?"

"Yes, I have."

"Fake ones, visa-hunting, I'm sure," Janey bristled.

*Uber-bitch, aren't you?* Veronica thought.

A man in a green velvet jacket suddenly appeared, gamely shook John's hand, and lowered himself next to Veronica.

"Hey, Norbu! Meet Veronica, our new Covergirl!" John beamed.

Veronica looked again. Was it—yes, he was the man from the Modern Antique Showroom, the one who caught her preening in the mirror!

John pressed into her shoulder and whispered, "Mr. Norbu's one of the richest art dealers in Hong Kong! He talked his way out of a Shanghai jail, then smuggled three Tang Dynasty Buddha heads into Tokyo and made a million dollars three days later. He's always got great jewelry." This was quite the resume. John was giving her that needy, anxious, please-flirt-with-him-if-only-for-my-sake look.

"I recognize your dzi bead." Mr. Norbu fixed a cool stare at Veronica, yielding nothing.

"We met at the Jarewallas' gallery."

"Yes. I remember both the dzi bead and your eyes."

"My eyes?"

"Yes. They have a strong color. Like a good gem."

"I see." Veronica couldn't help but smile and affix her violet eyes upon Mr. Norbu. "Do you live in New York?"

"I am just here for business. I live in Kathmandu." Mr. Norbu dipped his pipe into a tobacco pouch. Veronica noticed a five-pointed emerald gleaming on his left index finger. He then leaned back into his chair, lit his pipe, faced Veronica and commenced a full frontal Khampa X-ray. Speaking Tibetan was the only way Veronica could defend herself. She had tried and failed to survive a semester of Modern Colloquial Tibetan in college. Unlike Nepali or Hindi, where you could warble along with a few key phrases, once you attempted speaking Tibetan with an actual Tibetan, the Tibetan shot back incomprehensible sounds that left you mute, shamed, and perplexed.

"I lived in Kathmandu once, for a short time, a long time ago. It's, uh, phey yakbudu." There, the one line of Tibetan she could remember. Maybe that would throw him off balance.

"Aha, you know Tibetan?"

"Just a little."

"Tibetan is a very difficult language. It is not like Hindi, because it is tonal." The Khampa X-ray began snaking its way down her torso, toward her hips. Really, Khampas were worse than English rock stars.

"Tibetan has only three main tones, and three dialects: Kham-key, Am-key, and U-key, for Tibet's three provinces."

Khampas always did the X-ray in public so you had to pretend that you didn't notice, and they didn't actually touch you so you couldn't really say anything. She had to maintain a semblance of cool. She uncrossed her legs, flipped her hair, and resolved to take control of the situation. "I thought Cantonese had eight tones, more than Mandarin," Veronica replied. But it was no use, she could feel herself blushing furiously.

Mr. Norbu was now puffing contentedly on his pipe, enjoying her distress. "Thai has five tones, Mandarin has only four tones. I believe that Japanese has seven."

Veronica tried staring back at him to see what difference it would make—none, just as she suspected. She longed for the benign predictability of a coke-fueled European playboy. In terms of sexual self-confidence and all-around machismo, Mr. Norbu rendered Occo positively undergraduate.

Mr. Norbu then slipped a long cord of lapis lazuli over Veronica's neck and clasped it, in one swift gesture, lifting his hand off just before reaching her breast. "Take this. It's an old piece."

And then, on cue, the mysteriously clever Mr. Norbu embarked on a new torture technique, which was to ignore Veronica altogether and redirect his attention to a nubile Frenchwoman who had squeezed in next to John. This was Part Two of the Khampa treatment, highly effective because now Veronica was annoyed and wanted him to pay attention.

The Free Tibet people began passing out media packages in shiny folders. The press release read: "It's been half a century since China invaded Tibet. Half a century of economic, cultural, and environmental disaster. Now, you can take a proactive stance on Tibet's freedom. You can join our interactive Free Tibet dialogue. Find out more. Rangzen is what we're all about."

Rangzen, the Tibetan word for independence and the theme of countless songs, poems, and prayers, was no longer a sacred principle bequeathed unto a tiny fold gathered in tents, halls, and restaurants in a fragile diaspora scattered across the Indian subcontinent. Now it was an international movement, and a fashionable excuse for a party. Veronica had always mistrusted this missionary impulse to "save Asia's toiling millions." What effect did another season of black-tie balls and club fundraisers really have on Asia's toiling millions? What was next, a Prisoner of the Month Club?

"Shhhh!" a fierce blonde in red sneakers and an ill-fitting Tibetan chuba glared at Veronica and John's banquette, where the nubile French-woman was vigorously gossiping with Jet Lag Janey. The lights dimmed and one Mr. Todd Feele ascended to the podium. Todd's curly hair puffed above his brow whenever he emphasized a point of great significance. A lot of what he said was pure nonsense, such as, "In Tibet, it's a sin to kill even a fly!" If memory served, Winston's Khampa friends devoured steaks like candy and disdained the mere suggestion of salad. Todd then blathered on about "activism engenderment" and "power-sharing deliverables" and the "gender equality matrix." He detailed plans for an elaborate boycott of Chinese goods and instructed all present to "shop with a conscience" and think about "the karma of procurement."

Mr. Todd continued, "Now Tibet faces a new threat: China's growing wealth. As Napoleon famously said, 'When China wakes the world will tremble . . .'"

"Who's Napoleon?" asked a young Tibetan in the front row.

". . . This is a battle that I am proud to be a part of. It is a fight about truth, dignity, the definition of human values, the soul of man. It's about being change. It's about being right."

Veronica saw a deejay readying his turntables, and several rock 'n' rollers lurching near the podium. So this was the new PR methodology: Free Tibet through Rock 'n' Roll. This was something Veronica, and John, could support.

Mr. Todd finished his speech and joined them at the banquette. "We're doing some serious fundraising for our outreach initiative, so we really need you to put your money where your mouth is."

"And what is this campaign for?" asked Mr. Norbu.

"We're mobilizing on campuses. We want to develop an electronic dialogue with members, stuff like that."

"Don't you think you should listen to what real, actual Tibetans are saying?" asked Veronica. "It might help you to be a better advocate."

"Excuse me, but who are you?" Todd huffed.

"Veronica." She smiled at Todd, cool and precise. She was exceedingly familiar with his type; he was one of those humorless anti-globalization crusaders who knew much more than you about everything because he was so uniquely sensitive, and of course it was understood that emotion was more important than research.

"Well, Veronica, to answer your question, it's our job to be a voice for the voiceless, so we're conceptualizing some action initiatives which the Tibetans haven't been able to create independently."

"Just remember that it's easy for us to transplant ideas from the First World, but very often they don't work when you're back in Asia."

"Excuse me, Veronica, but I really don't see what you bring to the table."

"She comes from a very important family!" said Janey, unhelpfully.

"Okay, fine." Todd shoved papers into a file folder. "But you're a new face around here, so watch out." Todd skulked off to the bar. Just in case Veronica had forgotten the manifold charms of American boys from good colleges, Todd had most skillfully reminded her.

"I don't like the way he talked to you," said Mr. Norbu.

"That's right!" sputtered Janey. "Don't let him talk to you like that!"

"You know more than he does," said John.

"And what is he? Definitely a low-caste," added Mr. Norbu, who was now leaning back into his chair, twirling his prayer beads. He then fixed his gaze back on Veronica and announced, "Veronica should sing for us," knowing full well that under the heavy weight of the Khampa X-ray she would have no choice.

"Great idea!" cried John.

"Okay, okay, slow down—" Veronica gulped.

"Sing a Tibetan song!" someone shouted.

"Yes, sing a Tibetan song!" someone agreed.

"But I—"

"Come on, do it!"

Veronica felt all eyes settling on her as John steered her to the stage and put the microphone in her hand. John introduced her as Maya Smith. She was all alone now in the spotlight, and everyone was staring at her expectantly. She closed her eyes, willing herself to dive in headfirst. From somewhere, buried deep in childhood memory, came a song she had heard around Winston's campfire in Nepal, a song of the Old Tibet, a nomad's song of haunting beauty. When she opened her lips, the words and the melody came effortlessly and entwined with the deejay's lush electronica. Everyone in the room began to clap in time. By the time she finished the song, everyone, except Todd and the red-sneakered blonde, was standing and cheering.

"Sing another one!"

"Yeah, sing another one!"

"Free Tibet!"

"Yes, do it, Maya Smith!"

Veronica remembered her secret—that dance parties were the universal equalizer, and in the Golden Age of Globalization, the lingua franca of the five continents was rock 'n' roll. And there being no time like the present, why not just *make something up!*

"Here's a song I'd like to dedicate to—to all Tibetan Freedom Fighters. It's called—" In the far corner, by the banquette, she could see Mr. Norbu's green jacket and the silver-blue smoke rising from his pipe. "—it's called 'Khampa Boy.'"

*Got off the plane, went on a mission*
*I heard a story, I had a vision*
*I had to follow the boy with the long hair*
*But I looked everywhere, he wasn't there!*
*Escaped from suburbia I'm barely alive*
*You've been in the mountains so you survived*
*You're everything I want to be, oh don't you see*
*Baby I'm the refugee, you gotta rescue me*
*Khampa Boy—where did you go*
*Khampa Boy—you gotta let me know*
*Khampa Boy—I want to see you again*
*Baby you just gotta tell me when . . .*

When her song was over, the room erupted in screams and applause. Veronica bowed and smiled and floated back to the table and slid into the seat next to John, who was gleaming with paternal pride. She felt all eyes beaming toward her, including Mr. Norbu's, and it felt absolutely fantastic.

# Permanent Change

**"HERE SHE IS, MAYA SMITH!"**

"Hello, Miss Smith. We saw you perform at the Tibet Benefit last night."

"We thought you were fabulous! What language were you singing in?"

"English. And Tibetan."

"She speaks eight languages!" John piped in. He was sitting at the far end of the lunch table, watching Veronica field questions from the event promoter, the account executive, and the creative consultants and stylists who were planning the Superparty video shoot that John was coproducing.

"We'd like you to be in our Superparty video. We'll be shooting in Paris, next week."

"Next week?"

"I'm going with you," John said, as Tad examined details of the contract.

"We want you to do just what you did last night. The Tibetan thing, then that Khampa Boy song. Is that copyrighted?"

"And talk about your Disco Theory and Practice."

"World Peace through Dance!" "I love that—so practical!"

Veronica smiled. "I've written a song you might like. It's called 'Disco Darshan.'"

"Perfect. We need a theme song."

"What's darshan?"

"It's Sanskrit for holy vision."

"Holy vision!"

"But we don't want to alarm the Indian delegation—"

"Don't worry, we're billing you as Maya Smith."

"Let's make the case for globalization. It's under assault from the left and right and they're all wrong."

"We like your concept of the skyscraper as illuminated lingam."

"And rock star as demi-god. We love that."

"And the Intercontinental Party Girl Tool Kit—we love that too."

"So Veronica, we're putting you in the Davey Name sequence. As Maya Smith. The Tibetan Madonna."

John stared at her, dyed eyelashes quivering. "That was Mr. Norbu's idea."

"Mr. Norbu?"

"Oh, you have to invite Mr. Norbu!"

Apparently Mr. Norbu understood how to manage a successful double life. Which reminded Veronica that if she was soon to be flying to Europe, she'd need to replenish her international party girl supply kit. Quickly.

# Gemology

**DIAMONDS, SAPPHIRES, AMETHYSTS, ROPES OF GARNETS, GOLD** bangles, silver pendants, rubies from Burma, Nepalese turquoise, amber and coral, lapis from Afghanistan, Indian emeralds—they all sparkled and gleamed in Veronica's hands. Helena and Winston were in Washington for a state dinner so the Park Legend was penetrable. She found the Indian necklace with the blue sapphires and held it up to the light. It was her sixteenth birthday gift from Shanta's mother, the Rana princess. Helena had decided to keep it and wear it, for "security" reasons. In the farthest recesses of the bottom drawer, Veronica discovered the topaz necklace from Burma that Winston had been saving for her twenty-first birthday, an event that had come and gone without so much as a perfunctory dinner at the UNICEF cafeteria.

With a queasy mix of entitlement and guilt, she stashed the topaz and sapphire necklaces in her purse. She paused to study an especially radiant diamond brooch, given to Helena by a Javanese diplomat when the family lived in Jakarta. How strange that these iridescent little stones wielded so much power in human affairs. What was a diamond, after all, but a piece of charcoal under pressure, exhumed and sold to a beautiful woman in a European boutique? Veronica preferred jewels to money. Jewels, like beautiful women, were a valid currency on five continents, and you didn't have to exchange either at a bank when you traveled.

The clock hummed and chimed on the mantle. It was late. She had to go home and pack and meet John's limo, which would take them to the airport. Wu stood in the kitchen doorway, holding a towel and a silver candlestick.

"Hi, Miss Lonya. You stay here?"

"Hi, Wu. No, I'm going away."

"You go away?"

"Yes."

Wu yawned and nodded as Veronica went out the door and into the elevator. All the well-groomed, well-rested, healthy, respectable people with mutual funds, stock dividends, and health insurance stared at Veronica as she stepped into the elevator and out into the lobby. She strolled past the clothing boutiques with the sequined frocks and feathered jackets, the inadequate bookstore, the travel agency, to the Modern Antique Showroom. The space was thick with the mingled scents of jasmine, tobacco, and turmeric, and newly aglow with pink walls and a display of tantric paintings.

"Miss Veronica! You sang very well last night." It was Mr. Norbu, stroking his pipe and leaning against the doorframe.

"Oh well, thanks." She tried to smooth out her hair, she hated being caught unadorned and by surprise. "I hope you liked my new song."

"Khampa Boy! Very clever. My mother would cry to hear it." Mr. Norbu began to laugh, a sincere and reassuring laugh. "I didn't like those people. But we Tibetans are a small band of refugees so we can't always pick our friends."

"So how do you manage people you don't like?"

"You don't have to like someone to get something out of them. How do you think I built my business?"

"How did you build your business?"

"Always assume that your friend becomes your enemy and your enemy becomes your friend. You can only control your own luck—but only if you try very hard to protect your good luck. You never know where you will make it or lose it."

"It helps to wear a lucky stone."

"Of course. But first you must know which stones are lucky for you. Let's see what would work for you—which stones, which styles.

Everyone is different." Veronica allowed Mr. Norbu to dangle ropes of lapis lazuli, coral, and turquoise across her wrists and neck as he described various techniques of bronze casting and metallurgy; the reason why sapphires were unstable and diamonds were benign and rubies were preferred by some Asian royals over others. He brushed against her thigh as he slipped a topaz ring on one finger, an emerald on another. Shanta Rana was always talking about which gems were best to wear on the full moon and on the new moon, which for attracting and repelling men, and so on and so forth. Veronica wondered if it really worked, if such magic could be coaxed from a stone.

"So you believe in the power of—these rocks?" she asked Mr. Norbu.

"Of course. They help protect your good luck. There are three kinds of luck, la, sok, tse. You have to find out what kind you lack. I think . . . you need an emerald."

"I was born in July. I thought my lucky stone was the ruby."

"For you, I would say . . . diamonds are lucky."

"Why diamonds?"

"Because diamonds will protect your life force. You have it flashing out of you, too fast. Your eyes are a very unusual color. A shade of lavender. Like an amethyst. Maybe you need less beauty, not more. Too much will attract all kinds of pretas. Look here."

Mr. Norbu then pointed to a large eighteenth-century Tibetan painting in the center of the room. It was comprised of many small diagrams depicting the various planes of existence inside a wheel clutched by a vermillion-skinned demon, symbolic of maya, illusion, craving and desire.

"You understand what it is?"

"The Wheel of Samsara," replied Veronica like a good student.

"Now look closer." He pointed to a diagram of naked bodies writhing in the jaws of black demons. "These are pretas. The hungry ghosts. They have lost a human body so they can only satisfy their cravings for food and drink by attaching to those who have human bodies. It is the cause of drug and liquor addictions. They're very tenacious. You have to perform a special puja to get rid of them. I know you like to go to those kinds of places, to dance, so you should have protection."

Veronica could see exhausted patrons loitering about in a dark, unhealthy place, stalked by parasites. The image did resemble Travesty or Kitsch on a bad night. She could also feel Mr. Norbu's eyes roaming over her body, as if they knew she was carrying something valuable with her. She felt her hand reach into her coat pocket, lift out the sapphire necklace and hand it to him. He clutched it, and for an instant she feared that by some exercise of magic he would make it disappear.

"These stones are dangerous. They may cause an accident," Mr. Norbu said. "Don't forget that gems have a life of their own. They will outlive us, they will go through many different owners. It is said that they bring people together, or pull them apart.

"Well, well, Miss Ferris! Your mother has been purchasing some miniatures lately from us!" Mr. Jarewalla hung up the phone and swirled over to Veronica's side, rubbing his hands and radiating a businessman's specious joviality. His hair was longer and shinier and his cheeks a tad fuller, signs of prosperity. "Miss Ferris is most partial to our food as well." Mr. Jarewalla motioned toward the back room where frangipani incense was rising in thin gray sheets before the shrine. Mr. Norbu held Veronica's gems against the lamp to study the facets.

"Thanks, but I really can't stay—" Veronica snatched the sapphire necklace from Mr. Norbu's hands and ran into the lobby, into the ladies lounge. She locked the door and peered into the mirror, at her taut white skin, her auburn hair, and her strange lavender-blue eyes, which seemed to spin and twirl as they intersected shafts of light from the lamps and mirrors. They were her gemstones, and they would take her to Paris, out of Manhattan, where she could resume her double life and be alone with Davey Name.

# Dress to Confess

**MERYL LAY ON THE COUCH, TRIMMING HER NAILS WITH A**
sewing scissors while Veronica stuffed clothes into a duffle bag.

"So Veronica, you understand, right? You call me collect from Paris. The more details you give me, the better. I'll plug you a lot in the column. Are you flying over with Tiger?"

"Tiger Street?"

"Yeah. Do you know any other Tigers?"

"She's not going."

"Yes she is. She's really nice. We had lunch with her yesterday. She's covering the collections for *Page*. What, you don't read the papers?"

"No. I mean, sometimes. Maybe."

"Man, you are so not on the ball." Meryl threw the *Star* at Veronica. Page 3 showed a large photograph of Tiger above Meryl's story:

Tiger Roars for Penn! Who knows fashion better than Tiger the Cat? Nobody, says John Penn, who's putting the luscious London-born mannequin to work as fashion correspondent for his soon-to-debut Superparty TV show. Tiger wouldn't deny the rumor that she and rock warbler Davey Name are finally going to commence their nuptial countdown. "If I told you the date I'd be letting the cat out of the bag!" Tiger purred. Nonetheless, pals of the celebrity twosome say the Paris jaunt will be more than just a business trip.

Veronica neatly folded the paper and resumed packing. "Are they getting married?"

"Tiger and Davey?" Meryl began cleaning under her nails with the edge of the scissors. "She wants it really bad. We really connected at lunch so I thought I'd help her out by printing the rumor to nudge him along." She gave her cuticles a final shaping with her teeth. "She could give you a lot of advice. You should hang out with her."

"That might be a bit awkward since I'm sleeping with her boyfriend."

"You're sleeping with Davey Name?"

"Yes, I am."

"Why the fuck didn't you tell me before?"

"I couldn't tell anyone. If I told anyone I'd never see him again."

Meryl's brow relaxed into thoughtful concentration. "Yeah, I see your point." She leaned back and knotted her freshly manicured fingers under her chin. "So what's he like?"

"Charming, handsome, aloof."

"Is Tiger wise to this?"

"I don't know. I'd appreciate it if you'd hold the story until further notice."

"He's a bad bet. I've checked his files. Tiger's the first girl he's stayed with for more than a year."

"Davey's perfect."

"What do you mean he's perfect?"

"Rock stars should never get married. It's unfair to their fans." Yes, it was just *wrong* for any kind of professional sex symbol to appear monogamous, let alone have children. It violated all the rules; it was worse than watching them get old or fat.

"I'm telling you, get an agent. If we leak the Davey Name stuff in the right way it'll get you a lot of coverage," Meryl advised, grabbing a beer out of the fridge.

Veronica opened the envelope from John's office and examined the ticket and itinerary. Round trip, first class, Air France. Jet lag was a very small price to pay for hopping over the Atlantic Ocean.

# PART II

# A Long Weekend in Paris

# Superparty

**"NOW, THE IDEA IS THAT AFTER YEARS OF SEARCHING, YOU'VE** finally found it—the longest, wildest party in the world!" The director was earnestly motivating the crowd for the Superparty video while the assistant director provided an awkward translation for the European extras.

The event publicist guided a woman to John and Veronica's table. She wore a green corduroy suit and her perm had degenerated into a pale-blonde mini-afro, arising cloud-like from her distressed pink forehead. Veronica immediately pegged her as a tabloid matron.

"John, Veronica, this is Beth Armstrong from the *Mirror*. She's doing a story about Superparty." After the requisite shaking of hands Ms. Armstrong opened her notebook and aimed her tape recorder at John.

"Mr. Penn, why are you going into TV?"

"Because everyone's doing it."

"I see." Ms. Armstrong blinked and nodded, trying to figure out what she was missing. "I'm wondering how this show is going to innovate. What's going to make people stop the dial on Superparty and say, 'This is exciting, groundbreaking television!'"

"Because everyone likes to look at Davey Name, and Veronica wrote one of the songs."

Ms. Armstrong shifted her equipment and attention toward Veronica.

"So, Ms. Ferris, how do you write your songs?"

"With a pen."

"Oh." Ms. Armstrong twitched awkwardly in her upholstered suit. "So why do you write rock songs?"

*Oh please, can't you do better than that?* "Because people like them."

"Ms. Ferris, you've had a very privileged upbringing. You've moved in elite circles. You come from two prominent American families—the Ferrises and the MacDouglases are both in the Social Register. And here you are, with John Penn and Davey Name."

"Yes, isn't it wonderful?" Veronica smiled. Ms. Armstrong had misplayed her hand, had revealed herself to be a hostile force before luring out any choice details.

"Aren't your parents upset with your, ah, career direction?"

"Why would they be upset?"

Ms. Armstrong scowled, having anticipated a confession. "Well, because rock and roll is not something that an educated person, uh, woman would . . ." Beth's cheeks puffed unattractively. ". . . Rock is part of the drug counterculture—"

"Rock concerts have raised millions for all sorts of good causes. Do you object to raising funds for charity?"

"In your case I am sure that people wonder why you are more interested in spending time partying at clubs instead of doing charity work, like your mother."

"My mother went to plenty of clubs when she was my age." *These stupid questions, as if anyone cared. Why the hell do I have to explain myself to this overweight nobody?* Veronica lit her first filterless French cigarette of the day and donned a look of contempt. Ms. Armstrong twitched moodily and turned back to John. What was it about these tabloid people, crouched behind the protective armor of "the public's right to know?" They invaded your privacy, misinterpreted your remarks, gathered quotes from rivals, and forced you to lie to them. And they frequently looked awful, like this portly slattern, insensible of the effect corduroy pants had on her bulging thighs, yet they had the audacity to condemn you for not thoroughly combing your hair. It was infuriating to think how much power they had.

"Thanks for your time." Beth Armstrong closed her notebook and heaved herself off the chair. "Oh, Veronica, before I forget, Sandy Graver says hello. He's a very old friend of mine."

Oh, no—Sandy Graver! Obviously he had primed his esteemed colleague Ms. Armstrong, and this was his revenge for that night at Travesty, when the callous party slut Veronica Ferris locked him out of the VIP section after getting in on his ticket.

"Hey, John, the show looks great!" The jowly, nicotine-stained director took a seat next to Veronica. "Listen, let's cut party talk for a minute. I want you to tell me what you really want, career-wise, 'cause when I heard your song 'Disco Darshan,' I heard potential."

"She wants to be famous," John snapped.

"How famous?"

"More famous than Tiger Street."

"No, I don't!" Veronica interjected.

"Why not?" John looked wounded.

"How many songs have you got?" asked the director.

"My work habits are unpredictable."

"Veronica!" John jabbed her with his elbow.

"No problem, you only need three a year."

"Alright, turn it up!" the choreographer commanded from a go-go column. The lights, music, and smoke machines went to work. Everyone shrieked as Tiger Street entered, hair and limbs flashing, exploiting every opportunity to flaunt herself by adjusting a shoe, tightening her belt, pushing her blonde hair from shoulder to shoulder. Davey came dancing through the crowd, magnetizing all the women—and all the men. He slid his arms around waists, ran his mouth over necks and shoulders, pressed against hips, played with hair. He danced over to John's table and slid next to Veronica.

"Hey, Tiger's splitting tonight, so let's have dinner. Suite 508." Davey squeezed her thigh under the table and danced away, all hair and muscle and boots, grabbing everything he wanted. It wasn't fair to let sensuous, dramatic people get away with all manner of selfish, exploitive behavior, but what were you going to say to them? *No thanks, don't want to bask in your charisma for a few minutes, I'd rather do something dull?* Davey pulled a delicate, shabbily dressed girl to his chest, let his arms and lips travel up and down her body. Veronica saw Tiger's face twitch in pain. She was no longer the magnificent supermodel; she was just another unhappy woman with an unfaithful boyfriend. Davey continued carrying on with the girl, writhing against her and devouring her lips. Veronica felt no jealousy, just a vague irritation. After all, it was Davey's job to seduce the world with his sex appeal, but he wasn't even remotely gracious about it, was he? *To humiliate Davey Name, just once, now that would be a real accomplishment.* What was his fatal weakness? It had to be his vanity.

When the shooting wrapped, the crew and the extras and the hangers-on headed toward the refreshment table. Beth Armstrong ran after Davey and Tiger with her tape recorder. Veronica was heading toward the back exit when John came around the corner, hugging his knapsack.

"Veronica! You're going to be a star!"

"If you say so, I'll believe you."

"What, you want to be an extra? Not when you're old you don't. I'm leaving for New York tonight. Don't forget, you have to get back in time for your mother's benefit!"

"I will."

"Don't forget to call me!"

"I won't." She watched John's white hands and hair slide into the limo. And then he was gone. She took a deep, steadying breath. She was in Paris, with its glowing cafes, superior pharmacies, indulgent stationery stores, markets, gardens and medieval churches, and the crisp, chestnut aroma of the streets. There wasn't any reason to rush back to Manhattan, which was waiting, bored and filthy, to devour her. All the more reason to relax and have dinner with Davey Name.

# Dinner with Friends

EVERYONE IN THE RESTAURANT, EXCEPT THE ALGERIAN BUS-
boys, recognized Davey and Guy as the maître d' seated them at a table.
Guy, a French matinee idol, was dashing and weary, his skin stretched
tight over his cheekbones, exhausted eyes in perpetual battle with his
mouth. He'd brought a girlfriend named Yvette, who made a great
show of leaping up and down, ostensibly in pursuit of cigarettes or a
menu, anything that would provide an opportunity to show off her ass,
squeezed as it was into orange pants. Guy and Davey, the two superstars,
talked only to each other, leaving Yvette and Veronica to play with
jewelry and compare lipsticks. Actually, it was kind of tedious to be
around hugely successful people. They didn't need companions, just
cheerleaders.

"Veronica, what are you doing here?"

Veronica froze, cigarette and wine glass in midair, instantly sensing
that her double life was in danger. Exposed and powerless, she turned
and saw Bernard and Gail Hochst, two humorless neocon academics,
friends of the family. Gail was resolutely bland, with brown hair tucked
into an anachronistic bun. Bernard was uniformly round—glasses,
torso, shining forehead. They were ever determined to buck trendiness
in order to safeguard traditional values, such as long-term marriages
and short hair. Bernard had just published a book in which he blamed
rock 'n' roll and the Democrats for everything from America's declin-
ing auto industry performance to the demise of the Broadway musical.

And here he was, face-to-face with the enemy, Davey Name—the single individual, besides John Penn, chiefly responsible for the decay of Western civilization.

"Uh, Bernard Hochst, this is Davey." Veronica smiled miserably as Bernard bravely extended a hand toward the rock star.

"Sorry, I didn't catch your name?" asked Davey. Bernard stiffened; he assumed that everyone knew who he was.

"Bernard Hochst!"

"Pleasure."

"And this is my wife Gail."

"Hello." Davey shook Gail's hand and turned back to Yvette, who was asking him to please light her cigarette.

"Veronica, you've lost a lot of weight!" Gail exclaimed.

"She has?" Davey's interest perked.

"She looks too thin." Gail, the New York intellectual, was always the first to bring up issues like weight loss and skin trouble.

"You're the singer, aren't you?" Bernard blurted.

"I'm sorry?" Davey looked up. Yvette groaned.

"Aren't you the singer?" Bernard repeated.

"I sing on occasion." Davey turned to face Bernard squarely. A waiter barked at Bernard and Gail, who were stubbornly blocking the aisle. Veronica tried to fathom their motivation for refusing to go away. Either they were riveted by curiosity or they expected Veronica to ask them to join the table, a completely insane thought.

"Mr. Name, I mentioned you in my book." Bernard had decided that it was time to get professional. "I called your last album a 'meretricious exploitation of adolescent angst.'" Bernard glowed with pride as he quoted himself.

Davey smiled, politely. "Thanks for the news. I'm always curious to hear what the academics are saying. I rather thought you'd dismissed us long ago."

Having anticipated a fight, Bernard was at a loss. "Don't you feel a sense of responsibility for the mess your music has made of things?"

"I'm sorry?"

"The poor kids who get wrapped up in your cult."

"I'm not aware of any cult, Mr.—I'm sorry, what was your name again?"

"Hochst! Bernard!"

"No one is under any obligation to purchase any of my albums. They buy it if they like the way it sounds."

"On the contrary, your music has triggered a moral crisis!"

"And how is that?"

"Because you, I mean, your songs promote irresponsibility, sexual experimentation and . . . and . . ." Bernard was sweating. ". . . and you take liberties with the English language!"

"So I should . . . call the syntax police?" Davey grinned, brilliantly. Guy and Yvette laughed. Veronica wanted to kiss him with gratitude.

Refilling his wineglass, Davey continued, "I don't think the kids pay that much attention to the lyrics in any case. Shouldn't you be more concerned about things like selling nukes to Third-World dictators? Bit more worrisome, I'd say."

"Look, we're trying to eat, okay?" Guy waved at Bernard as if he were a dog looking for scraps under the table.

"Come on Bernard, let's go." Gail steered her husband away.

"Have a nice time in Paris!" Veronica called after them. She would have preferred to say something nasty or clever, but inspiration failed. Her double life now lay in a crumpled heap on the bistro floor.

"Who were those people? They were so mean to Davey!" Yvette gave Davey a supportive kiss. Guy gnawed on a steak bone. Veronica gulped the last of the Bordeaux.

Davey embraced Yvette with one hand and seized Veronica with the other. "Hey, Guy, let's go to that dance parlor of yours." Yvette squealed with delight as she and Davey slid out of the booth. Guy paid the bill as Veronica trailed glumly behind.

But once they reached the club Veronica's mood lightened considerably. Champagne arrived, as did tarts and groupies. Guy and Davey lit cigars and humored girls. An English groupie pushed her way onto Guy's lap. She had the requisite sexless body shorn of breasts and hips, and a lot of work had gone into her hair and nails, but her makeup was melting and she didn't have much of a chin. Veronica recognized her from the Superparty shoot. She was an extra who kept trying to get close to Davey. What was her name, Robin, Oriole? Something winged.

"So are you happy to finally meet your idol, Mr. Davey Name?" Guy pushed the girl off his lap. "Now you have to impress him."

"Just—tell me what to do!"

"What, you will sing for us?"

"Me? No, no, I can't sing—"

"Don't sing then, just tell us your name." Veronica smiled at the girl.

"I'm Lark."

"Hi, Lark. My name's Davey."

"Mr. Name, I love love *love* your music!!"

"Thanks. I like it too."

"So you can't sing," said Guy. "What can you do?"

"I love to dance!"

"So dance for us."

The girl stepped awkwardly from side to side.

"Come on, you can do better than that!"

"Take off your shirt!" said Yvette.

Veronica could see that the girl was trembling.

"Good idea," said Davey. "Take it off."

"But I—"

"You'll never get this chance again," Davey sneered. The girl timidly pulled her shirt over her head, exposing two limp breasts.

"Too saggy for me. Better go shag a roadie. Sorry." Davey smiled cruelly at the bird girl. Guy and Yvette laughed at her.

"Look at her!" Yvette giggled. "That's what happens when you're poor and ugly!"

"Let's go dance, shall we?" Veronica pulled down the bird girl's shirt, seized her hand and led her down the hall.

The girl was crying. Veronica pushed their way onto the dance floor, fixed the girl's hair, dabbed her face with a napkin.

"You were great back there."

"I was?"

"Yes. And you got away fast! Perfect!"

"Really? But—"

"Now you can tell everyone that you met Davey Name, and they didn't."

The bird girl couldn't help but smile.

As Veronica danced away, she thought of John Penn. He wasn't cruel to awkward young fans; he bought them dinner and gave them parts in his films. Perhaps Davey felt he'd earned the right to be cruel, because so many people wanted a piece of him. It would be so nice to humiliate him, just once. But how?

The deejay served up something ancient and priceless. Hoping this might redeem the evening, Veronica threw off her jacket and started flailing with abandon. A cute, drunk French guy grabbed her waist and kissed her. Veronica laced her fingers through his hair. How sweet he was, so young and obviously rich—look at his cufflinks! Now she had Davey's undivided attention, and Guy's and everyone else's. Suddenly, out of nowhere, Occo, whom she didn't even know was in Paris, was hurling arms and threats, met by fists and flashbulbs. Davey grabbed Veronica and pulled her out of the club and into a limo.

# Up-Close and Personal

**THE DISCO OUTING HAD PUT DAVEY IN A FOUL MOOD, BUT NOW** that he and Veronica were back at the hotel, he wanted sex. He turned off the light, pulled her onto the bed and began his usual routine—kisses over the face and neck, hands over neck and arms, undoing the necessary buttons and zippers and breathing heavily along the way. In recent weeks it had all become fairly routine, even a little boring. It was like watching a card trick that was intriguing at first, but less so after a few times.

He started kissing his way up her left leg . . . *Oh Lord, I'm really not in the mood. I'd rather be doing something productive, like rearranging my photo albums* . . . Now he was kissing her stomach and heading toward her breasts . . . *Oh hell, if he wants it this bad, why the fuck argue* . . . Having had his fill of breasts, he moved his lips southward . . . *Oh no, not this, he thinks he's so terrific at it* . . . Veronica lifted her head to observe what groupie hotlines the world over advertised as Davey's best number. His thin buttocks were hoisted toward the ceiling and his ribs made a weird canvas of his nacreous white skin. It was perfectly ridiculous. Having witnessed him thus, it would be impossible to care anymore whether he liked her clothes . . . *Oh Christ, now he's starting his coo and moan routine* . . . She burst out laughing.

"What's so funny?" He sat up, frowning.

"Oh nothing, just . . ." Oh God, the sight of him, the aging crooner playing the stud—without his tight pants it really was a *scream*.

"What the hell are you laughing about?"

"Nothing, um, important, it's just that . . . it was so funny . . ."

"What's funny?"

"Just meeting the Hochsts in the restaurant like that." This was the first and only alibi that came to mind. She could hardly tell the truth, that it was the sight of his bony ass in the air and his histrionic little love moans that were too nutty for words.

"They were your bloody friends!" He pitched himself onto his feet and pulled on a shirt, scowling.

"They are not my friends, they are merely my acquaintances."

Davey peered into a hand mirror and started playing with his hair. *Oh no, now he's worried about his hair and his crow's feet, oh the poor man.* She started laughing again with no hope of control.

The phone rang. Davey picked up, listened, hung up, cursed, paced the floor.

"Do you know what the hell's happened?"

"No I don't. Do tell."

"Seems I've been threatened with legal action by the management of that nightclub. When your charming friend Occo started pounding that retarded aristocrat. And I'm getting the rap for it!"

"So you're afraid that Tiger will find out we're in Paris together?"

"Look here, Tiger and I have been in and out of each other's scene for years. We're best friends, and I rely on her for lots of things."

"Yeah, she'll put up with a lot, I'm sure. By the way, you didn't have to be so nasty to that little girl who was so thrilled to meet you."

For an instant, Davey looked stricken. "You're a real mess, you know that? You're a real fucking mess! And I'm going to sleep!" Davey slammed the bathroom door. Veronica pushed her head into the pillow to smother more screams of laughter. It was fucking painful. The toilet flushed, the door opened, and Davey walked back to the bed and lay down with his back to her. Very soon he was asleep, and for a long while Veronica watched him in his valium-induced slumber, his black hair tangled about his cheeks and eyes, the distinct lines carved into his skin from years of singing and smoking. He would always look like this, and his women would get younger and younger. Maybe he didn't need a real girlfriend. The bond with his band mates and the adulation of millions was enough.

The room was overheated and Veronica couldn't sleep. She went into the dressing room, sat on the cushioned settee. She stared at her decaying boots, her depleted makeup, at all the other paraphernalia of vanity scattered across the floor and the bureau. And Davey's guitar, which she had carried for him once, when Tiger wasn't looking. Yes, it was true. Being a Penn Girl was absurd. Maybe she wasn't ruthless or disciplined enough to be a Professional Beautiful Girl. She felt stupid to be in a place like this with a man like Davey Name. You could only love Davey Name as your rock 'n' roll idol. You could have a moment with him, but you had to get away, fast, just as that poor little groupie with the weak chin had after she'd obediently debased herself for the rock-god.

It occurred to Veronica that Davey and Helena shared something in common: In both their worlds, beauty defined a rigid caste system, decreed by birth. Veronica's Willy Westwood photos had indeed served as visas to the Rock-God Realm. But this was a man's world where women merely served, and there were rows of ravenous groupies ready to claw their way inside. Meryl said that Tiger Street attacked groupies and sent bodyguards after them. So what would Tiger do to Veronica if she discovered that Veronica was alone in a hotel room with Davey Name?

Veronica had to get away, from Davey, from the hotel. It was 3:30 in the morning. There were all-night clubs in Paris but you had to know people to get in. Disco laws were universal. But it *was* Paris, so there had to be some kind of a bar open, somewhere. She pulled on clothes and slipped into the hall, down to the lobby and out to the street.

She followed a cluster of lights to an unkempt tabac where a few vaguely sinister patrons were smoking by the corner jukebox. She remembered hating Paris during parent-supervised childhood vacations; the torpid restaurant ordeals wherein she was repeatedly forced, at the point of Helena's butter knife, to ingest horrific animal parts and sit in enforced silence while the adults experimented with wines. It had rendered her a committed vegetarian.

A waiter came over with a tray of drinks. The coffee was bitter, the beer was cold. The effect of drinking one after the other was marvelous. The night air was laced with a cologne of tobacco, bread, and chestnuts. French bars really did feel cleaner and healthier than American bars. They kept the lights up and people didn't feel guilty about smoking and drinking. That was the essence of this country's charm; it respected hedonism. The French even had a proper word for it, jouissance. The Thais called it sanuk. And in India it was must. What was that famous Hindi pop song—*Must, to chiz bari hey must must* . . .

A man entered the tabac, bought a pack of Gitanes, then turned and looked straight at Veronica. It was Mr. Norbu.

"Well, hello, Veronica. May I join you?"

"Why not?" What a surprise. She was happy to see him, although she knew she wasn't having a Covergirl moment.

The waiter brought Nr. Norbu a drink. He took a measured sip as he scanned the room, and Veronica, with his Khampa eyes.

"You look like you were having a party."

"We were at a disco, earlier."

"Where is my friend Mr. Penn?"

"He's gone back to New York."

"So where are you going next, Veronica?"

"I don't know."

"You've got money then?"

"Actually, I don't."

"So if you don't have money, what do you have?"

"Charm and luck."

Mr. Norbu refilled his pipe and leaned back into his chair. He stared at her with a different kind of Khampa X-ray. "You'd better look after your luck."

"What do you mean?"

"You'd better not spend it all at once. We Asians believe luck is a form of morality. You think it will always be there to save you, protect you. And then one day your luck is gone. It has run out."

"So how's your luck?"

"Very good. I've learned how to feed it. Because I've lost it more than a few times."

"How?"

"It's a long story," Norbu replied, gauging her curiosity.

"Tell me."

"I'll tell you some of it . . ." Mr. Norbu leaned back in his chair and stared for a moment into his beer glass, then smiled, and began his story.

"In my childhood in Tibet, we were rich. My father was a chieftain. We had a huge estate, so many servants, animals, paintings, sculpture, jewelry, furniture. So many beautiful things we had. Our life was like a dream. Then the Chinese Communists came. First with smiles, then with gold, then with guns. They killed my whole family. I was the only one who escaped into India.

"I was trapped in a camp by the Indian border. So many Tibetans died there. It was so hot, so dirty. I never thought I would become a refugee and I didn't like it. I persuaded one of the Indian soldiers that I was much older than I was, and he assigned me to the special border patrol. I learned a lot there. I even learned how to parachute from a plane. But I saw my friends die, again and again. I knew that I didn't want to be a soldier for the rest of my life. I knew that I would have to make myself rich. In those days the Tibetan refugees were so desperate they would sell a horse or a gold necklace for a bowl of rice.

"I left the Indian army and went to Kathmandu. I worked as a sweeper at a hotel where European art dealers kept their boutiques. I made about ten rupees a day and I slept in a shack behind the taxi stand. I taught myself Hindi and English by reading newspapers. I was hired by a German art dealer to clean his store and make tea. I saw how much money he made selling Tibetan statues and thankas and dzi beads. I got mad, because he was a wealthy European, profiting from my culture, a culture that had been raped and ruined by a pack of thieves in Mao jackets. The Tibetan people who had made this art were beggars. I had saved a few antiques from my family shrine, so I took them to the German's hotel room and made my first hundred thousand dollars in three days.

"I bought a Nepali passport on the black market and started going to Hong Kong, Tokyo, and Europe. I worked very hard. My business grew and grew. I always took care of the people who worked with me, to make sure that I filled up my supply of luck. I took care of widows and orphans. Because then I might be taken care of one day. I learned how to keep money in different banks in different countries. I always have a supply of gold in case I have to run. And I protect myself from Miga. You'd better watch for Miga. You are too pretty, too famous."

"Me? Famous for what? What's Miga?"

"The Black Eye."

"Sounds like an after-hours club in the meatpacking district."

"Don't make jokes!" Mr. Norbu's eyes and nostrils flared. "It is very dangerous. It falls on you when people talk about you too much. When people look at you in a certain way. When they talk about you in their homes and across a mahjong table. It bleeds away your prana. Your chi. Your life force. My old aunt believed the Black Eye was cast upon her after her family lost all their wealth and became refugees. She feels it following her. She is convinced that people see shame and disgrace woven into the folds of her clothes. And she believes you get the Black Eye when you mix with foreigners. It is dangerous to be too much talked about. A girl like you, you have to be careful. Be careful in public, of the way you dance."

"What's wrong with the way I dance?"

"Nothing is wrong with it in your mind. It's other people's minds you have to watch. You give them too many bullets to shoot at you, too many reasons to look at you. Always confuse people if you can, so they can't corner you."

"Have a double life?"

"Maybe a triple life."

"In New York you have to be talked about behind your back to be worth anything."

"Whatever you want, it's your karma because you chose it. Like choosing a gem from a jewelry box. It brings you luck. Just not always good luck."

"So how do you know, when you're staring into the box, which gem to pick?"

"You do your research. Your friend Mr. Penn, he knows how to find the flaws in a ruby or an emerald. He likes sapphires. And Mr. Name, the singer, he likes diamonds. He is one of my best customers. He has a diamond in his tooth."

"Yes, I know." She noticed a bulbous ruby gleaming on Mr.

Norbu's right ring finger. She touched it, and felt a spark. "What's the Tibetan word for jewel?"

"Norbu."

"Norbu! That's you!"

"I know." He reached into his pocket and handed her a flyer. "This is my new project in Kathmandu. Why don't you come see it?"

"In Kathmandu?"

"Didn't you once live there?"

"Yes, a few years back."

Mr. Norbu glanced at his watch and stood. "I am afraid I have to go. I must leave for London in the morning. Will you be alright?"

"Of course, I'm staying across the street, at the hotel."

"Good-bye then."

Mr. Norbu exited the tabac. The waiter came over with another drink and some sandwiches. Exhaustion suddenly set in. Veronica's fingers went slack and her eyelids became unbearably heavy . . . *Yes, I always sleep better when Davey isn't around* . . .

# Wake-Up Time

**VERONICA AWOKE TO DAYLIGHT. THE TABAC WAS JAMMED, AND** an irritated waiter was standing over her.

"Mademoiselle! Nous avon besoin de la table!"

"What? Oh, the table, yeah you can have it." She fumbled in her pocket for some money and handed him a large bill, which he grabbed, muttering something vaguely abusive. *Where am I? Oh yeah, Paris. I'm supposed to be with Davey. Where are my sunglasses when I need them?*

Veronica stumbled out of the tabac and made her way across the square back to the hotel. She unlocked the door to Davey's grand suite and discovered that, while Davey was absent, her suitcase was not yet among the missing. She took a bath, ordered room service, and sank into the cool white bed linens, uncoiling the knotted muscles in her legs and arms.

"Alors, mademoiselle, levez-vous plus vite!" After a miserably brief fifteen minutes, the maids pushed her off the bed to change the sheets. Veronica ducked into the bathroom and locked the door. She put on a black Nehru jacket, tucked her auburn hair under a beret, circled her lavender eyes with black paint, and doused her face with white powder. It was always safe to go Left Bank circa 1975 when in France.

She opened the door and saw a concierge wheeling a flowers-and-fruit tray into the bedroom. Where did Davey say he was going next? Ulan Bator? Maybe he was in one of the restaurants or left a message at the desk.

She went down to the lobby and leaned over the reception desk. "Excuse me sir, did Mr. Name leave a message for Miss Veronica Ferris?"

"Non, mademoiselle. Rien."

"Nothing?"

"Nothing."

"Are you sure?"

"Yes, I am absolutely sure."

Veronica stood dumbly at the counter, unaware that her duffle bag had slipped off her shoulder and spilled its contents over the floor. Several bracelets had rolled toward the magazine stand and a bottle of purple glitter had broken. The bellhop was horrified. Veronica scooped up the glitter with a dollar bill and left it on the counter. The lobby swirled with people who had clear purposes and destinations, who had dinner reservations at good restaurants, who spent their summers in lovely seaside villas, who wore matching socks and had luggage with secure locks and zippers, and who had good credit ratings and plenty of traveler's checks and American Express Gold Cards. She watched them summon the bellhops, open and close their wallets, adjust their new coats about their trim and expensively maintained bodies. *Where do I get the right visa sponsor letter to live forever in a five-star hotel?*

"Miss Ferris, je m'excuse, there is a message for you." The concierge handed her a note scrawled on hotel stationary: "V—Urgent business in London. Back in two days. Enjoy yourself here. D." How nice of him to explain. The note was not hostile, so perhaps he'd recovered from last night's humiliation.

Now that Veronica had a suite again, the people in the lobby suddenly appeared charming and friendly, instead of rich and threatening. She sat down in the hotel cafe, ordered a salad, and proceeded to inspect the contents of her wallet. Two passports, one long expired, but perhaps could still slip past some customs officers. A card displaying John Lennon's image and vital statistics. Lyrics for a rock song. Calling cards from assorted strangers. Three Band-Aids. A calendar from a filling station. A picture of Sai Baba, or was it Sly Stone? Half of a New York–Paris–New York plane ticket. 230 francs. 140 U.S. dollars, and a few pennies. Great. She'd last about twenty-four hours with this stuff. Actually, she might hold out for a few days if she didn't eat anything.

"Now this is what I'd call fabulous place karma! Veronica Ferris, in Paris, with me!"

Veronica looked up—it was Jet Lag Janey, the notorious and invincible Dharma Hustler. "Oh, hi, Janey."

"Veronica, you have to admit, this is amazing. You and I have seeds from past lives sprouting up all over the place!" Janey sat down and plunged a fork into Veronica's salad. Doubtless she was hunting for a place to crash. Veronica was wary of Janey's aging-party-chick-on-the-make compulsions, her Bali gossip and dharma politics, but the sight of anyone besides the Hochsts was welcome, given the circumstances.

"How did you know I was here?"

"John Penn's office told me. You're so lucky to have a patron like him. By the way, I heard that Davey Name's staying here too. True or false? Rinpoche is just ever so eager to meet Davey, so I thought it would be just terrific if we could get those two together."

"Davey's not here, but his room is."

"Gosh, can we go upstairs and rest a bit? To tell you the absolute truth, I have felt better in my life." Janey sighed, twirling her enormous amber and turquoise necklace between vermillion fingernails. "Three-day dharma-boy binge. I've got a dreadful weakness for Tibetans. They've poisoned me for all other males. And they like to drink. So I've just learned to incorporate hangovers into my dharma practice."

"How does one merge hangovers and dharma practice?" This did sound promising. However, up close, evidence suggested that in Janey's universe the merger was as yet incomplete.

"Had I resisted that extra bottle of wine, I might not have a sore head. Karma, you see, is the law of cause and effect."

"So you know the universal party girl prayer?"

"No, please tell!"

"Dear God, if you take away my hangover, I will never ever drink alcohol again."

Janey blinked, in dead earnest. "Does it work?"

"Hey, Janey, let's go upstairs." Veronica reasoned that it would be less of a hassle to give Janey room access than to answer all the Where's Davey and What's John Penn Really Like questions.

When they entered Davey's suite, Janey swooned, mightily and predictably.

"Ronnie, can I use the phone?"

Why did Aussies and Brits always call her Ronnie? "Help yourself."

"Thanks. It's for the cause."

"Sorry, what cause? I forgot."

"Free Tibet, obviously." Janey dialed America, chatted, hung up, dialed again. Veronica lit a cigarette, leaned back into the pillow, stared glumly at her new suite-mate. *Wait a minute, I'm supposed to be famous. Famous people do not get stuck in strange hotels with creepy losers, right? Right, okay . . .*

"Is Danny there? Tell him Janey called . . . Yes, yes, *that* Janey!" She slammed down the phone, irritated. "This is when you've got sorry proof that one's karmic line-up needs a reshuffle. My travel agent won't return my calls. Mind if I plunder the minibar?"

"Go ahead." Presumably Davey was still paying. Janey took a Perrier and a chocolate bar. "Mmmm, fabulous. I know this must be expensive, but I deserve it—I've been so hard at work for the cause. Now we're doing time with the dharmites in Ko Samui, which is not really my favorite scene. I'm neither a Theravada nor a beach person. When was the last time you were in Ko Samui, Veronica?"

"Actually, never."

"Oh! And I thought you were an Asia person!"

"Guess I need to work at that." God, this woman was tedious. For a moment Veronica dreamed that she had a home, any home. Then she wouldn't be at the mercy of people who saw her merely as a means to a minibar.

"You know, this weekend Namkar Rinpoche's teaching the Diamond Sutra. Everyone's going. I could try to get you in. It's a bit late to register, but we could pull some strings. There's a reception at a Nepali royal's flat. Fifth quarter and fabulous." Janey was now helping herself to Veronica's clothes, trying on skirts, shirts, boots, leggings, and belts.

"Don't you have anything to wear, Janey?" Was she a thief, too? She had that free-loading aura of a hippie predator who poached your makeup, leggings, and money.

"I've got body parts that need to be camouflaged. When you're under twenty-five, I suppose all's slim and fine in the leg department. Take my advice: plan for the future! Start with the yoga now and only smoke when you absolutely must. You know, Veronica, I used to be like you."

"And how were you like me?" Good God, what did that mean?

"I was the Ultimate Backstage Pass Girl. The one who enters and exits mysteriously, clued to the scene! I still love going to restaurants and pretending I'm famous. Well, I *am* famous in select circles. But for years I relied on my looks to get through." This was the old sob story girls like Janey dished out when they wanted to ignite that aura of fame, that I-was-once-a-great-beauty-so-I've-seen-it-all bit.

"So when does the Beautiful Girl thing stop working?"

"All depends on geography. I love Kathmandu because there I'm still heavenly hot. It's a heaven realm for lonely First-World women who've suffered scorn in their native lands for being dealt a bad hand in the looks department. In Nepal they're showered with attention from dashing Khampas and Sherpas. Bangkok for Girls!"

"From guys who are looking for green cards and blue jeans."

"When you've been around as long as I have, dearie, it gets harder to flirt for your dinner. And I'm in debt up to my earrings. I can't borrow a baht or a pence or a rupee from any of our Golden Oldies." Janey rubbed tiger balm across her forehead and lit another of her Indonesian cigarettes. Veronica felt a grudging pity for her. How scary to end up a piece of trivia, too old to flirt for one's dinner. When did that start happening?

Janey sauntered toward the bathroom as if she were the girl who was secretly dating Davey Name, not a wrinkled Aussie in need of cab fare. Deciding she'd had enough of Jet Lag Janey for one day, Veronica left the room and took the elevator down to the lobby. She saw a cluster of saris and topis floating toward the restaurant where a Tibetan lama was seated at a large round table. It was Namkar Rinpoche, the famous Rock 'n' Roll Lama. He sat between a tranquil Nepali princess and a tiny Englishwoman. Namkar Rinpoche had a Dharma Center in Los Angeles, with dozens of actor-rocker-model followers. But Veronica had heard he was very gifted, spoke several languages, and disdained limousines. She leaned into the window glass to study Namkar Rinpoche. He had that strange, inborn beauty of a Tibetan holy man: copper skin, elegant brow and nose, a fine round head, and long, graceful fingers that emerged from the folds of his maroon robes. Veronica walked into the restaurant, toward Rinpoche's table, waiting for him to notice her.

"Bon nuit, miss madame!" A Nepali man in a topi hat of fluorescent pink and orange stripes saluted her with a glass of ginger ale. "We are in just the process of dinner. Please to join." He offered Veronica his seat. "We are felicitating Rinpoche. He has taken residence in our Nepal. You have seen our Nepal?"

"Indeed I have."

"Please miss madame, and what is your name?"

"Veronica."

"You are Janey's friend." Namkar Rinpoche was now staring at her, which was good. He spoke that antiquated boarding-school dialect of Indian English, which identified him as an exile, a multilingual hybrid who'd escaped with the Dalai Lama to take refuge in the southern continent in the land of Gandhi and Buddha. "Janey tells us you are a singer from New York."

"What else did Janey say about me?" His stare was unsettling, like that of Willy Westwood's, but could the lama see the accumulation of all her sins and faults and deceptions? Did he have the power to bless and purify?

"Janey called us here for dinner, but where the bollocks is she?" The tiny English woman was peeved and restless.

"Janey is always coming lately!" cried the Nepali man in the topi. "And she is always recommending such admiring places for fooding and lodging."

"Aha! Behold our little group!" Janey was now cleaned, pressed, and wearing one of Davey's shirts. "I feel like I've chucked off a thousand past lives with a single Jacuzzi. Am I late for the party?"

The man in the Day-Glo topi nodded serenely. "We are Nepali time. We do not believe in fast life."

"But I've missed the drinks service, oh gosh." Janey steered a chair in between the lama and the tiny English lady. "Rinpoche, please explain to Veronica why she should join the Free Tibet movement."

"Janey is trying to make you a freedom fighter?"

"Not really, but I would like to know what you think about the Free Tibet movement," Veronica replied.

Namkar Rinpoche stared at Veronica, his hands pressed together at his heart. "I know that the actual goal of freeing Tibet from China, that is maybe unrealistic. So the old Tibet has died. This is a terrible loss for the world, because so much knowledge and art has been lost, in such a cruel and terrible way. We must try to understand what Lord Buddha taught about impermanence. Here we sit, thinking about what to wear tomorrow, when every instant we are moving toward death, to the end of this precious human rebirth. We are creating karma every second, with the smallest thoughts and actions. Our selfishness sows the seeds of our own suffering. We can't blame other people for it. Whatever negative things we experience, we created them ourselves. That is why even the smallest act, if we do it with a pure motive, will multiply and grow, and create vast stores of good karma for us. Bodhicitta, Love, Compassion, is the magical elixir that can transform anything into pure gold. Have you ever taken the bodhisattva vow?"

"No, I haven't."

"You should. You vow to work for the liberation of all beings, vast as space."

"What if I fail to uphold the ideal?"

"You can take the bodhisattva vow again. You can take it many times, to strengthen your resolve to awaken universal love in your heart. Then you will never be afraid of anything, ever again. You will see that we are all trapped in samsara, in the wheel of karma, where nothing is permanent. We want to stay with our childhood friends, but we can't. We want to stay with our parents and grandparents, but we can't. They all die. And we die. So what do we do? We must awaken universal love, now, before Yamaraja, Lord of Death, appears, and we have lost our precious human rebirth, and once again we must wander in samsara, searching for our next rebirth. We must awaken bodhicitta, every day. It takes practice. You begin by taking the bod-hisattva vow."

Namkar Rinpoche held Veronica's eyes in a hard lock. She wanted to ask him more, to ask him if the bodhisattva vow would reunite her with her beloved grandparents Jack and Lilly. Rinpoche ate his dinner in silence. Very soon waiters were clearing plates, and the Nepali man in the Day-Glo hat was waving from the lobby and Namkar Rinpoche and the English lady were moving through the revolving door and into taxis, vanishing into the sparkling Parisian night.

# The Black Eye Blinks

**BACK IN DAVEY'S ROOM JANEY STARTED OPENING COMPLEMEN-**
tary bottles of facial moisturizer and cologne. Veronica lay on the bed,
scanning the tabloids. Lots of breaking stories—"Discos in Amsterdam
Reassert Themselves to Lure Clientele," "Chinese Premier to Visit the
Congo," "Footballers Dismayed by British Bust-up." . . .

"Gosh, you've made the papers!" Janey thrust forth a headline that
read: "Davey Name and New York Heiress in Disco Brawl."

"That can't be me."

"Take a look. It's you and Davey Name, who's so mysteriously out
of town. You didn't let on that you have a fabulous publicist! We've got
to get you to work on the next Free Tibet concert."

Veronica smoothed out the newspaper. The photograph showed
Davey grabbing an unfortunate young man in a headlock, in the club
they'd visited after being accosted at dinner by Bernard and Gail
Hochst. The greater portion of Veronica's thighs were clearly visible,
though her face was mercifully blocked by a clenched fist which appeared to belong to a bodyguard. The text, however, was painful:
"Rock maverick Davey Name's rivalry with Gilbert de Champioux,
cold cream heir, erupted in a violent fracas at the exclusive Vita Club in
Paris . . ." *Oh no, Gilbert de Champioux was the cute French guy!* "According to eye witnesses, the British singer lost his cool when the French
aristocrat paid too much attention to his date, New York socialite and
John Penn discovery, Veronica Furst."

"Janey, it's okay. They got my name wrong and I can only be positively identified from the waist down."

"Look, you've made it in three more tabs. You're on the wire services! With Davey Name! You lucky bitch!" Janey handed Veronica more papers. "This guarantees access to the best clubs for at least a week."

Veronica opened another paper and she saw herself, lurching knock-kneed toward Davey's limo, under the title: "Party Girls, Icons or Embarrassments?" Good God, is this how she looked, stumbling out of nightclubs at four in the morning? The piece was by Beth Armstrong, the puffy blonde in green corduroy who'd invaded the Superparty set. It read:

> Penn girl-of-the-minute Veronica Ferris loves the fast lane and doesn't care if she's heading for a crash. Heedless of the history of Penn Girls Past, Veronica's cool, with no plans to follow in the footsteps of her much-admired mother, Helena, food specialist and one of the most active fundraisers in Manhattan's charity circuit. If this is what a liberal education and the Social Register gets you, American values are seriously off track. The privileged elite of the eastern seaboard blithely glorify misspent youth as "cool," eagerly validating the drug culture and sexual experimentation. Go ahead, let's be oh so multicultural, it's all "ghetto-phabulous." But just think of the example they set to young Americans who don't regard our hard-won liberties as currency to be squandered in euro-trash discos, the young men and women who'll stand up for modesty and morality, restraint and gratitude, and, oh, a little hard work too. Too bad they never get on the covers of magazines.

Veronica let the paper slide to the carpet. So the petty tabloid journo was exacting her revenge for not being invited to the Superparty after party. Busted in a Parisian nightclub! And worst of all, with a terrible picture! How could she endure the nuclear fallout of Helena's fury? The jeers and scorn of the Dolly Seabrooks and the Tiger Streets! What would John Penn think? And Winston, how could she explain this to her adored father?

# GREEN CARDS AND BLUE JEANS

You meet lots of girls who come from New York City
You tell all of them you think they're very pretty
I know how to make you love me better
I'm going to write you one visa sponsor letter
we'll go dancing, yeah yeah

You say the visa is so hard to get
But you haven't kissed me or danced with me yet
I'm a girl with diplomatic immunity
Everything I want I get duty free

we'll go dancing yeah yeah
American girl, international world

Meh Amreikan larki hu
What does that mean to you?
I'm the girl of your dreams
I'll get you green cards and blue jeans

Ravi met a girl named Lisa
She got him a 5 year student visa
Now he lives in San Francisco
Every night he goes to the disco
Dancing, yeah yeah
with American girls, international world

Meh Amerikan larki hu
What does that mean to you?
I'm the girl of your dreams
I'll get you green cards and blue jeans

sara duniya meh dundh rehi hu
always looking for a boy like you
always looking for a boy who looks just like you
Oh my darling hum sath sath chelo
there are so many people you ought to know
Chelo chelo mera desh hum deko
there are so many places we ought to go
paiysa milegia, disco chalegiya,
paisa milegia, disco chalegiya

I'm the girl of your dreams
I'll get you green cards and blue jea...

Green cards & blue jeans
I'm a green card holder
Green cards & blue jeans...
it says so in my folder
I'm an illegal alien
I know how to have alot of fun
I know lots of Americans

Sometimes I even pass for one
I know a man at the embassy
I think he works for AID
Come on darling, I'll take you there
I'll even pay your scooter fare

Given the circumstances, maybe it was a good idea to have one nice, cold, stiff drink with a nice, hot, bitter Gitane. She opened a tiny vodka bottle and lit a brutal, filterless French cigarette. Last night she'd met Mr. Norbu in the tabac. He was talking about luck, that thing about the Black Eye. He said be careful of the way you dance! New York was filled with evil eyes, black eyes, angry eyes. She couldn't go back there. But now it seemed equally dangerous to stay in Paris! The paparazzi and the Hochsts in one night! Where could she go, where would she be safe? Where could she get a visa?

She emptied her purse over the bed. The two passports with a few long-term multiple entry visas. Very little money left. Winston always carried multiple currencies with stacks of hundred-dollar bills. The purpose of cash was to buy airplane tickets, which were more important than food. She did have a lot of good jewelry, which was more durable than cash. Never wear good jewelry on the plane. Carry it wrapped up in your handbag—*never* in checked luggage. Makeup—vital for customs. An address book and an international calling card with dialing codes. Then she could find her old friends. Maybe Miss Tanaka had never returned to Tokyo from Jakarta! Was Heidelberg Henry still in Bombay? Or was he in Goa full-time now? And was Red-Faced Jerry still running that shop in Sydney called Honky Tanka?

A small flyer slipped from Veronica's purse. The paper was cheap, the printing inexact. It read: "Help Poor Children of the Himalayas." Mr. Norbu had given it to her at the tabac. It shone in her hand like a talisman that conjured her magical childhood.

She heard Janey singing, off-key, in the bathroom. What a marvelous gift for Davey. A rabid hippie looking for a clean place to crash. It was good karma all around, Janey would get to meet the rock star, and he'd get some unconditional love.

"Hey, Janey, I'm going out for a bit. Make yourself at home."

"Don't worry, I'll look after everything. I ran the most fabulous guest house in Bali for donkey's years." Janey had already dislodged a half-bottle of champagne from the minibar, turned on the TV, filled the Jacuzzi with bubbles, lit an Indonesian cigarette and propped her feet on the gold soap tray.

"If you see Davey, please give him my best."

"I certainly will do. And if you run into Rinpoche's translator, invite him up. He needs a nice rest."

Veronica pushed open the door to the Modern Antique Showroom on Rue de Seine, hauling luggage and dripping with rain. It took only twenty pleasurable minutes to sell the topaz necklace with a clause to repurchase, and buy a round trip ticket to Kathmandu.

**THREE DAYS LATER JOHN SAT AT THE VIP TABLE AT TRAVESTY** with Tiger Street, Suki Dean, Dickie Drake, Venice Beach, Jerry Dollar, Tad, and Bennett. John snapped photos of the Benefit Ladies and Real Beauties and the New Girls in Town while the uninvited pushed against the ropes to get a better view of the thin, rich, and famous. Veronica's face, hair, and eyes and Davey's arms, legs, and lips filled the oversized screens that played the Superparty video deep into the night.

# PART III

# In the
# Buddha
# Valley

# Purify Me

**VERONICA SAW THE GOLDEN ROOF OF PASHUPATHINATH, THE**
Shiva temple. She slammed the taxi door and ran past cows, pigs, monkeys, pujaris, sadhus, colored smoke pouring from the mouths of temples, stone lingams, monks and stupas, crows, hippies, beggars, filth, splendor, chants, bells, barks, cries, flutes, drums—all the old familiar sights and sounds. The sky was pulsing that pure, wild Himalayan blue, that blue she had dreamed of for years. She ran down the temple steps to the Bagmati River—it was still there, washing sin and giving life. She threw herself into swirls of brown water. She was back in the Asia of her long-lost magical childhood.

After she booked a room at the Potala Palace Hotel, drank a cup of chai, smoked a bidi, read the *Kathmandu Post*, and made friends with the bearers and porters and waiters, Veronica walked into the bazaar to touch the foot of a stone Buddha and buy a Free Tibet tee shirt.

# Spin Cycle Goes Global

**VERONICA SLEPT FOR SIXTEEN HOURS AND SPENT A FULL AF-**ternoon lying in bed, watching a Dev Anand Lifetime Achievement tribute. Bikash, the house boy, set a lime soda on Veronica's nightstand. She gave him fifteen rupees. He blushed, and hovered in the doorway, hoping to be asked to rearrange furniture or fix the radio. Veronica pretended to have a headache and gave him ten more rupees to go buy some aspirin.

Veronica opened her window and inhaled deeply the Asiatic scent, that weave of dung fires, incense, cooking oil, and marigolds, the scent of her home continent. The lilt of prayers floated from a hidden temple, mixed with Bollywood disco. There were no tabloids, no sinister friends here. New York and the First World seemed very far away. Thank God she was still lucky. And thank God for her intercontinental party girl tool kit. She still knew how to get on an airplane. Pity the poor party girl who had nowhere else to go but Luna Ticks on an off night. Tonight she would celebrate her return at an ex-pat bar, but first and foremost, she had to rescue her double life, and locate a telephone.

There was an international dialing center behind the Potala Palace, operated by Mr. Topden, a cheerful fraud in a polyester chuba and a huge, completely bogus Khampa headdress.

"Hello to Madame! May I know your good name?"

"Veronica. And yours?

"I am Topden! Topden from Tibet!" Mr. Topden's beaming countenance bespoke mountain peaks and mystical romance, buffed and polished to attract foreign clients infected with Shangri-la Syndrome; but his Punjabi accent and the prevalence of Hindi film star posters in the back room confirmed that he was an exile, born and raised in India, for whom a Saturday picnic at the Hotel Radisson was probably a rugged nature outing.

"I have to call the USA. Right now."

"Surely! Please to continue." Topden handed her a grimy telephone, and she dialed.

"Hey, Meryl, how's New York?" Topden's elbows were inching across the counter while his crimson Khampa headdress teetered off kilter.

"Forget New York! Your Parisian disco brawl sure as hell made news. So what really happened?" Veronica heard Meryl readying her keyboard. "You could've spun that right-wing loser Beth Armstrong a lot better. Tiger Street went nuts when she heard about you guys in Paris. She's given Davey some kind of ultimatum. She's getting great press out of it, so in reality she owes you big-time. Are you still partying in Paris?"

"No."

"Why not?"

"Because I'm in Kathmandu."

"What the fuck are you doing in Kathmandu?"

"I'm volunteering—" Veronica pulled Mr. Norbu's flyer out of her purse. "At an orphanage."

"Okay, so what kind of orphans?"

"Tibetan refugee orphans."

"Oh, well, that's fairly hot. Last week the Tibet benefit at Travesty totally killed the global warming thing at Luna Ticks. They lost money and the party planner got fired." Veronica heard the tapping of Meryl's keyboard. "So what's your job description? Party coordinator? Fashion consultant?"

"The Tibet cause has at long last gained international attention, so it's an opportune time to gather more support for the Tibetan people, victims of genocide, population transfer, religious persecution."

"I got some Free Tibet flyers here, I can fill in that stuff. Any other celebrities working at this orphanage?"

"It's not—that kind of orphanage."

"I've never been to an orphanage, so give me some visuals."

Veronica peered at the flyer, which offered little more than a grainy black-and-white photo of a square building with four rows of uniformed children standing in front. "It's a simple place. I was invited here by Mr. Norbu. I met him with John Penn. They're very old friends."

"That's a twist. Tell me more."

"He's a famous art dealer and collector. He persuaded me to do this, given my Asian background."

"And your mother is the Queen of the Benefit Ladies."

"She is indeed. I've learned so much from her."

Twelve hours later the AP wires ran Meryl's story, "Penn Girl Returns to her Roots, Finds her Inner Mother Theresa, and Tibetan Kids Get a Helping Hand," with a photo of Mr. Norbu's orphanage spliced into an alluring yet thoughtful headshot of Veronica from John Penn's camera.

The Modern Antique Showroom was besieged with calls for Mr. Norbu. Helena was heaped with praise for her daughter's commitment to humanitarian service in the Third World. Winston's UNICEF deputy invited John Penn to design the logo for a globalization conference in Bangkok. Winston and Helena's supremacy in Manhattan was secure. Veronica was back in Asia, home again. Once more, her luck had held out.

# Evening Prayers

KATHMANDU WAS SAID TO HAVE MORE TEMPLES, FESTIVALS, AND holidays than any city in the world, but now it also had factories, traffic and gridlock, water shortages, garbage dumps, and a collapsing infrastructure. The World Bank, with fervent assistance from the Nepali royal family, built dams, sold fertilizer, got the government into debt—the usual thing. They claimed that poverty alleviation was their mission, all evidence to the contrary. Veronica never really understood the development dudes, Winston's innumerable protégés. They were forever shuttling from Bangkok to Manila, from Kathmandu to Jakarta, attending conferences, meetings, dispensing grants, reviewing projects. Some of them thought they were saving the world. The smart ones had wonderful careers as partners and teachers. Some were missionaries in bush shirts. They all appeared to be having a good time, with their business-class tickets and per diems and hotel credits, and visa sponsor letters. Yes, the development dudes had visas to the Golden Age of Globalization.

Veronica passed sleeping dogs, stone goddesses tangled in marigold garlands, sunrays fading on warmed patches of red, purple, and orange-colored earth. She stopped to buy incense and perfume. She saw a temple belonging to White Machendranath, guardian of the Kathmandu Valley. The brass lattice above the shrine was fretted with cobwebs, the brick walls were coated with emerald-green moss. A Sherpa monk handed her a candle. She touched it to the altar flame and prayed that

Machendranath would protect her as long as she was in his realm. Winston had taught her, years ago, to always pay respect to the local deities, whomsoever they may be.

On every street corner children burned small fires and fished through garbage. This reminded Veronica of many a Ferris cocktail party and dinner party conversation. Diplomatic wives were fond of reciting Asian horror stories of professional beggars who deliberately mutilated their own children to increase their earning power, proof of the inferiority of Eastern civilizations. This would spark a predictable, inconclusive cocktail hour debate about which was worse, professional begging or the development of the hydrogen bomb, the caste system or antebellum slavery. When Veronica tried to argue the case for Mahatma Gandhi, Helena proclaimed that India had more starving children than all of sub-Saharan Africa, which nullified whatever was left of Gandhi's legacy. Then Jamie would break in with a defense of vegetarianism and Grayson would scream about constitutional democracy, and at last Winston would advocate tolerance and the benefits of education while Veronica would attempt to finish off the Pinot Noir before someone else got to it.

Veronica's taxi pulled up to a spare, treeless compound, where a sign read: "Himalayan Transit School Mission, Boudhanath, Tinchuli, Kathmandu, Nepal. May Lord Buddha Shower You With World Peace." A gang of children gathered round the taxi and followed Veronica into the clinic. Inside the office three nurses sat at a table, sorting through medicines. The room was clean and spare, with an enormous Korean refrigerator grumbling loudly in the corner and a small TV showing a fearsome Hindi villain and a shrieking maiden in a wet sari. Behind a desk sat a handsome Indian woman in a pale blue nurse's sari and a white cap, reading the *Hindustan Times*.

"Excuse me, I'm a friend of Mr. Norbu's. Veronica. From America."

"A friend of Mr. Norbu's, our glorious patron! Please to sit down. I am Sujata. Head nurse. Take tea!" Sujata poured a cup of semi-rancid butter tea into a chipped pink cup. "So miss, what is your aim?"

"Excuse me?"

"Your aim? In work for here?"

"Oh, I, well . . ." This was a confusing question. "I want to help with—with assistance to the needy." Did that make sense?

"Our children are needing sponsors for school fees. Here is young Lopta. He is a Tamang child. His mother is lately a widow so she cannot be caring for him. He is needing a sponsor-mother."

Sujata summoned a small boy, who hovered behind his mother's skirt. His mother wore a faded pink tee shirt, a gold nose ring, small gold earrings, and a glass necklace. She told Sujata that she wanted to leave Kathmandu to go to her brother's village. She didn't want the boy to go to boarding school, nor did she want him to be left alone. Sujata sympathized with this, but could see that there would be no future for the boy unless he went to a boarding school. But what of the school fees, cried the mother. The father has died, leaving us only gambling debts! What to do? The mother stared into her lap, the boy glanced anxiously from his mother to Sujata to Veronica. Veronica paused, lifted three thousand rupees from her purse and handed it to Sujata.

"I hope this will help with his education."

"Oh, Madame, this is very kindly! Thank you kind Madame!"

As Sujata explained Veronica's gift, the mother fell to her knees and sobbed, "Thanks to kind Madame, thanks to kind Madame!" The boy looked bewildered. Sujata gave him a lollipop and told him to watch the Hindi movie. Veronica smiled at the boy, who blushed and clutched his mother's skirt. How simple it was, to reach out to him.

Veronica filled out the sponsor information card, and felt the weight of many eyes upon her, the eyes of other children who had no parents and needed a sponsor-mother. The children stared with hushed fascination at the fair-skinned, purple-eyed apparition with the strange clothes and jewelry and the thousands upon thousands of rupees in her purse, which could change the course of a life.

"Miss Veronica, please to come again. When Mr. Norbu is back from his travels."

"Mr. Norbu isn't here?"

"No, no, he is coming lately. After the festival. We wish to show him our progress!"

Yes, Veronica wished to show him her own progress, from rumpled disco patron to refugee case worker. She was infinitely grateful to him for bringing her here.

"It is time for evening prayers. Please to be going to Great Stupa! It is just ahead."

Veronica didn't want to leave. She wanted to remain with the Nepali family and watch the children play, but the chowkidar and the assistant nurse were ready to clear everyone out and lock the compound gates. Sujata dutifully walked Veronica to the gate. Veronica waved good-bye to the children, who laughed and waved back.

# Wandering in Samsara

**AS VERONICA PUSHED THROUGH THE TRAFFIC OF COWS, GOATS,** rickshaws, and motorcycles, she saw the gold and blue eyes of Amitabha, Buddha of the Western Paradise, filling the earth and sky with a promise.

The pilgrim stream moved round the stupa's base, a human prayer wheel of monks, nomads, housewives, shopkeepers, beggars and lepers, a rare Buddhist monk from Southeast Asia, and of course, the dharma bums. Veronica spotted two excellent specimens staring dumbly at the golden spire. They were in a daze of rapture, hands lifted in prayer, babbling and sputtering, on the verge of tears. Identifying new dharma bums was an endlessly satisfying pan-Asian entertainment. Veronica and Jamie competed in various categories—length and depth of sartorial absurdity, cultural inaccuracy, histrionic weirdness. Most fun was inventing nicknames, such as Nose Ring Nutcase, Past Life Patty, Too Long At The Bong. Veronica wondered what it was these people saw when they stared at the stupa. Asians were expected to show due reverence to holy places, but when a French teenager in an ersatz turban and hiking shorts moaned and sobbed and writhed in the dirt, it was ludicrous and highly entertaining.

Following the advice of three Swiss trekkers, she walked up a flight of stairs and into the Double Dorjee, which, if memory served, was an old haunt famous for its superior location and putrid menu. It had the usual Kathmandu restaurant decor: the requisite portraits of the Dalai

Lama and Nepal's king and queen, and a poster from the Tibetan Freedom Concert of the Beastie Boys and Tibetan Monks with guitars and
fists heaved skyward.

Veronica slipped into a chair, exhausted and grateful. The air bore
mingled scents of earth and moisture, charcoal and rose, dung fires and
mud. She was wearing her black-and-red Free Tibet shirt and a green
velvet Moroccan jacket, a gift from Winston. She caught her reflection
in the window glass; her lavender eyes shone brilliantly in the Asian
light, her hair seemed thicker and darker. Yes, she was on her continent.

She saw a man take a seat by the window, yank off his motorcycle
helmet, wipe his cheeks, and shout for beer. She studied his shining
black hair, his long eyes and angled cheekbones, his polyester trousers.
Was he a Tibetan or a Sherpa? Hard to say. He slouched against the wall
and stared into the pilgrim stream that swarmed through the evening
dust. Veronica wanted to talk to him. She could pretend to be a tourist
looking for a meditation class.

"Can I join you?"

"Me? Why?"

"Sorry, I'm bothering you—"

"No no, please, sit down."

"Can I have one of those cigarettes?"

"Sure."

She glanced at the package. "What does Bijuli mean?"

"Lightening."

"Oh yes, I remember these. The cheapest of all cheap Nepali cigarettes, more toxic than a hundred Gitanes, but tasty nevertheless." As she
took one and allowed him to light it for her, her dzi bead rolled out
from under her shirt and caught the light.

He stared at her necklace. "Where did you get that?'"

"This? In Solokhumbu. A long time ago."

"Are you a Buddhist?"

"No, I worship at the altar of Sony Discman." He didn't laugh.
"What I mean is, I like to dance."

"Oh, I see."

In the late afternoon light rays she could see the hazel hue of his
eyes, the rich tone of his skin. He was, in fact, exceptionally handsome.
"Where are you from?"

"Kham. That's in Eastern Tibet."

"Oh, yes." Of course, he was a Khampa. This was Kathmandu. Bangkok for Girls.

"What's your name?"

"My name? Sonam."

"Sonam, who's that man, the tall one? He's standing by the gate."

"Oh, him. Driver Dawa. He's a smuggler. He does runs from here to the Tibetan border. He's supposed to be a Chinese spy. He acts like one."

"How does a Chinese spy act?"

"He's always got Chinese money. He uses blackmail. He punishes anyone who crosses him. I think he killed my neighbor."

Veronica peered at Driver Dawa, at his baggy polyester Beijing trousers and leather coat. He had a cruel face, deeply lined and lightly pockmarked. A small, wiry man, also dressed in Beijing trousers, approached Driver Dawa and handed him a package. The transaction looked thoroughly illegal.

"What's he doing?"

Sonam laughed. "Maybe he's ordering a horoscope. Tibetans won't do anything without consulting the astrologer or the lama or saying prayers. But I don't pray anymore."

Prayer, Veronica thought, had not wrested Tibet from the Communist hordes, or rescued her from the choking tedium of a college campus, not that the two were in any way comparable. She peered at Sonam, her chin upon her hands. His detachment rattled and aroused her. "Where do you work, Sonam?"

"At a carpet factory. Not a nice one. We only make cheap modern carpets. It's not what I'd planned on."

"Why not?"

"I went to college in Delhi, and I won an art scholarship at a university in England. But my father died, so I came back here to look after my mother and my younger brothers and sisters."

"Why couldn't you go to England later?"

"Tibetan society does not look kindly on elder sons who abandon their family duties for things like education or travel."

"So you liked living in Delhi?"

"Of course! I still miss those debates in the canteen about socialism and capitalism and chaos theory, listening to the Beatles and reading Alan Ginsburg's India diaries. In my world, inquiring minds are punished. You westerners want so much to believe in—what's it called?"

"The Shangri-la Syndrome." This was the Tibet theory that Jet Lag Janey and the other Dharma Hustlers so fiercely promulgated. It had proven, over time, to be an effective fundraising tool. "The dharma bums believe Tibetans are genetically enlightened, endowed with rare and mysterious powers."

"Oh really!" Sonam laughed and pushed back his chair. "So where are those rare and mysterious powers when a Tibetan wakes up with a hangover? Or owes money to a Nepali landlord?"

"Listen, I just arrived, from America—well, I stopped in Paris on the way. I want to walk around the stupa and light some butter lamps. Could you show me where to go?"

They paid the bill and went down the stairs and stepped into the pilgrim stream. The light was fading quickly. The Tamang priests had started the evening invocation to Ajima Ma, the Grandmother Goddess.

Veronica noticed a crowd swarming over the North Gate, past which she could see a large Tibetan man screaming outside the Tasty Amdo Restaurant. He was wildly drunk, his shirt unbuttoned, his tongue lolling in his cheek. A beggar boy had been hovering near the man's leg, fishing for his wallet, when the man seized the child and starting choking his neck. The boy was struggling for air. Then the man pulled off his belt and began to whip the child's face. No one was doing anything; they just pointed and stared.

Veronica was jet-lagged and mildly drunk among strangers, but this was an outrage. She pushed through the crowd, pulled the man's silver hair and slapped his face. The man was stunned. He let go of the beggar boy, seized Veronica's arm and slapped her right back, hard.

Someone threw two bricks from the Tasty Amdo. One crashed against Veronica's shoulder, and the other landed squarely on the head of Detective Basnet of the Nepalese Home Ministry Civility Control Division, who was striding toward the disturbance with his billystick and walkie-talkie in hand. The supine and wounded Detective Basnet cried for his men to seize the culprit, whoever he may be. The drunken man tried to flee and knocked over several timid Nepali policemen, whereupon Detective Basnet tripped him with his billystick and ordered that the miscreant be handcuffed and hauled off to Boudha Police Station. Finally, Detective Basnet got to his feet, hoisted a megaphone and ordered all present to evacuate the crime scene.

Sonam steered Veronica to his uncle's antique shop, where they sat on the cot in the back room.

"Where are we?" Her head was spinning.

"In my uncle's shop."

"Who was that man who was beating the beggar child?"

"His name is Romi. He is extremely violent, especially when he gets drunk. I apologize."

"Why should you apologize?"

"It's embarrassing when people in my community behave so poorly." Sonam lowered his eyes as his cheeks blushed crimson.

Did he know how handsome he was? Veronica slid her hands underneath his jacket, across his back. He seized her face and kissed her. His hand went into her blouse, over her breast; she kissed his ear and his neck. Trembling, he reached down to the hem of her skirt and pulled it up to her hip, where he felt the elastic band of her stockings. He pushed her back onto the bed . . .

Then they heard the shop door groan open on its weary hinge.

"Sonam! Are you there?"

"Just a minute!"

"Who is it?" Veronica whispered.

"It's my uncle! Wait here!" Sonam struggled with his pants, flushed and agitated. He made it to the front room before his uncle barged into the back. This was a timely reminder that in most of Asia there was no concept of personal space—only of clan, wherein everything, even ideas, were community property. Veronica pushed the door open a crack to watch.

"What happened to foreign girl? The police will make inquiry!"

Veronica accidentally pushed against a chair, causing a pile of wooden artifacts to plummet to the floor.

"A cat! Bad luck before Losar! I'll go get Jampa!"

"Don't!" Sonam shouted. "I've got it under control. Go home and tell Mother I need some fresh tea. I've—I'm feeling sick, and I need tea."

"Sick? Yes, yes. I tell Mother. Sick tea." Uncle Thondup stumbled out the door. Sonam rushed to the back room. Veronica sat on the bed, her clothing, to his obvious despair, fully restored.

"I must take you to the clinic. You're hurt."

"No, I'm fine, really. I just need some fresh air." She did want some fresh air, but she also wanted to take advantage of happy hour.

Sonam's face twitched miserably as they walked outside. Maybe it was cruel to flirt with him. He probably had all those Asian man problems that inhibited romance, such as sharing a cramped apartment with his mother and his younger sisters who needed dowries. But she liked the way he stared at her, and his kiss was wilder than Davey Name's. She had to find out where he lived.

They walked toward the taxi stand. Sonam kept looking left and right, as if they were being followed. "Please tell me where you're staying."

"The Potala Palace."

"I'll come here tomorrow, in the morning. I'll wait for you here, by the gate." She wanted to invite him to join her for dinner, but his uncle had surely alerted his mother that her eldest son needed Sick Tea and if he didn't get home soon his mother would send someone out looking for him.

# Local Heroine Meets Hippie Elders

**VERONICA STEPPED OUT OF HER TAXI IN THAMEL, THE LATEST** incarnation of Freak Street, where the Hippie Elders had first colonized the Himalayas in the mid-1960s. There were lots of new pubs and clubs with neon signs and techno hits, packed with Japanese hipsters up from Puket, Aussies from Annapurna, dharma bums in from Dharamsala, beggar-hustlers working the corners and, as Jet Lag Janey promised, lots of deadly, sexy Khampa boys, stalking for conquest, speaking in code, flattering tourist girls.

She was rattled after her twilight visit to Boudha. She had been prepared for tranquil prayer, not child abuse and a mini-riot! It outraged her the way that vile drunk had hit the beggar child and no one did anything about it. She must have blacked out, because the next thing she knew, she was lying on a cot with a handsome Khampa boy. She felt sorry for him, thinking he must be lonely.

Veronica followed three lumbering trekkies down an alley, up a staircase, and into a teeming pub with Hendrix shrieking, lights blinking, girls flirting, boys plotting, beer flowing, dialects of Swiss, Italian, German, variants of Tibetan, Hindi, Mandarin. Stirred by perverse curiosity, she ordered a piña colada, since it was late winter in the Himalayas and logical to assume that coconut juice might be in short supply. She knocked over the ashtray, which summoned the handsome, ever-smiling waiter with a replacement ashtray. She spied a tall hippie cowboy, complete with boots and hat, approaching with drunken gallantry.

"Since we folks from that table over there have anointed you our newborn hero, we would like to buy you a drink."

"How am I your hero?" Veronica was perplexed, wondering how she could be a hero to anyone but a Davey Name groupie.

"You busted Rotten Romi, in full view of all of Kathmandu!"

"Is that the drunk who was beating the child?"

"I'll say! My name's Passport Pete, and I and my pals would like to buy you several drinks."

"Can't say no to that." Indeed the sight of the Hippie Elders erased all residual jet lag and the unsettling incident at Boudha. The Hippie Elders were still alive and well, reenacting their nocturnal dramas of drinking and smoking and conniving and hustling—rituals fixed in her child's eyes from years past, viewed from doorways and from beneath tables.

"Just so you know, Miss Super Hero, Kathmandu is a nickname town. May I introduce Temporary Rick, Randy Andy and Tent Tom, Original Chris, Bangkok Bill, Saudi Jack, Suitcase Pam, Available Edie, he's the manager of Drugs in Rugs. And that's Raw Sex Richard waving from the corner."

"Mr. Raw Sex Richard, what does he do?"

"You can ask him that yourself. And this is, uh, what's your name again, honey?" Passport Pete slid his arm around a dewy brunette.

"Jenna. I'm here on the Wisconsin Junior Year Abroad program."

A Germanic woman in a purple turban evaluated Veronica with narrowed eyes—seeing her as young, beautiful, and American, a thing to be destroyed. "So vat is your real name?"

"Veronica," she replied, stifling a laugh. If she could survive Tiger Street and Beth Armstrong, this withering ex-pat was merely practice. The smiling waiter handed her a piña colada that tasted at least fifty years old.

"Hey, it's all in the brotherhood!" said Passport Pete. "She's wearin' a Free Tibet tee shirt! We're in Kathmandu. The Rock 'n' Roll Raj! Bangkok for Girls!"

The American student withdrew a notebook and pen from her gigantic book bag and asked earnestly, "What's Bangkok for Girls?"

"Keep doing the Gwailo Shuffle as best you can."

"Vat is Gwailo?" the Germanic woman asked.

"Cantonese for Honkey."

"We gotta take Miss Super Hero to meet Stupa Joe!" exclaimed Passport Pete.

"Stupa Joe?" Veronica asked, amazed to hear he was still alive and well.

"Yes, the most famous ex-pat in the Himalayas!" Veronica followed the Hippie Elders to the alley where they ignited motorcycles and drove to Stupa Joe's compound. Joe's gleaming silver Mercedes convertible kept court with Enfields, Harleys, Volkswagens, and Marutis. The white dome of the Great Stupa was visible above a dark line of trees and prayer flags.

In the first of many rooms was a long Chinese table covered with silver ornaments, tantric masks, art catalogs, magazines, bronze vessels, smoking paraphernalia. There was a slim ledge for the elbows and drinking cups of the many guests who came to proffer jokes, joints, and art pieces. At the head of this table sat Stupa Joe, the nexus of this self-generating party universe, rolling a cigarette with graceful, explicit fingers. He wore gold rings, wire-rimmed spectacles, and a Mandarin shirt with a silk vest. His hair was now three-quarters gray, as was his moustache, which curled over his ever-mirthful grin. Veronica scrambled through her mental archives for his bio-data: English gentleman, married a former Ms. Thailand; had an Olympian capacity for smoke, drink, and parties that astonished even the most hardened Patpong survivors; spoke at least seven languages, was once arrested for icon smuggling, but had reportedly talked his way out of a Chinese jail. Surely he must be acquainted with the notorious Mr. Norbu.

"Take a look at this, latest in Chinese propaganda. I collect the stuff. It's the acme of high camp." Stupa Joe held up a magazine entitled *China's Tibet*. It was thick and shiny, with the usual puerile Stalinist illustrations of rosy-cheeked cadres, eyes shining with imbecilic devotion, features drawn with a decidedly Caucasian cast. The back page had a faux-Chagall tableau of smiling maidens tilling the soil. "Does anyone here know those new Free Tibet computer people? I saw them taking pictures of my friend's shops last night." A young woman in lavender salwar-kameez glided through the room with a tray of drinks. "They came round here asking me all sorts of questions about my business—legal angles and so forth. I don't trust them. They made me unwrap fifteen carpets and didn't even buy a pencil holder. They're fishing for information. Please don't bring them over, any of you. I have no use for journalists or charity hunters."

An astonishingly handsome Khampa hovered in the doorway, studied Veronica for a brief, tantalizing instant, then vanished. Bangkok Bill bumped Passport Pete's arm and sent the spliff flying over the antique carpet.

"Hey, that's early nineteenth century, Central Tibet!" Stupa Joe swatted the ashes off a complicated Dragon-and-Phoenix-patterned carpet.

A Hippie Elder with a snow-white ponytail yelled from the hallway, "Hey Joe, where the fuck is 'Please Mr. Postman'?"

"The same place it's been for the last twenty-five years. In the drawer that says 'Oldies.'"

"Oh, yeah, I forgot."

"Hey, Joe," said Passport Pete, "Allow me to introduce you to Veronica. She just accomplished the impossible."

"What's impossible in Nepal, besides knowing which of the many Mr. Anils one should bribe at the Home Ministry to get one's visa extension? I fear the day when my Mr. Fixit, Tinky Rana's uncle, retires or dies, for I'll be forced to work my Thai connections with unimaginable ferocity."

"Joe my friend, this young lady, newly arrived from New York City, just got Rotten Romi arrested."

All hands around Joe's table momentarily ceased lifting beer cups and rolling joints.

"What the hell happened?"

"He was hitting a child," Veronica replied calmly. "So I hit him back. The police came and handcuffed him."

"Hitting a child is neither new nor criminal in Nepal," Stupa Joe replied. "But getting Rotten Romi arrested is nearly miraculous."

"Pardon me," Veronica ventured, "but who is Rotten Romi, and why is everyone so afraid of him?"

"Romi," replied Stupa Joe, "is one of the richest Tibetans in Nepal. Rich from his antiques business. A lot of us deal in antiques, so we've had to deal with Romi. He's a wanted man in India and Tibet for stealing icons from temples and swapping them with excellent fakes. He's even sold fakes to Sotheby's and Christie's. If he thinks you might expose his racket, he'll make sure that your male staff gets the living shit beat out of them and the women are raped. I believe he had one of my couriers murdered. I don't know what you did tonight, but we can breathe freely and business will thrive, 'cause the bastard's behind bars. Amazing!"

Veronica noticed a faded photograph dangling behind a lacquered skull cup. It was a campfire shot of several Khampas with Sherpa porters, and Winston.

"Where did you get that picture?"

"That one?"

"That's my father."

"Your father? You mean Winston Ferris? He used to buy Bhutanese silver from me, cases at a time. My goodness, this girl is Himalayan royalty." Joe raised a silver cup. "Welcome, Miss Veronica from Manhattan!"

Veronica raised her cup to Joe's, as assorted guests divulged tales of the Himalayas, old and new, true and false. Winston's chivalric grin and crest of white hair beamed from the old photograph as a blessing.

"Please Mr. Postman," exhumed at last, boomed from the speakers. Joyous Hippie Elders were soon merrily writhing to selections from the rock 'n' roll hymnal. Veronica felt blissfully happy. Her college rivals were somewhere in First-World purgatory, attempting to whittle copious thighs on a treadmill or licking envelopes for the Alumni Association Empowerment Breakfast, while she was on a dance floor in Kathmandu with the Hippie Elders and Khampa boys.

At 2:30 A.M. Veronica wandered into the garden in search of the taxi that Stupa Joe had promised would soon appear. An animal rushed across the lawn. She jumped toward the wall, where she saw Sonam, staring at her from a broken window behind Stupa Joe's garage.

# Universal Language Lessons and Double Life Indemnity

**THE NEXT MORNING VERONICA WENT TO THE DILAPIDATED** communications center behind the hotel and called New York.

"Hello, John? Hi, it's Veronica."

"Oh, wow, Veronica! I read about you in Meryl's story! But you missed the Superparty premiere, what happened?"

"I had to come back home."

"But I thought you were a New Yorker!"

"How is New York?"

"It's great, but you're missing everything. Davey's wondering where you are."

"Really? How nice to know."

"He told me that you left him alone in Paris, with a Dharma Hustler."

"I'm sure he lived to tell the tale."

"Hey, your Dad's office invited us to a globalization conference in Bangkok. You should meet me there! Why don't you start a new band for the Bangkok event? Think of a name."

"How about the High Nomads?"

"The High Nomads! That's really great. Keep working on some songs."

They said good-bye and Veronica hung up the phone, utterly relieved that John still loved her.

# Getting to Know the Neighbors

**THE BATTERIES IN VERONICA'S AGING DISCMAN GASPED AND** died. No music! This was a genuine emergency. She went into the bazaar, where she tripped over a sleeping pig. What day was it? Tuesday? Wednesday! Sujata, the lady from Mr. Norbu's orphanage, was hosting a tea party! Veronica was not only invited, but expected! She had to appear like a respectable refugee activist, advocate supporter. Which meant appearing in a blue chuba with a Free Tibet pin.

Sujata hosted a weekly tea party for the South Asian Women's Association where ladies in the community gathered to discuss welfare projects, fund raising drives, and other matters of general interest, such as engagements, illnesses, who had just gotten an American visa, and who had to settle for Canada. Veronica arrived a respectable thirty minutes late in her best chuba and jewelry. She sat on the edge of one of the many chairs in Sujata's sitting room and met the other assembled guests, which included Mrs. TseDolma and Mrs. Sumitra, whose husband was a retired undersecretary of tourism who presently operated a golf course behind the Austrian embassy and hosted ladies' lunches every third Sunday, or so Veronica was told.

"Veronica lived in Kathmandu, in her youth," Sujata said. "And she is studying our language." A chorus of Hellos and Welcome to Nepals followed, then the ladies grinned and nodded and stared blankly into tea cups. Veronica fidgeted with her notebook. More tea was poured and more cookies proffered. The women stared curiously at Veronica's chuba, which actually fit, unlike the nylon mishaps of most foreigners. And on her wrists were silver bangles, old and rare and expensive!

Veronica managed a few queries in Nepali and Tibetan on basic bio-data, which petered out after about two minutes. The ladies, Sujata explained in English, were engaged in an ongoing debate over the promise and peril of modernity. The young people, the hope and future of Asia, were a regular topic. Many a youth was wasting away in casinos and snooker halls. Those pernicious, corrupting Hindi films, cried Sumitra, glamorized blue jeans and cigarettes and discos! Sujata clucked in agreement, and reminded all present that there was a Shashi Kapoor double feature special on Star TV at 7:00 P.M. Asian youth have no direction, they just want to go to America, sighed Mrs. Suchitra, whose husband had spent hundreds of thousands of rupees on visa-puja that the swami assured would procure a five-year multiple entry to America, but, she sighed, had failed to "procure the needful."

"We should encourage our Tibetan youth to go to Tibet," said TseDolma, "and be real Tibetans."

"But what would they do in Tibet," asked Veronica, "since they don't speak Mandarin?"

TseDolma's lip curled with disgust as she glared at Veronica. Veronica studied the older woman's severe brow and chin, her shining plaits of hair, her turquoise and coral ornaments set in gold and strewn across her dark chuba, from which her hands mysteriously withdrew amulets, bangles, boxes, keys, and lipsticks. What did Veronica's Tibetan teacher once advise? *No matter how good your language skills are, never forget to play dumb.*

"So Veronica," said Sujata, "I think it would be for you very nice to visit TseDolma. Theirs is a real Tibetan home, not like my modern office."

"Is it okay?"

"Of course. We of Asia always treat guest as family member. So please go to enjoy."

The tea party concluded, and so Veronica followed TseDolma to the ground floor of a four-story concrete structure. A stout, unsmiling Tibetan woman appeared in the doorway. Inside, and under a flickering ceiling light, a timid servant girl unloaded a tray of tea and sugar cookies. A toxic cloud of dust, smoke, and incense hung in the air. TseDolma sat on the couch, drinking tea. A phlegmatic uncle with a cheerful, toothless grin perched upright on the edge of the couch to gape at Veronica, this creature of unfathomable strangeness.

"Hello, Madame! I am Thondup, from Tibet!" He pushed closer, his prayer wheel twirling at a hefty clip. At once, she recognized him from the shop where Sonam had taken her.

"Tibet is very beautiful," Veronica replied, pointlessly.

"Yes! Pure Tibet!" Suddenly the conversation skidded to a deathly halt. The stone on the tail of Uncle Thondup's prayer wheel nearly whacked Veronica's tea cup from her hand. TseDolma coughed, trembled, fingered prayer beads. The unsmiling Tibetan woman sat on the couch, picked her nose, and yawned.

Veronica took a deep breath. "It seems that Nepal has changed very much in the last few years."

"Oh, yes."

Silence.

"There seem to be lots of visitors here nowadays."

"Yes."

More silence.

Uncle Thondup and TseDolma then proceeded to ignore Veronica and chat in Tibetan.

"What—what are you doing here?" Sonam stood in the doorway, staring at Veronica.

"Oh, hi, Sonam!" she replied.

"You are knowing Sonam?" TseDolma frowned.

"We met at—at the stupa. So you have met my mother, and my wife, Lhamo."

Lhamo, the stout, heretofore unsmiling woman on the couch, made a peculiar smile which pressed her cheeks up into her eyes. "Sonam and I are married for five years already," Lhamo stated firmly.

Veronica saw a large photograph on the bureau, between the two Chinese paintings. It was Sonam's wedding portrait. He wore a brocade, fur-trimmed hat and she wore the elaborate wedding jewelry of a Lhasa bride.

Sonam gulped a lukewarm tea as two small children wandered into the room. Lhamo grabbed a child, withdrew a flaccid breast from beneath her blouse and slid it into the child's mouth. Uncle Thondup mumbled prayers as Lhamo nursed the child. So this was Sonam's house, where he lived with his mother and wife and children and uncle, and God knew who else. It must have been an arranged marriage. The fresh smiles in the wedding photograph were gone; now they were just trapped in a dimly lit room filled with family junk. Pure treachery, what marriage did to innocent, unsuspecting youth.

Sonam cleared his throat. "Veronica is doing so much, helping the new refugees at Sujata's clinic."

"My father works for UNICEF," Veronica offered. Normally the UNICEF reference would induce smiles and nods, but TseDolma's scowl grew deeper and longer. She did not approve of seeing American generosity wasted on dirty newcomers who made trouble for the old-timers.

Sonam's twin daughters started crying. The servant girl asked about dinner. Veronica thanked everyone with a polite bow, and felt Sonam watching her from the doorway as she disappeared into the alley.

# Winston Pays a Call

**"AMERICAN TELEPHONE, MADAME!"**

"Go away, I'm asleep!"

"Telephoning to you only, Madame!"

"I need some privacy!" In Asia privacy was something you had to pay for at a hotel. Wasn't she in a hotel and wasn't that what she was ostensibly paying for?

"Please to answer! Phone call for Miss Madame!"

"Okay—okay—" She fumbled for the receiver.

"Veronica!"

"Oh, hi, Mom." Even half a planet away, Helena was her reliably bellicose self. Amazing, too, how she had traced her errant child to a crummy hippie hotel in the Himalayas.

"John's deeply disappointed in you for missing that film premier. He was wonderful in it but you looked distracted. Veronica, what in God's name are you doing in Nepal, of all crazy, self-destructive choices?"

"Didn't you read Meryl's story?"

"All of New York read Meryl's story. The phone hasn't stopped ringing. I don't know what to say anymore! Young lady, you are to get on a plane and fly to New York at once! Do you hear me?"

"Gee Mom, I though you'd be thrilled to get me out of Manhattan and out of your way."

"Don't be flippant. This is a breach of protocol!"

"Can I talk to Dad?"

"*No* you may not!"

"Fine, I'm hanging up."

"Wait!"

After much murmuring and shuffling Winston got on the line. "Veronica dear, are you there?"

"Hi, Dad."

"I'm going to be in Kathmandu for three days for a UNICEF conference. The conference is at the, Helena, will you give me that paper—no, yes, that one—at the Yak & Yeti. Where are you staying?"

"I'm about to switch hotels." Better not let Helena know anything.

"So you know where I'll be and we'll be dining together in a matter of days. You're sure you're alright?"

"Yes, I'm fine."

"Really? Good then. Veronica, hold on a moment—what? Salad, your mother says don't eat any salad, and go to the embassy infirmary to get a gamma globulin shot. Immediately, she says. See you soon dear—Helena, please, not now—and looking forward to it."

It was clear that Winston was using the UNICEF conference as a pretense for retrieving Veronica from the multiple perils of the Third World. But she wanted to assure him that what she was doing here was so much better than what she'd been doing in Manhattan.

Veronica experienced profound cultural dislocation upon entering the Yak & Yeti lobby, where a turbaned sweeper was cleaning the floor to a disco medley. The marble interior was filled with jeweled, languid women leading trails of frantic children. A UNICEF banner swung from the ceiling. UN delegates marched in and out of conference rooms. Veronica stepped into the coffee shop and found a nameless marine and the perennially annoying Aaron Eastman awaiting her. Aaron rose warily to his feet.

She slipped into a chair, favoring the nameless marine with a generous smile. "So, Aaron, how did you get invited?"

"They call me King of the Junkets." Aaron grinned and smoothed his tie. At the next table a party of upper-income, neo-suburban Delhites were finishing lunch. The youth, hopelessly bored, toyed with silverware while the women talked about clothes. The fundamental things in life, like family outings, were the same the world over.

"Veronica, your father said—oh, here he comes." Aaron leapt to his feet as Winston strode toward the table, trailed by four UNICEF delegates. She watched her father nodding and smiling, radiating wisdom, authority, the rule of law. With what dazzling ease he moved through Asia, always in a perfect suit, with his ruminative gray eyes and his silken white hair. Winston's fame was less volatile than John's or Davey's. It was Winston's job to dispense reason and forbearance, whereas it was Davey's job to arouse lust and hysteria, yet both wielded considerable influence on the world.

"Hello, my dear girl!" He kissed Veronica on both cheeks. "Now if you don't mind, I'm going to monopolize my daughter for a bit, so you fellows go and have yourself some lunch." The marine saluted. Aaron crept off with an obsequious half-bow. Winston ordered baguettes and omelets and drank tea. He did not broach family issues easily, so Veronica decided to make it easy for him.

"I'm sure you're wondering what I'm doing here, Dad."

"Well, in fact, yes, your mother and I were rather curious about it." Helena had obviously prepped him with all kinds of charges, which he was struggling to remember. "Your mother said that Mr. Penn had given you a very good part in his film project and that you just left him without any explanation."

Shame flooded Veronica's being. "You should be relieved, Dad. I escaped from the tabloids and spared you and Mom."

"Oh my, well, I hadn't . . ." Looking pained, Winston placed his glasses on the bridge of his nose and opened his date book. "I always liked your friend Mr. Penn. He's not a silly man, not at all. He's dead serious about his humor. And he encouraged you. Now tell me, dear, what is it that you want to do in the months ahead?"

"I don't want to go back to New York."

"And why is that?"

"It's not my world."

"Maybe Asia wouldn't look so beautiful to you if you were a low-caste Hindu woman. You can love it because you're from New York City."

Of course he was right. She loved her foreign-woman-in-Asia status, floating through places with that ex-pat's cultural immunity, where the rules did not apply.

"I love Asia, of course," Winston continued, "but I see its fault lines. It has the world's richest and deepest cultures, weighted by some of the worst corruption. I have many colleagues who believe that corruption is a natural condition of our species. I do know that there are some things you can correct, but not too many in the end."

"Such as?"

"Well, a small dose of literacy can produce minor miracles. And a stable income, even a small one, helps a child grow. Though now we have too many children on this planet, and not enough air or water for all of them." His eyes grew sad, as he thought of a single heart in pain, somewhere beyond rescue. "I know how you feel my dear girl, when you walk into a little room, or a village. Your heart grows. But you must try to do something practical for people, not just feel for them. We can never take peace for granted. Never assume that the miracles of our age are secure. We live in the time of the broad, sunlit uplands, after the great wars. This peace was hard-won. It created the UN, which has been my life's work. There is a reason that the UN is headquartered in New York. New Yorkers are supremely tolerant people. They have a great concern and delight for worlds other than their own. But my dear, that is not the same as getting into the business of fighting other people's fights. Be careful about getting drawn into the politics of what makes someone a refugee or a beggar, and what keeps them there. In this business remember that refugees may be your friends, but they lie too."

"Dad—" Veronica blew her nose into the stiff polyester cocktail napkin. "I feel so much safer here than in New York."

"I know you do, but Nepal is a strange country. It's not like Thailand or India. One feels that it could blow apart in an instant. It's poor, very poor, and filled with very active temples, with a surfeit of black magic. There was never a Gandhi here. Oh, before I forget—" He withdrew an envelope from his pocket. "I shan't have time to find a gift for your mother, or for my dear secretary Barbara, so would you pick out some nice things? You can send it to New York with Justice Rajan,

I believe he's soon to join us at the General Assembly. And please, dear girl, buy yourself something very special. You might need it someday."

Winston was always so generous with everyone. He was famous for his huge, thoughtful tips; he would send cash gifts with handwritten notes, in English, for the gardener, the laundry man, the cook, and the assistant cooks! The grateful recipients spent the money and displayed his letters proudly, often on family shrines. So no one ever forgot Winston, and when he came back to Manila, Jakarta, Dacca, Bangkok, or Kathmandu, as he so often did, he would be showered with garlands and tikka and kata and blessings.

"Dad, remember the Christmas Dance in Jakarta?"

"Oh yes, my dear, and St. Patrick's Day in New Delhi!"

"And the Balinese Germans on water skis!"

Together, they began to remember and laugh once more about the mad bearer and the singing cook and the poetic gardener and the time they had lunch in Kashmir, in the woods, and the faux-kidnapping in Borneo that was foiled by the Australian ornithologist.

"How wonderful that you remember everything so well." Winston's glasses slipped to the end of his nose. "But may I remind you, dear girl, if anything you do involves anything illegal, please do me one favor." Winston removed his spectacles and looked straight into his daughter's eyes.

"What?"

"Don't get caught. Remember all the trouble your brother Bradley caused when he tried to smuggle those icons out of Thailand for that collector friend of his?"

Winston made a note in his date book and tucked his pen into his shirt. Veronica admired his shining, meticulously trimmed fingernails. "The Ranas have invited us to a party tomorrow night. They still have that marvelous bungalow behind the King's Palace. We shall go together, at eight." Winston slipped his date book into a pocket and stirred a packet of sugar into his tea. Veronica could see that his attention had already moved on.

"So Dad, what's your trip schedule?"

"Mine? I'm going to Hong Kong and Manila for a few days."

"What for?"

"Oh well, just the usual business of trying to keep the world from falling apart, that's all." Aaron signaled from the door. "If you'll excuse me dear, I'm expected in a conference."

She watched Winston glide toward the door, dispensing a tip, retrieving a briefcase, and admiring his driver's forehead, freshly painted from a visit to the Shiva temple.

# Dr. Rana Throws a Party

**THE FOLLOWING EVENING, WINSTON, VERONICA, AND AARON** arrived at Dr. Rana's bungalow at 8:15. Dr. Rana came forward, arms outstretched, wearing a cream-colored Nehru jacket with ruby buttons, Bangkok loafers, and milk-white trousers.

"Winston! Let me have a look at you! Just the same, no, your hair's whiter, a sign of good health!"

"My dear Winston!" A tiny, exquisite woman in beige silk floated into Winston's arms and kissed him on both cheeks. "Don't tell me you've come without Helena, how could you?"

"I've brought a substitute!" Mrs. Rana clasped Veronica's hands and bathed her in a radiant smile. "How wonderful to have you back in our Nepal. Shanta will be heartbroken to miss you, but our Tinky and Papu are here and just aching to show you around. Tinky! Come and say hello."

Tinky Rana stepped forward, scented, bejeweled, and swathed in iridescent green silk. The Asian guests sparkled in saris and ornaments, but there were plenty of diplomats on hand to keep the scene safe and dowdy. Aaron Eastman grabbed two kebabs from a passing bearer and chewed noisily. Ah yes, this was just what America needed to improve its international image, another supercilious carnivore in taupe polyester.

Aaron tapped Tinky Rana's shoulder. "Tinky, would you do me the kind favor of pointing out persons of especial interest? I'm still 'on duty' you might say."

"Of course! Please meet Mr. Ajit Manswani from *Asian Business Weekly* and Mr. Bikesh Bhandari from Asian Development Bank."

Aaron crossed his arms to indicate that he was about to flex his intellect. "You're all persons of considerable distinction in your respective fields. I'd like to know what you think are the most serious challenges facing Asia today."

"The most pressing issue caused by modernity is a preponderance of unqualified astrologers!" declared Mr. Bhandari. "It is havocking marital unions."

"Population pressures in the north are causing deforestation, which creates soil erosion and flooding at the coastal regions," offered Mr. Manswari. "Last month one hundred thousand Bangladeshis died in flash floods, but in only twenty-four hours ten thousand Bangladeshis are born."

"How efficient, the rest of us require nine months!" quipped Aaron. Veronica tried to hide behind her wine glass.

"Veronica darling," said Tinky, "we read in the papers that now you are on a mission to free Tibet, so you should meet our uncle, Justice Rajan. He has taken a great interest in the Tibet Question."

Tinky steered Aaron and Veronica into the library. The room brimmed with travel artifacts that described the course of the family's diplomatic postings. Veronica noticed a Union Jack wastebasket, a Zulu spear collection, faded posters of Tokyo pop stars; bookshelves heaving with dictionaries, lexicons, encyclopedias, the complete works of P.G. Wodehouse and Barbara Cartland; and, inexplicably, three copies of *Portnoy's Complaint*.

Justice Rajan, an austere, white-maned Brahmin, with a full dhoti billowing about his ankles, was seated on a velvet settee, sipping a glass of Ayurvedic mango juice.

"Uncle, meet our two American friends, Aaron and Veronica."

Justice Rajan blinked at Tinky, and continued sipping his mango juice.

"Justice Rajan, we were hoping to discuss with you a matter of long-standing personal interest regarding the Chinese occupation of Tibet," Aaron said.

"On the subject of Tibet, just say some prayers."

"Could you be more specific?"

"Say some prayers and Tibet will become free. In about ten years' time. That is all." Justice Rajan frowned and blinked, and sipped more juice.

"We, I mean, I—" Veronica ventured, "I have many Tibetan friends."

"Of course! Tibetan people are so friendly. Please to take holy prasadam from the temple of Lord Shiva, Pashupatinath. It has been blessed this morning only." Justice Rajan extended a silver plate bearing hideous clumps of orange-pink sweets. Knowing there was no escape from the holy candy of Lord Shiva, Veronica grasped a sugar ball and swallowed it whole. Aaron slipped his sugar ball into a pocket, whereupon the orange goo leaked pitilessly over his white trousers. Aaron then slipped the orange mush into a flower pot.

Justice Rajan glared at Aaron with the full force of his Vedic authority. "I see that the holy prasadam of Lord Pashpatinath has shifted from your hand. If you do not consume it the Lord will take offense. That is not a wise course. You must eat, or you will become unlucky!"

"Certainly can't risk that, now, can we!" Aaron fished the dreaded candy, now coated in dirt, from the flower pot, and under Justice Rajan's watchful eye, washed it down with a glass of Limca.

"Come, let's leave Uncle to rest," Tinky said, handing Veronica a glass of duty-free Merlot as a cluster of Middle Eastern delegates busily argued issues of East versus West, rich versus poor, man versus woman. There followed a heated debate about whether or not hepatitis B was floating around the Everest Hotel. And did that Mexican water purification expert really get typhoid at Mother Theresa's?

Tinky's Merlot had taken effect, flushing heat through Veronica's cheeks. Antique '60s pop music trickled in from the dance floor on the outside patio. The party teemed with Asian royals and development dudes. In the diplomatic corps, a double life was a prerequisite for survival. To hell with nuclear leakage and debt relief packaging, everyone was going to have fun, dammit!

Stupa Joe was extemporizing about one of his favorite topics, marriage and saving face. "Tibetans have a tribal approach to marriage. They practice polygamy and polyandry. I know a very rich Tibetan family here where one woman is married to five brothers. It keeps the money in the family. My Tibetan secretary once said, 'Never become emotionally involved with your husband, it ruins your love life, because husbands will always cheat, so if you care for him, it will hurt. Save it for your lover.' Very practical. Aha! Here's a man who's an expert! Mr. Norbu himself!"

Veronica swerved round. Yes, there he was, Mr. Norbu, wearing an elegant black chuba with a white silk shirt, his hair and skin smooth and gleaming, a new ruby gleaming on his left middle finger.

"Well, hello, Mr. Norbu!"

"Welcome to Nepal, Veronica. I understand you have met Miss Sujata at the orphanage."

"It's a wonderful place you've created."

"It's simple but it has a lot of happiness in it."

"Norbu my friend, what were you doing in Beijing?" Stupa Joe asked.

"Looking for statues. The Chinese have stolen all the good ones, so I've gone to buy them back."

Across the room Veronica saw an American in an ersatz bush jacket, not the genuine thing as a Brit or a Canadian or even an Aussie would have worn. And he was wearing inflated, triple-toned shoes, always a sign of approaching danger. What was he, diplo, journo, or import-export? He turned around—oh hell, it was Todd, the sanctimonious Free Tibet creep from that party in New York, with the red-sneakered blonde! The blonde had radically upgraded her look, and was wearing a navy blue kurta pajama with a proper pair of chappals.

Tinky Rana steered the Free Tibet couple over to Veronica. "You have to meet my fabulous new friends, Todd and Angie! They've just come to Nepal to start—what's it called?"

"The Free Tibet Millennium Initiative."

"I think we've met, before." Veronica smiled and shook Todd's hand.

"We have?" Angie looked surprised.

"In New York. At your benefit at Luna Ticks. I sang karaoke and John Penn made a contribution to your group."

"Oh, yeah, I remember now."

"Veronica and I have been friends since our fathers were ambassadors together!" Tinky exulted.

"Your father's an ambassador?"

"He's the distinguished chap with the snow-white hair." Tinky pointed to the buffet, where Winston and Dr. Rana were deep in discussion with a diplomatic elder in lederhosen.

"Oh, yeah. Wow." Todd's face went white. Aha, the truth was out, they had dismissed Veronica as a wacky hippie, and now they realized that she was a wacky hippie with a UNICEF connection. Todd and Angie's body language visibly shifted. Veronica inhaled a Bijuli and savored her triumph. *Now you know who I am and I'll never let you forget it.* John was onto something with his star theory.

Mr. Norbu joined their circle, cocktail and pipe in hand. "So what brings you two to Nepal?"

"Todd and Angie have a fabulous project called Free Tibet Now, something like that," said Tinky. "Mr. Norbu has a fabulous gallery and runs one of Nepal's biggest carpet factories!"

"Have you been tested for child labor?" Angie glowered, suddenly in full interrogation mode.

"Tested?" Mr. Norbu laughed. "Tested for what?"

"I built the website for Rug Watch, which monitors child labor abuse in the carpet industry. I know a lot about it."

"Ah, yes, I've heard of you," Mr. Norbu replied. "Thanks to your efforts, more than half of the carpet factories in Nepal were shut down and all the children and women they had employed went into prostitution."

"How do you know?" Angie reached for a kebab. "It's really hard to get solid stats on that kind of thing."

"I employ over twenty thousand people in this country," Mr. Norbu said, now turning toward Todd. "I see your type come and go. You want perfection and you're outraged when people are grateful for survival. When foreigners meddle in these things it risks angering our host nation. We could lose our businesses and our homes. What do you think all the Tibetans would do if they were kicked out of here? Will you put them up at the Potala Palace?"

"That won't happen," Todd asserted.

"How do you know it won't happen?"

"Because—because we're down with the Nepalis!"

"Excuse me?" Mr. Norbu was genuinely baffled. It melted Veronica's heart that he didn't understand Todd's slang. Mr. Norbu peered calmly at the young Americans, who glared back with tense jaws and burning eyes. "What gives you the right to speak to me about being a Tibetan businessman in Nepal?"

"Sorry, man, but I just have some issues about your level of commitment."

"Please explain what you mean. I'm afraid I don't understand."

"You've sold out! You just think about your own survival! My credentials are pretty solid."

"I spent every day of my life serving my community, often in poor, dirty, difficult situations. I sincerely doubt that your sacrifice is in any way equal to mine."

"Okay, sorry, I'm trying to help!"

"If you've never been hungry a day in your life what makes you think you know what's best for people who are starving? Why don't you go back to America and take care of your own beggars? We can take care of ours."

"So you encourage begging?"

"I believe in giving to beggars. Eliminate the middle man!" Stupa Joe laughed. "I always give to beggars to enhance my luck. I accept that life is a cruel and dreadful affair. You should enjoy every ounce of good luck you get, because it'll expire soon enough."

"Let's cut." Todd yanked Angie away to the garden.

Stupa Joe wove an arm through Mr. Norbu's. "Will someone please explain why professional altruists are intolerably rude, whereas criminals are deeply charming? Perhaps it's because criminals work hard, take risks, and put themselves on the line."

And then Winston appeared, flanked by Aaron, Mr. and Mrs. Rana, a nameless marine, and three elegant Gurkhas. He clasped Veronica in a loving embrace. "Veronica, my dear, I must go. We are flying to Hong Kong in the morning. I haven't had time to buy something for your mother, so please don't forget. A piece of jewelry. Why don't you visit Mr. Norbu? He always has marvelous things."

Veronica followed Mr. and Mrs. Rana, Tinky Rana, Stupa Joe, the nameless marine, and the three Gurkhas into the driveway as Winston waved good-bye.

# Jewel Hunting

VERONICA STEPPED INTO THE TANTRIC TREASURE GALLERY, which was, according to his calling card, Mr. Norbu's Kathmandu contact address. Three men hovered by the counter. A plump Tibetan woman in a pink sweatshirt marched behind the counter, ordered the men out, parked herself on a stool, chewed a chocolate bar, and opened a comic book.

Veronica traced a hand over the silks, woolens, silver, bronze, and copper flowing from shelves and baskets. She spied a small photo of the young Mr. Norbu, sleek and chiseled like the contemporary Mr. Norbu, but with a more serious, pensive look. Stupa Joe had told her that Mr. Norbu once had a Tibetan wife who had long ago moved to Berlin. This allowed him to pursue women freely, unlike his beleaguered partner, who had a jealous wife who chased him out of bars and parties when she suspected intimacies with younger, prettier women. Stupa Joe said that Mr. Norbu kept mistresses, but kept them hidden, always careful to save face. It was the privilege of the rich Tibetan Durbar Marg Art dealer to enter casinos and fly to Paris and New York and Hong Kong for weekends and enjoy any kind of sex life he wanted, as long as it wasn't on public display. She studied the family photo shrine for pictures of women, but there were only babies and grandmothers.

"Welcome to my little shop," Mr. Norbu appeared behind the counter, leaning on his elbows, twirling a pipe in his bejeweled, graceful fingers.

"Oh, hi. I was just looking. . . . You did a good job with those Free Tibet people last night."

"Yes, I enjoyed that."

Veronica noticed the plump Tibetan woman in the pink sweatshirt glaring fiercely at her from the doorway.

"I need to buy a gift for my mother. A piece of jewelry. She likes earrings."

"So I hear you got my rival, Romi, arrested!"

"Where did you hear about that?"

"You think everyone doesn't know about that? It's made you famous."

"Famous! But—I've come here to get away from fame."

"You must watch yourself when he gets out of jail."

"I heard that he's in for five years."

"Let us see. He's a rich man."

"What does that mean?"

"That he won't have to serve as much time as a poor man. Look at this piece, the painting is very good." He moved to a swirling thanka of a multi-armed and multi-headed green goddess. He described in detail the iconographic complexities, the unusual shading technique used for the sky and clouds, the fine gold work on the tips of the lotus petals, the excellent condition of the silk binding.

Then Mr. Norbu touched her lower back, sending shock rays racing through her abdomen. "So Veronica, are you glad to be back in Nepal?"

"Of course. It's my dream. My Himalayan dream."

"Just beware you don't pay too high a price for your Himalayan dream."

"What's that supposed to mean?" She wondered if he was cruel, like Davey Name, or just arrogant. Arrogance in Mr. Norbu's case seemed warranted. Khampas had only to narrow their eyes and start talking in their impenetrable language to transmute commonplace, pedestrian qualities like arrogance into virtues, unique and marvelous to their race.

"Veronica!" Sonam stood in the doorway. He looked angry to find her leaning over Mr. Norbu's countertop, examining a metal vajra.

"Hello, Sonam." Mr. Norbu offered Sonam a handshake and a chair. "And how is the family?"

"They're fine." Sonam slid into the chair, his eyes darting from Veronica to Mr. Norbu to the fat Tibetan woman in the pink shirt.

Veronica was charmed, as ever, by Sonam's handsome, troubled eyes and his long black hair, which fell over his brow. Mr. Norbu, by contrast, kept his hair combed and smoothed behind his ears and kept his inner life deftly concealed. Mr. Norbu also wore a gold necklace, and gemstones set in orange gold on his elegant fingers. Sonam didn't wear anything, not even a wedding ring.

"Hey, are you Miss Veronica?" A Nepali hipster in distressed leather pants entered Mr. Norbu's store. "I'm Topper Singh. I was just reading about you." Topper held up a newspaper with Veronica's photo and Meryl's story, which had landed in the *Kathmandu Post*, courtesy of the international wire services.

"That's you?" Sonam stared at the photos. "When did you do this?"

"In New York."

"Veronica is a very good singer," said Mr. Norbu. "She has written a song called 'Khampa Boy.'"

"Khampa Boy! Too cool!" Topper Singh was getting excited. "We're organizing a Himalayans for Human Rights Concert. Here's the plan."

While Topper Singh walked Veronica through the details of the concert, Sonam and Mr. Norbu talked rapidly in Tibetan. Guy talk, like gossip and drug deals, had universally discernable inflections. Veronica pretended not to feel the attention as she chatted about pop stars with the ever-eager Topper Singh. She wondered how Tibet could produce sublime Buddhist masters and deadly sexy criminals, both. And handsome men  like Sonam, who were lonely and weary and in search of love.

"I've got some song ideas, musical ideas, which might work very well for your project. Let's see . . . here are some of the song titles: 'Khampa Boy,' 'Disco Darshan,' 'Inji Party' . . ." Veronica offered.

"So why don't you all come by our office? It's right behind the Cosmic Karaoke." Topper handed her a flyer which read, "Cosmic Karaoke, A Cool Place to Meet People."

"Sonam, let's go together."

"I can't!" Sonam snapped. "I'm busy."

Mr. Norbu peered at Sonam through a wreath of pipe smoke. "We don't see you out much these days. Busy with the carpet factory?"

"No, no, that goes on, always the same. My wife's cousins are here from Dalhousie. Every night they want to go to the casino to play mahjong. It is an evil game, it stole Tibet! The Chinese addicted us to mahjong to make us weak and stupid. Anyone who plays that game is a traitor! Like my stupid relatives."

"So forget them for one night and come with us."

Ignoring Mr. Norbu, Sonam stormed out into the street, leaving the boutique door open.

"I do not understand Sonam," said Mr. Norbu. "He allows that family to keep him a prisoner. *He* is the head of the household. Before he was married he was so passionate, so energetic. He was a hero to our community. He was our most active freedom fighter. He once spent ten days in Thribhuvan jail for throwing a tomato at the Chinese ambassador's limousine."

"Do you have a family, Mr. Norbu?" Veronica asked.

"I had one, once. My son died very young. We were not lucky that way. I let my wife move to Germany and marry another man. She did not want to stay with me after our son died. She said there were too many ghosts in our house."

Mr. Norbu turned to Topper Singh, who wanted to know the price of a turquoise necklace, and then helped Veronica pick out some antique silver pieces for Helena.

# Chance Encounters

**AT THE POTALA PALACE, PILES OF NOTES FOR MISS VERONICA,**
all penned by hand, grew like yeast:

*Dear Mrs. Veronica, I am addressing your kind favor to please consider the plight of a poor refugee. I am knowing of your good works with refugees and I am not doubting that Lord Buddha will smile upon you with favor for your good duty. And so it is with a low heart that I beg your penning one visa sponsor letter for myself . . .*

*Dear kindly Madame Veronica, Please to be thanking you much for your wish to lighten the burden of us poor Nepalis in our daily sufferings and blights. However, if you could please to consider one letter, given to the American Embassy, for myself to obtain one Visa only, your good name would be prayed upon in every temple . . .*

*Dear Veronica. Hello, I am Tempa. I see you at the bar and you are cool. Maybe one time you go disco me with. We have a big fun. I like American, it is good for me . . .*

Veronica tossed the letters on the floor, shut the curtains, and went back to assembling a large and eclectic collection of used clothes, books, CDs, cosmetics, and magazines for the orphanage. But first, she had to jot down lyrics for a song that Topper Singh might find useful for his Himalayans for Human Rights Concert:

*You know lots of girls who come from New York City*
*You tell all of them you think they're very pretty*
*I know just how to make you love me better*
*I'm going to write you a visa sponsor letter*
*You say the visa is so hard to get*
*But you haven't kissed me or danced with me yet*
*I'm a girl with diplomatic immunity*
*Everything I want I get duty free*
*Meh American lerki huh (I'm an American girl)*
*What does that mean to you? I'm the girl of your dreams*
*I'll get you green cards and blue jeans*

Veronica took a taxi to Sujata's camp. The lane was flooded, and Veronica struggled with her sandals and handbag as she climbed over the mud and sewage to Sujata's clinic. A group of seventy refugees had just arrived from the Tibetan border. Sujata and the assistant nurses were trying to clean them, feed them, and interview them. The children greeted Veronica with screams and cheers, and the assistant nurses brought tea and cookies. Even the chowkidar got excited when the bags were opened and the gifts distributed. Sujata asked if she could keep a purple spandex shirt. Two girls fought bitterly over a lipstick. Veronica had also purchased a boom box which she donated to the orphanage, occasioning a dance party. This was the kind of charity Veronica wholeheartedly believed in—the dance party. Wasn't the quest for a good party one of life's primordial drives? She felt a simple tranquility, sitting on the floor, watching the children play with her old clothes. Maybe real charity was just showing up, or just showing up in a good mood.

After the bags were scoured and the drinks and cookies finished, Veronica went to gaze upon the human prayer wheel spinning round the stupa. A cluster of nomad women from Mustang, in woolen shawls and rubber sneakers, encircled the Ajima Ma shrine. Two goats joined the pilgrim stream while a vast Brahma bull slept in a cup of sunlight.

The bazaar teemed with puddles, bicycle rickshaws, wet dogs, music. She noticed an astrologer sitting in his clean, modern storefront, drinking tea and reading *Asia Week*. His sign read: "V. L. Rajalingam, Astro-Consultant, Expert Advice on Gems, Matrimonial, Promotion, Unsuccess, Foreign Tour, Old Diseases, Etc. President, All-Nepal

Tantric and Yoga Ass. This Predictor of World Fame Will Help Attain Cherished Desires. Highly Appreciated by Eminent Persons and Foreigners." Astrology was useful when the predictions were good and you needed a boost, but today Veronica was blissfully content. Why ruin the present worrying about the future?

She stopped to buy incense, kajal, and perfume, turned a prayer wheel and lit a butter lamp, and wandered past more restaurants and tiny shrines and alleys that encircled the stupa. She came upon a shop filled with Chinese velvet, Bhutanese weaving, Lhadaki copper, Varanasi silk, Nepali topis, and a collection of Korean radios. The proprietor cut a jaunty figure in his neatly ironed pants, trim moustache, and eyeglasses, presiding over his showroom. He was working on two German ladies who were puzzling over a Kashmiri shawl, and soon, having successfully subdued the German buyers, he affixed his fine brow and canny eyes upon Veronica.

"May I know your good name, Madam?"

"Veronica. And yours?"

"I am Textile Taring, the only and the one! Today I have got some excellent Kulu shawls. Good for cold." He lit a cigarette. How handsome he was! God, it was difficult, so many bloody attractive men on every bloody street corner and in every bloody shop. "Please to sit, here, and take some tea." Mr. Taring handed her a cup and then deftly attended to three Australians in khaki shorts.

Veronica settled on a rickety stool with a view of the gleaming face of the Great Stupa. She felt a gentle pressure on her leg. She looked down and saw a beggar child, crouched in the dirt and holding a tin cup. It was a girl. Her mouth was taut, her eyes pleading. There were wide scars on her cheeks and scalp. Veronica wanted to give her something. Fumbling in her pocket for money, she saw how the girl's eyes followed her hands, hungrily. Veronica remembered that she was wearing a slim gold bangle, one of Helena's, a gift from a Siamese royal. She slipped it off her wrist and handed it to the child. Veronica saw that her arm was cut off just below the elbow. When the girl realized that Veronica was staring at her stump, she quickly covered it with her ragged shirt, as her eyes welled with tears.

Textile Taring shouted and tossed a brick at the girl, who grabbed her tin cup and fled.

"Why did you do that?"

"These beggars are havocking our customers. Please not to mind."

"I mind that you scared her away! Where did she go?"

"Go? Back to the gutter. There are so many like that. Such dirty people."

"Fuck you!" Veronica kicked over Mr. Taring's stool and stormed toward the North Gate. She cut through an enormous pack of camera-wielding Europeans—what the hell were they doing here at this hour! She collided with a cluster of towering Goloks from Eastern Tibet. Goloks had fierce tempers and carried knives and it was dangerous to push them or even brush against them. The Tasty Amdo restaurant was closed. A swarm of Indian pilgrims glutted the North Gate. This was where the boy had tried to pick Romi's pocket. Perhaps this was where the beggar girl had fled, but Veronica couldn't see anything but smoke and heads and elbows.

Veronica followed the crowd down the lane. It stank of rotting food and manure. Two dogs fought over a dead chicken. A buffalo groaned in its pen. Down another alley Veronica saw three girls trying to wrest a necklace from a body that lay in the gutter. The children spied her and vanished into a nearby compound. Veronica peered down at the body, which lay twisted over a pile of garbage. It was an old woman in a thick, frayed chuba and an ancient pair of leather boots, adorned in the Khampa style. From beneath a faded red cap two long silver braids uncoiled over her chest, where her crippled hands clutched a heavy silver charm box. She was crying, softly, and trying to slide the charm box into her chuba. Veronica touched her shoulder. The woman then tried to speak, but there were sores around her mouth. Veronica heard a thunder clap and felt rain. She slid her arms around the woman's torso, pulled her to her feet, and steered her toward Sonam's house.

Sonam opened the door, and saw Veronica, dripping with rain.

"What can I do for you Veronica?" He asked coldly.

"I need your help."

"What for?"

"I need a translator."

Sonam pushed aside the door curtain. The old woman hovered in the shaded hallway, afraid to be seen or heard. Veronica led her out of shadow, into a dim pool of light. The woman stepped timidly into Sonam's living room. She peered at the aged black-and-white photograph of Sonam's family. She pointed to Alo, Sonam's father, and asked where he was. Sonam replied that he had passed away five years ago. The woman gasped softly and began to weep. Sonam helped her to the couch, gave her some water, and asked her some questions which she answered through tears.

"Sonam, what is she saying?"

"Her name is Lhanzom. She comes from Bathang. It's near to Lithang, where my father was born. She says he looks like her brother."

"Where is she living?"

"She doesn't have a place to live. She came here looking for her family but she says they are gone. She has never been to Nepal before. She says she is lost."

"She just came from Tibet?"

"Yes, somehow she escaped. She looks so much like my aunt, this one—" Sonam pointed to a woman in the family photo, who also wore a charm box and a small cap. "My aunt, she died last year."

Sonam handed the photo to Lhanzom. She stared at the face and traced her fingers around the frame, as if to summon the old spirits from Lithang. She started to murmur what sounded like a prayer, a mantra.

"She is saying a Tara prayer—for the dead. And now she says we can call her Auntie, because my aunt is dead and I must be missing her."

"Auntie Lhanzom."

"Yes."

"Sonam," Veronica said, "I have a tape recorder. Can you ask her to tell us how she got here?"

"Yes, I will." Sonam spoke to Lhanzom, pointing to Veronica, who handed her the tape recorder. Lhanzom stared quizzically at the machine as Veronica showed her how it worked. The old lady smiled and nodded and asked for more tea. Veronica inserted a tape and placed the machine on the edge of the table. Auntie Lhanzom began to speak, in the strange and marvelous tones of far eastern Kham, slowly at first, and then faster . . .

I was born in Batang. My father was a chieftain. I was the youngest of my family. We lived in a beautiful house near a large monastery that I would often visit. I remember sitting there and staring at the paintings and the colors in the room, the red walls and the large golden Buddha in the center. One day a lama was asked to do a divination and he saw something very bad, about Tibet. I didn't understand it, but I remember seeing the lama crying.

I was just fifteen when the Khampa revolt broke out. I remember Chinese pouring into our region. They captured all of our leaders and took all of our knives and swords. They imprisoned many monks and lamas and sent clan leaders into China for re-education. We heard that the Chinese often came in the night to take away the heads of the household.

One night the Chinese surrounded our home, firing bombs. I saw my mother and father shot and killed. My brother was shot in the leg and couldn't walk, he was crying in pain, blood was everywhere. I tried to carry him but I couldn't, I was too small. We had to run. We had to leave many behind, we had to leave them to their deaths. We hid in the forest for weeks. We had no food, we were starving. We had to get something to eat.

We came to a village. We asked for food. Suddenly, dozens of Chinese soldiers came out of the woods. They grabbed us and shoved us against a wall. Who are you, they shouted. I said we were just beggars. They said I was lying. I was made to kneel and bow my head. They accused me of many crimes. I was slapped, kicked, and punched. I was gang-raped by all the soldiers. They held my head over a fire. For two years the skin on my head was like black leather and my hair didn't grow. They accused me of hiding treasures in the forest, of stealing from the people. But I was a young girl, I had done nothing.

I signed a false confession and was sent to a prison. I was not allowed to speak to anyone. I was kept in a small cell and beaten every day by the guards. The guards were Tibetans, they'd been recruited by the Chinese, or they would never have beaten a young girl. But they only had Tibetan blood, not Tibetan hearts, not any more.

I was often beaten because I was often caught praying. We were told that Buddhism was a poison, so prayer deserved punishment. In dreams I would see Lord Buddha circling my family house, I knew he was trying to protect me. I had a recurring dream of an old monk. Whenever this monk appeared, the next day I was beaten and tortured. I don't know what these dreams meant, but it always happened that way.

We had to work in a mine, hauling rocks. We were given a cup of soup and a stale bun, twice a day. It was like hell, like being in one of the hell realms I had seen only in thanka paintings. When people collapsed from pain and hunger and the guards would beat them with sticks and belts, sometimes they died from the beatings. We weren't allowed to speak to each other, to look at each other. Most of the people in that prison died one by one. I think many people went mad, and died from madness. I thought I would, too; it was only my prayers that kept me from dying. I really don't know why I didn't die, maybe Lord Buddha wanted me to live so someone could tell this story.

One day they released me. I was never told the reason, the release papers were written in Chinese, I couldn't read them. I went back to my village, but my village was gone, it was filled with Chinese buildings and strangers. Everything I had loved was killed. So I went to Lhasa. A truck driver gave me a ride. I had nowhere to stay, I slept in doorways, I begged for food. One day I went to the Potala Palace, but they wouldn't let me inside; they said it was part of the old serf system and they were going to use it as a prison. I wondered what we Tibetans had done in past lives that now such terrible karma was ripening.

Then I met a man from my village in Kham. He said that my brother was living in Kathmandu. It was the first time I had any news of my family. I had no idea whether they were dead or alive. This man helped me find a guide who could take people to the Nepal border. I was caught by Nepali border police and put in jail. They treated me very badly. They made fun of my old clothes and they tried to steal my charm box. They hit me with sticks, but I wouldn't give up my charm box, it was the only thing from my childhood that had survived the labor camp. It is a symbol of my family.

When they let me out a Khampa bribed a policeman and he paid for me to take a bus to Nepal. Nepal is so crowded and dirty and I don't understand what the people are saying. I was so happy when I first saw the stupa. I found my brother's house. But when I got there the people said that he had died last year. They were not friendly at all, they didn't even let me into the house. They gave me some food in the servant's quarters, but that was all. I was so sad to learn that my brother was dead. I don't know why Lord Buddha has kept me alive. That was when the nice foreign lady found me, lying in the alley, trying not to think anymore . . .

Veronica watched in silence as Auntie Lhanzom's sobs merged with the rain pounding in the garden. Soon the rain subsided and the last echoes of thunder receded. Sonam pressed his cheek into Auntie Lhanzom's knees, and he began to cry, as she stroked his hair and brow.

# Auntie Lhanzom

**EVERY DAY, VERONICA VISITED AUNTIE LHANZOM AT SONAM'S** house. She brought chocolate from the Swiss bakery, incense, sweaters, medicine, even European magazines that she thought Auntie Lhanzom might like to look at. Whenever Auntie Lhanzom saw Veronica, she would seize her hands, press them to her heart and begin praying to Goddess Tara for Veronica's long life. She wouldn't let go of her hand or let Veronica leave her side.

Sonam called the Nepali doctor who gave Auntie Lhanzom medicine for her stomach and antiseptic cream for the sores on her hands and feet. Sonam often sat with them, translating for Veronica and answering Auntie Lhanzom's questions about the exiled Tibetan world, the travels of the Dalai Lama, and the myths and fears people had about life in Tibet under Chinese occupation.

Sonam's mother and wife, TseDolma and Lhamo, resented the attention given to Auntie Lhanzom. They didn't want an old, dirty refugee woman taking up space in the household, but Sonam insisted that Auntie Lhanzom stay with the family. It then occurred to TseDolma that Auntie Lhanzom could be leveraged for status within the community, so she began to host tea parties for the South Asian Women's Association to present Auntie Lhanzom and her saga of suffering, in order to elicit further sympathy for her own family's plight. But Auntie Lhanzom didn't want to meet anyone; she wanted to sit with Veronica and watch Hindi movies on the television and drink tea and pick apart the Swiss chocolates. Sometimes she pulled a shawl over her face and shook her head and then asked people to leave. She only felt comfortable with Sonam and Veronica.

In the afternoon Auntie Lhanzom liked to walk to the Great Stupa. When she saw the golden spire rising into the gray-white sky, she clasped her hands in prayer, steadying herself on Veronica's arm. Veronica would take her to Textile Taring's shop and buy her a sweater, a shawl, and a pair of socks. The old lady liked to sit on one of the small wooden stools and study the fabrics that had come from Tibet, Bhutan, Sikkim, and Mustang. Veronica would serve Auntie Lhanzom tea, and gaze at her contorted hands and her soft eyes, which grew brighter each day as she received more food, medicine, and care.

One afternoon, as they sat in Textile Taring's shop, Veronica saw Mr. Norbu walk out of the Tasty Amdo and pause by the North Gate to talk to a man who looked very much like Driver Dawa, the smuggler who worked for Romi. No one had seen or heard from Romi since Veronica had gotten him hauled off to Thribhuvan jail. Stupa Joe said business was thriving as a result, and had even promised Veronica a commission, to be paid in antique Tibetan carpets. The man wore baggy polyester trousers, sunglasses, and a Chinese cap. He smoked and argued as Mr. Norbu proffered an envelope. A large European tour group blocked Veronica's view, as Auntie Lhanzom asked for tea. Veronica poured tea into Auntie Lhanzom's cup and settled a Kulu shawl over her lap, then turned to find Mr. Norbu standing in the doorway.

"Veronica, will you introduce me to your friend?"

"Oh, yes, her name is Lhanzom. We call her Auntie Lhanzom."

"I know. I have heard about her story." Mr. Norbu knelt on the floor beside Auntie Lhanzom. "I think that maybe she would have known some of my relatives from Tibet, they were also from Batang."

Mr. Norbu spoke softly, as Auntie Lhanzom listened and nodded, and then answered, her hands moving rapidly through the air. Mr. Norbu shook his head, Auntie Lhanzom spoke faster. Mr. Norbu dropped his head into his hands and began to cry. Auntie Lhanzom patted his shoulder. Mr. Norbu withdrew a turquoise necklace from his jacket and placed it in Auntie Lhanzom's hands. They touched foreheads, in the old Tibetan style, then he stood up, wiping away tears with a silk napkin.

"What did she say?" asked Veronica.

"She was telling me about—about some Khampas that we knew.

They are all dead now. The Chinese were their most disgusting and cruel to the Khampas. They punished us for fighting back, and for saving the life of the Dalai Lama. They enjoyed killing people slowly. They would hang a man upside down and slice off his fingers, then his toes, then his limbs. They would do this over three days and make his family watch as they did it. They would make children kill their own parents. We Khampas say that a torturer is a coward. If you are going to kill, just shoot once, or cut a man down in battle. The torturer enjoys himself when his victim cries. When I was a soldier I liked to win, of course, but I never liked to watch the blood when it came. At least we know that in samsara, in the endless wheel, you can never escape karma. So these Chinese who tortured so many Tibetans to death, who kept this poor lady as a slave for so many years, and laughed as they did it, well, in their next life they will wake up in the hell realms. That is some comfort."

Mr. Norbu stared at Veronica, as if searching for what motive made her cleave to Auntie Lhanzom. "You want to help her, I can see that."

"Of course I do."

"Just be careful."

"Of what?"

"Just mind that you listen to her."

"I do listen to her." What did he mean?

"Make sure that she gets what she needs. What she wants. She has been through so much."

Mr. Norbu then bowed once more to Auntie Lhanzom and disappeared into the pilgrim stream.

That night, alone in her room at the Potala Palace, Veronica wrote a song about Tibet:

*I come to you searching for the sacred*
*I throw myself into your waters, lay myself across your stones,*
*take your soil into my hand, take it back, take the Pure Land*
*I come as a pilgrim, I weep as a drunkard, I beg as a child*
*Give back the land, give back the wild . . . purify me*
*My people exiled, my temples defiled, holy waters desecrated, poisoned*
*   by the creed of hatred*
*A chi la du, Lhasa machak Lhasa chak, A chi la du . . .*

# The Black Eye Blinks Again

**EVERY DAY AUNTIE LHANZOM GREW STRONGER, AND SOON SHE** was able to move her hands and legs without feeling pain. The sores around her mouth healed and her headaches diminished. Veronica insisted on paying for the doctor and the medications. Sonam had initially resisted but under pressure from his mother and wife he accepted Veronica's money. Auntie Lhanzom slept in the living room, which irked TseDolma and Lhamo who were accustomed to having regular mahjong parties in the afternoons and now had to shift the card games into one of the bedrooms. Auntie Lhanzom said that she didn't mind having all the mahjong contestants in the living room, as she liked to spend the afternoons going to the Great Stupa with Veronica.

Auntie Lhanzom held Veronica's arm, stopping at every shrine that they passed, giving coins and chocolate to the beggar children, feeding the cows that loitered by the North Gate. Veronica steered her away from Golok monks and curious tourists and made sure that she stopped to rest when her gait slowed down. The Nepali calendar was filled with auspicious and inauspicious days, and some days were marked for special tsok offerings wherein masses of rice, flowers, and sweets were piled before the shrines of the protector deities. Auntie Lhanzom had never seen tsok offerings before and marveled at the strangeness of the scents and colors and music that accompanied the ritual.

One day a wealthy Nepali businessman commissioned an especially elaborate offering for his deceased mother. Ten priests sat in a circle, playing horns, drums, and bells as they tossed flowers, cookies, chocolate bars, lentils, kidney beans, and rice in a small mountain before the golden form of Ajima Ma, the grandmother goddess. Auntie Lhanzom squeezed Veronica's hand and pointed at the priests. Sonam wasn't there to translate so Veronica didn't know how to explain it.

Veronica was taking Auntie Lhanzom toward the North Gate when they bumped against Todd and Angie, who were stalking pilgrims with a video camera.

"Hey, Veronica, who's your friend?" Veronica saw the predatory glint in Todd and Angie's eyes. Surely they were wondering what she was doing with an authentic Tibetan elder, other than trespassing on their territory.

"Her name is Lhanzom."

"She looks like she just came from Tibet."

"She did."

"Wow." Angie's eyes traveled over Auntie Lhanzom's weathered hands, her charm box, her Khampa boots. "She's really amazing."

"Yeah, she's for real." Todd raised his camera and adjusted the lens. "All of Tibet's there, in her face." Todd's shutter clicked and whirred, flashes exploded. Auntie Lhanzom covered her eyes and pulled at Veronica's hand.

"You're making her uncomfortable."

"She's perfect."

"Can you stop taking pictures for a minute?"

"Sorry." Todd put down his camera. "What exactly is her story?"

"It's a long one." Veronica clasped Auntie Lhanzom's hand and led her away, back to Sonam's house.

A few days later Veronica arrived at Sonam's house to discover TseDolma, Sonam, Angie, and Todd in the midst of a tea party. Angie addressed Auntie Lhanzom in slow, deliberate English, translated by Sonam.

"So what have I missed?" No one offered a chair, so Veronica lowered herself onto the floor. Uncle Thondup had parked himself on the couch and was twirling his prayer wheel as if to stir up some wind in the stuffy room.

"We're just getting to know Auntie Lhanzom," said Angie. "And her story, well, it's heavy."

"Yes, you could say that." Veronica glared at Sonam, whose eyes flickered from Angie to Todd to Auntie Lhanzom. Angie wore an ill-fitting chuba and the red sneakers. Todd's hair was tamed under a headband, and his jaw was clamped tight.

"We think Auntie Lhanzom would be the perfect spokesperson for our interactive video conference," Angie said. "We've got a potential sponsor who's asked us to find a human rights victim who tells their story. Lhanzom not only has a story that is powerful, but she comes across as totally credible and is a really effective storyteller."

"She's not telling a story. She's describing her life."

"We understand what she's been through," Angie continued. "I've discovered, in doing our Oral History Project, that the act of remembering is a healing process."

"I'm not sure if I think telling such a painful story in an interactive video conference is a healing process," Veronica replied.

Angie reached for a sugar cookie. "But we can coach her so she understands what's happening."

"She need operation!" TseDolma spat out. "So you give money for operation first!"

"The sponsor has offered a significant amount of funding for this project. We will pay Auntie Lhanzom for her time."

"There are other Tibetan labor camp survivors who have been rehabilitated, who have already written books and done international tours," said Veronica. "Why don't you ask one of them?"

Angie glanced at Todd for support. "But people have already seen them. They're, like, done. Auntie Lhanzom is a new face. No one's discovered her yet."

Veronica's cheeks burned. "Do you always treat newly discovered labor camp survivors like something to be marketed and sold, like soap and vitamins?"

"In today's media market you're competing with every other issue on the planet. You have to be strategic." Angie refilled her teacup. "The Tibet issue needs something fresh and intense, like her."

TseDolma wheezed and glared. She wanted to stop all the tea party chatter and get right to the point, which was how much they planned to pay for the privilege of broadcasting the Khampa's collective tale of woe on international television.

"We should ask Auntie Lhanzom her opinion," said Veronica.

"We already did," said Angie. "And she really wants to do it, for the cause. When we got here Mrs. TseDolma translated for us, and Auntie Lhanzom is really excited about it."

Veronica gasped. Sonam then queried Auntie Lhanzom, who nodded her head and said this was the reason Lord Buddha had saved her life, to tell the world what she had suffered.

Sonam turned to Veronica. "Auntie Lhanzom said she wants you to help her write down her story."

"It's really important that the story gets told, you know, right." Angie was now using her best professional consultant voice. "I promise you, this will be effectively marketed and will get results, for Tibet."

Veronica stared at the girl, who smiled primly at TseDolma. Auntie Lhanzom seemed energized. Maybe this was what she wanted. Veronica wanted to kick Todd and Angie out of Sonam's house and have them deported back to Manhattan, but Auntie Lhanzom turned to Veronica with an eager, fragile smile. Veronica remembered what Mr. Norbu had said—*Listen to her.*

"Of course I want to help her. If this is really wants she wants."

"Wow, that's great!" Angie beamed and squeezed Todd's hand.

# Tell Your Story Once

**EVERY DAY AUNTIE LHANZOM SAT WITH VERONICA AND SONAM** to impart the details of her life story. Sonam translated as Veronica wrote and asked questions, with dates, names, places, and details. It was difficult for Auntie Lhanzom to recall many parts of her life. Sometimes she collapsed in tears and had to lie down, but she always kept going, with extraordinary detail and emotion, remembering all the Tibetans who had died and could not tell their stories.

Sonam and Veronica worked feverishly on the transcript, which came to 450 pages. Veronica typed the entire manuscript, made computer disk copies, and delivered the entire package to Todd and Angie's office. Todd and Angie sent off the manuscript to the corporate sponsor who was so impressed he wanted to organize a North American tour for Auntie Lhanzom to tell her story. And since Veronica had a family tie to the UN, she could help with meetings and conferences and interviews, which would start a network of support for other Tibetan survivors.

Veronica found Sonam in the Double Dorjee, drinking a beer and smoking a Bijuli, with his feet propped up on the table.

"Sonam, have you heard the amazing news?"

"Yes. Angie told me. We are taking Auntie Lhanzom to America."

"Aren't you pleased?"

"It's good news for Auntie Lhanzom."

Sonam's eyes followed the strings of colored flags twisting in the wind, then focused on the human prayer wheel, which spun day and night around the holy mound. "Look at my world. The whole community is on display. No privacy, no escape. It makes you very lonely."

"Too much freedom and privacy makes you lonely too."

"Everyone in Nepal dreams of going to America. They think it'll make life easier, richer, better, freer. My schoolmate married an American called Betsy and got a green card. He wrote to say how easy it is to find jobs, girls, cars, no parents watching over you. Oh, but his sad return, and his confession, behind closed doors, of what it's really like to live over there! No friends, no fun! No one to borrow money from except the bank! He warned us, 'If you go to the West, don't go with a foreign woman. Let your uncle arrange it!' But he could never admit this in public."

"Why not?"

"He had too much status riding on his green card. And saying so might attract Miga, the Black Eye."

"I see." The Black Eye again. "So you believe in the Black Eye?"

"Whether I believe or not, everyone else does." Sonam stared at the ancient, bronzed faces of his tribe, praying, kneeling, scowling, gossiping. He knew their pride and their fears, what kind of secrets and jealousies they nurtured, the ideals that ennobled them, and the prejudices that crippled them. He knew too much to care when he saw an elder turn a prayer wheel or light a butter lamp, because these ritual gestures had long ago ceased to awaken faith or instill peace in his mind and heart. Why then, did he remain a prisoner of his world? Why didn't he break free, like Mr. Norbu, who was still very much a Khampa?

"So what are you trying to say, that you don't want to go with us?"

Sonam stared into the faded painting of the Potala Palace above the counter. "And do what? Join all those people who entertain themselves by shouting 'Tibet for Tibetans!' 'Chinese Go Home!' 'Oh Tibetans, Fan the Undying Flame of Freedom!' It's so dishonest. Seducing people with false hope."

Veronica searched Sonam's hazel eyes, probing for what had so shamed and angered him. "You always say you gave up everything for your family. What have they given up for you?"

Sonam frowned, and crushed his Bijuli into the plastic ashtray. "That's not a proper question."

"You're educated, you lived here in exile, not like Auntie Lhanzom. You don't have to work in that carpet factory forever." Or stay with his cold, resentful wife.

"So I should act like Norbu and his gang, and sell statues and fly to Hong Kong for the weekend?"

Was he jealous of Mr. Norbu? "You act like you're powerless."

"What will happen to Auntie Lhanzom when it's all over? When people lose interest and move on to the next tragedy? There's plenty to choose from."

"I can take care of her."

"You'll be too busy. So many of you people come and go, promising all kinds of things you can't give. You can never understand our world when you're just visiting."

"You don't know me well enough to know what I will or won't do."

He stared at her coldy, then turned toward the window. "I've seen so many like you come and go."

"Fine, then I'm going." Veronica strode to the stairway and down into the street below. Why didn't he act like a real Khampa, seize her, abduct her, at least kiss her! She pushed through a swarm of Hindu pilgrims, toward the taxi stand, to the spot where they had parted on that first night, after they had kissed in Uncle Thondup's store.

Veronica slid into a taxi when Sonam suddenly jumped in beside her, slammed the door, seized her and kissed her. She could feel how desperate he was, in his loveless marriage and his dull job. His skin smelled of sandalwood, his hair was so soft. The taxi jostled over the cracked road—was the driver watching in the rearview mirror?

The taxi pulled up in front of the Potala Palace. Veronica gripped Sonam's hand. "Come with me."

"I can't."

"Why not?"

"Because—because it's not possible."

"Are you afraid of your family?"

"I'm not afraid of anyone!"

"Yes you are. Afraid of the Black Eye! Some crazy superstition!"

"*You* don't understand about the Black Eye! How people will talk, how it attacks your life force! You can leave this place, but I live here!" Sonam leapt from the taxi and vanished into the tangle of people and cows and smoke.

That night, alone in her room at the Potala Palace, Veronica felt a strange melancholy when she let go of the idea that Sonam could take care of her.

# Waiting for the Night

VERONICA AVOIDED BOUDHA AND DURBAR MARG AND ANY place where she might run into Sonam. She also checked her messages several times a day to see if he had called. But he didn't call, or send a letter, or appear anywhere.

As Veronica walked through the bazaar she felt people staring at her, with curiosity mixed with jealousy and disdain. She could feel them searching ravenously for something famous or scandalous. *Look, there she is!*—they would point and stare, and measure their expectations against the real thing. It happened in college when she danced too wildly or got drunk and dragged her wounded, poisoned self into the dining hall the next morning. It happened to Covergirls, who were scrutinized by the unchosen from behind the velvet ropes. Maybe Sonam's wife had seen them kissing in the taxi. Maybe someone had read Beth Armstrong's hatchet job and spread the word. What exactly she had done wrong she had no idea, but she knew that someone somewhere had branded her a fallen woman, a disgraced girl. The Black Eye was following her, and she felt the pain.

To her temporary relief, Topper Singh persuaded Veronica to attend a brainstorming session at the Cosmic Karaoke, a spangled, noisy trekker's pub behind the King's Palace. The place was filled with development dudes, climber guys, and Israeli hipsters in Ganga tee shirts. She was seated next to an anxious Ph.D. scholar of anthropology from New Zealand—short of stature, pimpled and shy, but fluent in Chinese, Thai, and Lao. He was advising the concert organizers about Asian media markets. To her right was a Kyoto punk duo, with nose rings, leather pants, and pink hair, who were helping with the light show. The house drummer, a perpetually stoned Tamil hipster, kept whistling and tapping his feet, while Tinky Rana handed out press packages for the concert.

Veronica opened the press package and saw images of Tibet's beauty, the mountains and lakes melting into ruined, charred temples, military barracks, the haunted faces of child refugees. There were many photos of Todd and Angie at the refugee camp, kneeling next to an assortment of refugees, looking pained and earnest. But there was no mention of Sujata and her many overworked and underpaid nurses. Across the collage, the text read: "Today the Free Tibet Movement has gone global. Everyone's getting on board. And so can you. Help expose the continuing crimes against humanity perpetrated by the most populous nation on earth, America's Number One trading partner. Become a doer, not a talker."

Veronica turned a page and saw, to her horror, Todd's photos of Auntie Lhanzom, framed by a collage of images of torture and hard labor and icons of Tibetan deities. It read: "Auntie Lhanzom is a face you'll never forget, a lady you'll want to meet. She survived 35 years in a Chinese Labor Camp, but she has the courage to smile and to share. Auntie Lhanzom needs your help. Every dollar you send will pay for her to visit the United Nations in Geneva and New York, to let her people know that we're watching." There were more photos of Todd and Angie with Auntie Lhanzom, and even a couple of TseDolma smiling for the camera, but nothing of Sonam and Veronica's transcript of Auntie Lhanzom's story. And then came the final indignity: an advertisement showing Auntie Lhanzom next to a photo of an expensive sneaker.

Veronica swallowed another whiskey sour. She knew that her cheeks were flushed and her hair was damp and splayed about her ears, but she didn't care. She felt a violent rage rising from her gut and flooding her brain. Where was Sonam? Trapped in his joint-family compound with his wife's cousins!

She ran outside, and wandered into a silent courtyard. In the corner she saw a stone goddess, smeared with blood and marigolds. She saw a crippled beggar crouched in the gutter, holding up a withered hand. She dropped a hundred rupees into the beggar's lap, as the creature wailed and bowed in response. These gestures of recompense to the poor made one feel so terribly powerful. It was such a cheap, easy way to redeem oneself. She leaned against the pillar where a Sherpa hustler sold hashish.

"Cigarette, Madam?"

A stream of pilgrims pushed her against the wall. "Where are all those people going?"

"To temple. Full moon puja. High day for soul cleansing."

*High day for soul cleansing.* Yes, that's what she needed. She pressed through the anxious pilgrim swarm, the spinning prayer wheels, the cows and goats. A narrow hall led to a large courtyard, where hundreds upon hundreds of butter lamps threw their light upon deities with multiple limbs, heads, and eyes; bodies of vermillion, green, turquoise, black, orange, white; riding upon clouds, waves, animals. The chanting of monks was punctuated by the sound of cymbals, drums, trumpets. She saw Buddhas with hands raised in mudras, protector deities encircled by fire, goddesses and gods, kings, pilgrims, and demons. She saw the wheel of life, the infinite details of blessings and torments. A lama sat on a throne, three monks stood to his right, another monk held an offering plate to a gold Buddha.

A pristine sun ray illuminated the lama's robe and face and the golden arms of the Buddha. She watched the lines of his hands in mudra, invoking the deity, the lama's eyes fixed on the Buddha, the monk turning to face him, holding his hand in the shape of a conch. He had taken the bodhisattva vow. He was not afraid of universal love.

She floated back into the bazaar, upon the pilgrim stream. A man seemed to be following her. He looked like Driver Dawa, with his pockmarked face and nylon pants. She ducked into an alley and waited for him to walk by. He kicked a sleeping pig, spat in the gutter, and got into a car. On the wall, Veronica saw a poster for the Himalayans for Human Rights concert, with photos of local pop stars, Todd, Angie, and Auntie Lhanzom, crowned with a fake halo.

Veronica's bag slipped from her shoulder and bills of several currencies scattered in the gutter. She pressed her hands into her eyes and envisioned John Penn's studio with the Mayan funeral urn and the inflatable Oreo cookie stool; his pale, clever hands, his blue eyes and dyed eyelashes. She missed him terribly. What would he tell her to do? Certainly he wouldn't allow defeat. Maybe it was too late to stop the concert, but it wasn't too late to disrupt the marketing of Auntie Lhanzom as a Human Rights Covergirl.

# The Big Night Approaches

**VERONICA FOUND A COMMUNICATIONS CENTER AND CALLED** Manhattan. John Penn answered the telephone.

"Hey, Veronica! Someone is trying to steal your songs! When are you coming back?"

"Very soon. I have an idea for you. What's Davey doing next weekend?"

"I don't know. I'll ask him. He's got a new record. I think he's in Japan."

"Japan? When are you going to Bangkok?"

"I think next month. You have to join me."

"I will. But maybe you and Davey can join me here, in Nepal."

"But—oh, wow—when?"

"There's going to be a concert, Himalayans for Human Rights. You can join us right from New York. On an interactive video hookup."

"Oh, yeah, Jerry Dollar is doing a lot of that!"

"I want you and Davey to do it."

"Wow—okay, we will. Talk to Tad."

After she negotiated and finalized the details with Tad, she thanked him, hung up the phone, and went back to the Potala Palace, savoring her triumph. There was no bigger star in the world than Davey Name, and neither Todd nor Angie had access to his manager.

# A Change of Plans

**WHEN VERONICA OPENED THE DOOR TO HER ROOM AT THE**
Potala Palace she saw Bikash, the houseboy, serving tea to Auntie Lhanzom and Sonam. Something was wrong. Todd and Angie's brochures
were scattered over the floor. Sonam looked unkempt and unshaven.
He wouldn't look at Veronica. He bowed his head and let his black hair
fall over his eyes.

"What happened?" Veronica knelt beside Auntie Lhanzom, who
was anxiously kneading her prayer beads. "Is everything okay?"

"Auntie has come to say good-bye."

"Good-bye?" Veronica felt a rush of fear and jealousy—that Todd
and Angie had stolen Auntie Lhanzom and were going to whisk her
away to the West to make her their poster girl, their mascot. She
couldn't let that happen! "I'm going back to New York with her. We
can travel together."

"She says she doesn't want to go to the West."

"Why not?"

"Auntie says that she owes so much to you for your kindness, and
for trying to help her. She is most thankful to you for taking time to
write her story. So she wants you to understand, and she wants to say
she is sorry, but she cannot go to the West."

"But I will take care of her."

"She says she will not be happy there. She is not even happy here in
Nepal. It is too different from everything she knows."

Veronica clasped Auntie Lhanzom's hands and gazed at the old woman's silver braids, her knitted red cap, and the charm box dangling from her weary neck. She had wanted to help this woman. It had been the one true, uncorrupted impulse of her life. She racked her brain for some kind of understanding of Auntie Lhanzom's world, of her true needs, of how she could stay alive and find some lasting comfort. But maybe she could never understand Auntie Lhanzom's universe. Maybe all she could do was listen, and wonder.

"Where will she go? And who will take care of her?"

"She doesn't know. She doesn't want to ask anyone here for help. She says they don't want her in their house."

Veronica knew that TseDolma and Lhamo wouldn't want Auntie Lhanzom around. She attracted all the attention, the sponsors, the visa letters. Of course she couldn't stay with them. And she brought bad luck; after thirty-five years in a Chinese labor camp she attracted ghosts and the Black Eye. She was not welcome there.

"But she has no money."

"She says she will sell her charm box. It is an old piece, she can get a good sum for it."

"No, no don't sell that—she needs it." Veronica opened her jewelry box, withdrew the blue sapphire necklace and handed it to Auntie Lhanzom. "She can sell this. It's a gift, from me."

Sonam gasped, as Auntie Lhanzom peered quizzically at the blue gems sparkling in Veronica's hands. Veronica poured the jewels into Auntie Lhanzom's lap and pressed her face into the old woman's knees, praying for her blessing.

# The Big Night Out

**THE HIMALAYANS FOR HUMAN RIGHTS CONCERT AND INTERAC-**
tive video conference was getting unprecedented international press
coverage. Reporters from Japan and Germany were flying in for it.
Meryl and John Penn's *Page* staff were covering it from New York.
Aaron Eastman had expressed interest in submitting Auntie Lhanzom's
story before the United Nations Human Rights Commission. Helena
and Winston sent a brief letter conveying their goodwill and best
wishes for a successful weekend.

Gareth Meeks, a London emcee, was warming up the crowd of international journalists, trekkers, students, dharma bums, human rights
activists, women's issues policy makers, refugee advocates, and even
some actual Tibetans, who poured into the Shangri La ballroom.
"Thank you, thank you all, for being present at the Creation." He sputtered from the podium. "We are just thrilled to be broadcasting the first
Himalayans for Human Rights Concert. We have satellite feeds on all
continents. We're hooked up to an interactive video conference which
will debut a life story that will touch hearts and minds around the
globe. We are here to break the mold with a multicultural, interdiscipli-
nary approach. We seek to harness technology to promote democracy.
We seek solutions as we delve into contradictions. Art and genocide.
Light and dark. Can the two be reconciled? That is our mission. Let the
festivities begin!"

No one was paying attention to Gareth because Todd and Angie

walked in with some second-tier model-actresses, imported from Los Angeles. There was even a right-wing congressman, escorted by an aid from the American Embassy and, of course, the corporate sponsor, who was a dead ringer for the famous TV anchorman from Helena's parties.

"Well, well, Veronica Ferris!" It was Jet Lag Janey. Of course she would show up just when the big party had started. "I knew you'd miss me sooner or later, so that's why I'm here!" She went round the table air-kissing the assembled guests. "Last time I saw Veronica we were in Paris, where she left me all alone!"

"In a nice hotel, as I recall. Did you have fun after I left?"

"I most certainly did! Davey has just the best taste in wine and clothes. And what are you charming fellows doing in Nepal?"

"We're going to film the concert for Zee TV," said Topper Singh, checking out Janey's saffron spandex pants, which were more of a rarity in Nepal than one of Mr. Norbu's antique dzi beads.

"I see . . ." Janey proceeded with her well-rehearsed ritual of opening a packet of exotic tobacco products, arranging her hair, and surveying the opposition. Veronica noticed that her figure had assumed new angles and allure, hardly a small achievement, considering her age and frequent state of inebriation.

"And look, here's the press package." Tinky handed Veronica a crisp, glossy folder. "You should really be involved. It's going to be fabulous."

"I am involved."

"You are? How?"

"With Auntie Lhanzom. Sonam and I transcribed her story."

"Really? How terrific."

"And this is Gareth Meeks, from the British Cultural Counsel."

"Miss Veronica, I've heard tons about you from Tinky! What's a real live Penn Girl doing in Nepal?"

"I'm—I'm not a Penn Girl any more."

"Oh, no? What a shame. It's what makes you interesting."

"Excuse me?"

"Let's get some drinks!" Tinky snapped his fingers and summoned five waiters who spread drinks, food, silverware, and cigarettes across the table. Clearly the privileges of royalty were never to be underestimated.

Gareth returned to the podium and announced, "We proudly present the singing sensation Viki Wow, creator of such timeless hits as 'Goan Dancin' and 'Love Marriage.' Elvis incarnate in the high Himalayas!"

The band played a rousing intro as the energetic Mr. Wow leapt on the stage. He wore a white vest with a billowing pink shirt and perhaps the widest bell-bottoms in history. But it didn't end there; supporting the package was a pair of platform shoes that deserved a circus prize. He did indeed bear some resemblance to Elvis, though not the virile, untamed Elvis of "Jailhouse Rock," but rather midcareer, Vegas casino Elvis. Veronica stared incredulously. American popular culture was an extremely dangerous substance which should only be used by qualified professionals. Of course, the same could be said of Eastern religion, Veronica thought, noting a table of dharma bums in saris and hiking boots.

Tinky summoned Viki over when the set was finished. "Viki, meet Veronica from New York."

"Peace!" Viki winked. "Hey, I really love your American music."

"Who's your favorite American singer?" asked Veronica.

"Definitely Simon Garfunkel. That guy's got soul!"

Veronica spied several dashing Khampa men in black chubas seated among the many guests. And then she saw Jet Lag Janey aiming for the VIP section, but one of the dashing young men intercepted her and led her away from the action that swirled around the rock stars, the models, the corporate sponsor, and the right-wing congressman, past the lesser mortals at the center tables, to the irrelevant mortals who were exiled to the back. Stirred by perverse curiosity, Veronica moved over to Janey's table and sat to her left. To Janey's right was a genial balding American lawyer, who was chatting to a charming teenager.

"Veronica," Janey whispered, "I'm so glad you're here. This is totally and completely unfair! I'm furious!" Janey was in a hell realm, as the friendly lawyer left the table without a parting word and was soon three tables away, pumping hands with a heartily rotund couple oozing just-been-trekking tans and smiles.

"It's everything that's wrong with the movement!" Janey gaped at the cool people laughing, talking, eating with the famous and the beautiful. "I mean, we deserve to be seated at the front table with the Guests from the West!"

Veronica blinked at Janey, and felt wonderfully superior. "Where's Davey? I thought you said you were going to get him to come."

"Well, Veronica, why didn't *you* call him?"

"I did call him. He's coming later."

"He is? So where's he staying?"

Veronica saw a golden ring flashing on Janey's hand, and it looked mighty familiar. "Hey, Janey, where did you get that ring?"

"This? It's great, isn't it? I—oh—" In that instant, they both knew it was Veronica's ring, a topaz that matched the necklace Veronica had sold to the Jarewallas, which was underwriting her Himalayan adventure.

"That looks just like my ring."

"What kind of ring are you talking about?" Janey was clearly nervous, and shifted her cigarette to her other hand, but Veronica grabbed the stone and held it up to the light. Then she scanned Janey's arms, ears, and neck for proof of additional larceny.

"I know that's my ring. You must have found it when we were in Paris." She'd caught Janey in a lie, a lie about a theft. What else had she taken when Veronica left her alone in the hotel room in Paris?

"Did I? Well, maybe I did."

"Can I have it back, please?"

"Right here?"

Veronica held out her hand. Janey balked. This was a refreshing new experience, to catch a dharma thief in the act and watch her squirm. "Just give it to me, before I post this news on the Free Tibet newsletter."

"I must have found it in the wash basin. And very good karma that I did, 'cause otherwise you'd never have seen it again." She twisted the ring off her finger and tossed it casually in Veronica's direction. "Relax, Veronica, you are one of the most careless people I've ever met."

Veronica froze, whiskey sour in midair. *You are one of the most careless people I've ever met.* It stung to hear this. But why should she care what this fraud, thief, and liar said, even if it was true? Veronica stood up, walked toward the stage, and leaned against the wall by the exit. Todd and Angie sat on the stage, next to a large screen.

When the hundreds of folding chairs were filled at last, Todd stood at the podium and spoke into the microphone: "Hey, I'm Todd, and this is Angie. It's awesome to see so many people. We want to show you what dedicated activism can accomplish. Check it out." Todd pressed a button, and the screen filled with Todd and Angie's montage of Tibet's mountains melting into labor camps. Todd and Angie were smiling and waving and soaking up the wild applause. Todd beamed with cringe-inducing, fake humility. It was his Coverboy moment and he was having it all. *Just wait, you prick.*

There was a brief stir among the audience, calmed by Angie, who asked for everyone's attention. The screen filled with a stark black-and-white photograph of Auntie Lhanzom's anguished, beautiful face, which told the whole story of Tibet. The drone of a Tibetan flute floated through the room, then melted into some kind of weird techno fusion. Auntie Lhanzom's face splintered into a collage of different faces.

Then Gareth strode once more to the podium. "We have a very special surprise guest tonight. Someone everyone's heard of. Someone everyone loves. Someone, may I say, who imparts to all of us a rare kind of universal joy! Someone who's at the top of his game, beamed into us, live from Tokyo! A big round of applause please, for *Davey Name!*"

And there he was on the video screen, Davey Name himself, looking cool and gorgeous, holding a mike and singing "Get Up, Stand Up." Everyone screamed and cheered. To Veronica's infinite delight, Todd and Angie fumed and squirmed. After all, who was going to give a fuck about two midcareer human rights hustlers when Davey Name was in the room?

Veronica watched Davey moving across the video screen, taunting the girls with his hips and eyes, singing brilliantly, seething charm and making everyone in the room feel special just to look at him. This was where he was supremely generous, where he dispensed unconditional love. Veronica peered around the ballroom and saw all kinds of people, who spoke all kinds of languages, singing in unison along with Davey Name and gazing at him in rapturous adoration, while flirting with their friends and neighbors. Davey was one of the high priests of globalization. Maybe he had earned the right to be cruel, because millions of people wanted to devour him. Yes, she could only love Davey Name as her rock 'n' roll idol. And miraculously, she could rely on him to come through when she needed him most.

When the song was finished, Davey peered into the camera and said, "Just want to say hello to everyone in Nepal. And thanks to my friend, Miss Veronica Ferris, for hooking me up with your party tonight." Davey winked and blew a kiss. Veronica felt all eyes in the room turn to her—and it felt fantastic. Yes, being a Penn Girl had its perks after all.

The lights came up on the stage. Now it was time for Auntie Lhanzom to come up for the interactive video conference. Todd and Angie stood with the corporate sponsor and the right-wing congressman, who held a silver plaque and a bouquet of flowers for Auntie Lhanzom. Topper Singh readied the camera crew for the close-up.

But Auntie Lhanzom did not come.

Angie signaled to one of the dashing young men in the black chubas, and he went behind the curtain. Veronica could hear murmurs and shuffles off stage. The right-wing congressman smiled gamely for the cameras.

But Auntie Lhanzom did not come.

The Tamil drummer played air guitar. The man in the black chuba walked back on stage and whispered something to Angie. The right-wing congressman smiled for another photographer.

But Auntie Lhanzom did not come.

Angie leaned into the microphone, "Pardon the delay, it seems that Ms. Lhanzom isn't here. If anyone knows where she is, could they please come forward?"

Sonam stood up in the back. Veronica could see that he was drunk. "Auntie Lhanzom isn't coming!"

"What do you mean, not coming!" Topper Singh yelled. "We're on a satellite feed to twenty-five markets!"

"She's gone!"

"Gone where?"

"Gone!"

"Did the Chinese kidnap her?"

"She didn't want to do this," Sonam said, pointing to the camera.

"What do you mean she didn't want to do this?"

"*You* made a joke of our freedom struggle!" Todd roared at Sonam.

Sonam ran to the stage and punched Todd in the face.

The corporate sponsor stormed off. Angie made a futile plea for everyone to remain calm and stay in their seats. The right-wing congressman shouted for help, security guards raced toward the stage, clutching billysticks and walkie-talkies. The lights went off. Everyone started screaming and grabbing their bags and darting toward the exit signs.

Veronica could feel all hell breaking loose. She ran though the kitchen, down the stairs, to the path behind the hotel. The streets were no longer a maze of redemption, walks back in time—no, the streets were haunted. The gardens and temples seethed with disease and danger. All the enchantment was gone. Luck was draining out of her, like coins accidentally dropped into the gutter. She tripped on a rock and fell into the mud. Her left heel had come loose. She heard a rickshaw and a cow moaning in the distance. She couldn't see a way out; she would have to go back the way she came. She felt so utterly ashamed of this dream, this fantasy of saving Auntie Lhanzom, saving the world—she couldn't even save herself. She was just a foolish, stupid girl, with a broken heel and muddy hands. She suddenly wanted to go back to New York, back to Travesty, Galaxy, Meryl's couch, anywhere in New York.

"I've been looking for you." A man appeared at the end of the alley. He looked drunk, and very angry.

"Me?"

"They told me you were here."

"But what do you want with me?"

"You're the one who got me arrested," He growled, approaching her. She recognized Romi.

"That wasn't me—"

"Oh yeah? Everyone knows it was you. You can't hide anywhere, everyone knows it was you!"

"I—I'm working for you—for the Tibetans!"

Romi laughed. "So what?"

"So we shouldn't fight!"

"That doesn't mean anything to me, that you work for the Tibetans. So do I." Romi was nearly upon her, his arms tensed and ready to strike.

"I'll give you money," Veronica blurted out in desperation.

"Give me money? You don't have as much money as I do." He laughed a nasty, oily laugh. "What about the time I spent in jail? You can pay me back for that?"

"But—you got out."

"I had to pay a lot of money to get out. So you want to pay me back for that?"

"I have a lot of jewelry."

"So I hear."

"I'll give it to you."

"I see." He came closer. "No, I don't want money or jewelry. I want something else."

"We—we can talk about it." Her heart was racing and she felt sick.

"It's my reputation that you damaged. And my luck."

"You can get that back, your lungta, right?"

"So, you know about lungta? Explain it to me."

"And—and your—yang!"

"Aha, not bad. What else?"

Veronica saw lights approaching behind him. "What's that? Police?"

"What police? I know all the police." He lunged for her neck, but she kicked him hard in the knee and he fell into the mud. She ran down the alley, behind the hotel, toward the King's Palace. Dozens and dozens of policemen poured from blue police vans, thin, awkward young men in ill-fitting uniforms, all carrying machine guns, all ready to shoot to kill.

"Get in." Mr. Norbu grabbed Veronica's arm and pulled her into his car.

They swerved around the King's Palace, and back toward the hotel. Ten policemen blocked Mr. Norbu's car, the timid Nepali driver slammed the brakes, and suddenly four rifles were jammed through the windows. Mr. Norbu addressed the policemen calmly. The man in charge blinked at the quaking driver and at Veronica, then waved them on.

Mr. Norbu wiped his face with a napkin. "The police in Nepal are not like your nice police in New York City. There will be quite a few arrests in the next few days."

"Arrests?"

"Yes. What do you expect? You come walking into an ancient place that's crippled by tribal feuds that you know nothing about. What were you people thinking?"

"I'm not one of those people—"

"No? Then what were you doing with them?"

Veronica felt hot tears of shame sear her eyes and cheeks. It was humiliating to cry in front of him. He made no effort to comfort her. He said something to the driver, who steered the car into an alley. Mr. Norbu grasped her hand and led her up a staircase and into the small bedroom that adjoined his gallery. One of his many servants handed him a stack of papers. He locked the door, poured a glass of Scotch and lowered himself into an armchair.

"What happened to Auntie Lhanzom?" Veronica asked.

"She's safe. She's with my courier."

"Where are they?"

"By now, they must be just over the border."

"What?"

"Yes, she's in Tibet. They went overland, in my Land Rover."

"Why would she go to Tibet, where she was tortured and imprisoned?"

"I know you cannot understand why she would want to go back to a place where she suffered so much. She wanted to go back to Tibet to die. When my time comes, I hope that I'll have the good luck of dying in my homeland, not on top of a slum in a hot, dirty country like Nepal. Lhanzom told me that she is glad she came to Nepal and that she saw her brother's family, but she didn't like it here. So I arranged for my courier to take her to my house in Lhasa. She will be safe there."

"How do you know she'll be safe?"

"Because I pay my monthly bribes to the police on time," he laughed. Veronica felt utterly foolish. What sort of callow hubris had led her to think that she could ever know anything about this place? "In this part of the world, bribery will get you everywhere. Those Americans with the project made a very serious error. They bribed the wrong officials."

Veronica thought it impossible to pin more crimes on Todd and Angie.

"Look at this, more trouble from those human rights people." Mr. Norbu handed her the *Kathmandu Post*, which read:

Idol-Lifter Nabbed—Dawa Topden, alias "Driver Dawa," a notorious dealer cum smuggler, has been arrested in Nepal on idol-lifting charges. Mr. Dawa was kingpin of a notorious smuggling ring that removed religious relics from temples. Mr. Dawa has made for himself a tidy sum in plundering the dazzling artistic and cultural heritage of his native homeland, Tibet, in a brazen, nefarious, and illegal manner for some time now. Representatives of the Tibetan Autonomous Region of the People's Republic of China and of the Kingdom of Nepal have jointly declared that Mr. Dawa will be regarded without pity for his dastardly actions. A spokesperson for the Historical Relics Department said, "this is a day of victory for the religious art heritage of the Himalayas." Todd Feele, spokesperson for the Free Tibet movement, provided authorities with several other names from the ring of iniquity, but according to Detective Basnet of the KTM Police, the miscreants are still absconding.

"What does this mean?"

"It means Stupa Joe will have to leave town. Our businesses will all collapse. But it is no problem for those Americans. They can leave any time. They have American passports."

"Mr. Norbu—"

"Why do you call me Mr. Anything?! Please, I am just Norbu!"

"Is it too late, to, to—"

"Save Tibet?" Mr. Norbu suddenly looked very sad. "No, it's far too late for anything to make a difference. So much damage has already been done. It's safe to plan and argue when it's just a dream, when it's someone else's dream."

"Mr.—I mean—Norbu, is it too late for me to go back to New York?"

"Too late for that?" Mr. Norbu laughed, a surprised, reassuring laugh. "Your family will always take you back. They have to. But with other people, you can use them up. And then when you change your mind, it's too late. You've made your choice. It's like choosing a jewel, now it's yours. Maybe you picked the wrong one. The fake. But it's too late, the trader is gone, and now you have to wear it."

Veronica went into the bathroom to wash her hands. She looked into the mirror and hardly recognized herself. Her hair was a tangled wreck. Her face was gaunt and sallow, her eyes ragged and bloodshot. Where was her natural beauty? Had she ruined it? Now she was free to cry—there was no point in worrying about the Black Eye.

"Veronica, sit here." Mr. Norbu handed her a shawl and steered her to the couch, where she lay down. "Don't shake like that. And don't ever cry in public. It hurts your lungta." He slid a hand around her waist and pulled her into his chest. She felt immense gratitude and relief. She couldn't imagine anything worse than being alone.

# Good-bye My Friend

"Please, I feel sick." She pressed a pillow over her eyes.

"I had my driver get your things from the Potala Palace. You had a lot of mail. This is from your father. Here, take it." He handed her a fax, written in Winston's distinctive hand. She held it up to the light and read: "Hello, my dear, I hope this finds you well. I have some sad news for you that you may have already heard. Your friend Mr. John Penn has died. There seems to have been some mistake in the hospital and it happened very suddenly. There is going to be a memorial service."

"John's dead!"

"Yes. It is sad that our friend John Penn has died. But the disturbance caused by those Free Tibet people has drowned out everything. You might want to see their latest. Here." He opened a flyer with a photograph of Auntie Lhanzom beneath the caption, "MISSING."

"What does this mean?"

"It means it's time to get out, if you can. I'm going to Hong Kong."

"Hong Kong! But—"

"I can't take you with me, even though I would like to. But you can't stay here."

She pressed her face into the pillow.

"I'll get you to New York. You have to say good-bye to Mr. Penn. If you don't, you'll be sorry, more than you are right now." He walked to the window and lifted the curtain. He was, as always, beautifully dressed, his hair was combed and oiled, his skin a smooth, deep gold.

She pulled herself out of his bed, into the bathroom. She stood under the shower, letting herself cry—this time for John.

She managed to dry her hair, put on clothes and follow Mr. Norbu to his car. The gardener, the cook, and the houseboys gathered in a crooked circle. The head bearer touched Mr. Norbu's feet. The servants gazed in silent rapture as Mr. Norbu handed each one an envelope filled with cash and a piece of Swiss chocolate.

Mr. Norbu and Veronica got into his car and drove toward the airport, past herds of cattle, rickshaws, dogs, temples, stupas, monks, hippies, filth, and splendor. The clouds parted above a ring of snow-white mountains. A beggar child ran to the car window with a tin cup. Veronica felt her hands reach for her dzi bead—she had nothing else to give, and she didn't want it anymore.

"Don't do that." Mr. Norbu reached over her to drop a hundred rupee note into the child's cup. "You'll make it worse for them if you do that. The ring leader will take it away and the other beggars will beat him up."

The beggar child grabbed the hundred rupees and vanished.

"Don't look so sad. You still have some luck."

"How do you know?"

"Because I have this for you." Mr. Norbu held up her mother's topaz, the one she'd sold in Paris so she could escape to Kathmandu, and the blue sapphires she had given to Auntie Lhanzom. "I bought the topaz from Shastri. I know it's a special piece and you'd want it again. It was very kind of you to help Auntie Lhanzom, but she wouldn't know how to sell it in Lhasa. I bought it from her when she was leaving. I gave her a very good price. Remember what I told you, gems have a life of their own. They often decide where they want to go."

Mr. Norbu placed the jewels in her palm and wrapped her hands around them. Then he laughed and pulled Veronica to his chest as the car pulled through a swarm of dust and soot and passed the first of the many security check points that took them to the departure terminal.

And as the plane rose into the sky, Veronica waved good-bye to the ice-toothed ridge of the Lantang Himal, Ganesh Himal, and Manasalu, to the blue Himalayan sky, and to the Buddha Valley below, so green and gold, crippled and pure, turning, spinning, in and out of death and life.

# PART IV

# The Magical Island

# A Funeral and a Party

**THE SCENE OUTSIDE ST. PATRICK'S CATHEDRAL LOOKED LIKE A** club opening, which was how John would've wanted it. A police barricade held back crowds as the honored guests swarmed the entrance. Veronica found a seat behind Suki Dean and Venice Beach. She was drained from the twenty-seven-hour flight from Nepal, and ashamed of the dirt under her fingernails, her frazzled hair, and all the tears and creases in her old jacket. The church was filled with neat, clean, well-dressed mourners who discreetly scanned the pews to see who was sitting where, whisper in each others' ears, and nod and wink at friends across the aisle. Helena had to be somewhere up front, just where she belonged, with all of John's very dear, very old friends.

Dickie Drake, the first speaker, launched into a pretentious ramble about John's contribution to the world of art. Veronica lifted her hand to her neck for her dzi bead. The string was bare, the stone was gone. Gone! After so many years, gone, like John! Tears poured down her cheeks; she sniffed and coughed, totally unable to control herself. Suki Dean nudged Venice Beach to take in the delightful sight of the ragged and disheveled Veronica Ferris wiping her nose on her shirt sleeve. Veronica knew she was making too much noise and disturbing all the clean, graceful people seated nearby, but the tears came in a flood, as she thought of John Penn, his black turtleneck shirts and his clever, generous smile, and she realized that she would never see him again.

After several more people spoke and prayers were read, the service was over. Two *Page* employees seized Veronica as she was leaving the church. There was a special private funeral after party at Jerry Dollar's new club and Veronica could get them in because she was a Covergirl. Veronica had no strength to shake them off. What the hell did it matter now? *Go ahead, suck my blood, let me be your host this afternoon while I'm still worth something.*

They flagged a taxi and drove to Jerry Dollar's club. Sure enough, there was a door policy, since everyone in New York had heard about the party and word had leaked out about where it was. Tad, standing guard with a guest list, saw Veronica and waved her through.

To honor John Penn's legacy, Jerry Dollar had organized a real party. The walls were pasted with *Page* covers. Rock 'n' roll blasted on the PA system. Food and drink circulated, women laughed and flirted, men raised toasts and exchanged business cards. The place was teeming with new and old starlets, cast-offs, Covergirls and Coverboys, Real Beauties, New Girls In Town, former employees, and posthumous groupies who'd never met John but wanted to get in on the action while there was still time.

Veronica saw her *Page* cover over a banister. Her fingers curled around the empty string that had held the dzi bead. People glanced at her with cold, hard eyes. What were they thinking? *Look, there's a Covergirl, what happened to her?* Maybe she'd been gone too long. Maybe she wasn't beautiful anymore. But what did it matter now?

"Veronica Ferris!" A girl tugged her coat sleeve. "You were so hot in the Superparty video. Then you dropped out of sight."

"Not completely." It was Bennett, her old college friend, with long, newly blond hair and a blue leather jacket. "John loved your music. Take a look." Bennett opened the last issue of *Page.* Veronica saw photos of herself, taken by John, with her song lyrics, "Khampa Boy," "Inji Party," "Bombay Superstar," "Disco Darshan," attributed to Maya Smith.

"Who's Maya Smith?"

"She looks like Veronica Ferris."

"Veronica Ferris! Wow, she's the one who got Davey Name to sing in Kathmandu! Look!" The girl opened a tabloid to a huge color photo of Davey filling the video screen at the Shangri La Hotel in Nepal.

Veronica quickly read the text. No mention of Todd or Angie and the Tibet Millennium Initiative. "How did you *do* it?"

"Yeah, how did you do it?"

"I just called John."

"That's it?"

"Oh my God, *look!*"

All heads turned as Davey Name and Tiger Street made a grand entrance. She wore black, he wore white, they moved through the crowd, bestowing smiles and hellos. If they had genuinely grieved for John they'd done it last week or yesterday morning or had yet to fit it into their schedule. Davey floated toward the photographers as Veronica let the party traffic push her back against the wall.

The cameras shed another wave of light as Helena entered, flanked by Dickie Drake and Dolly Seabrook. She was dressed like a royal widow, black cape, diamond earrings, hands and eyes moving in series of bereaved gestures which informed all present of her cosmic distress. Anxiety and jet lag were curdling Veronica's stomach; she had to find someplace quiet to lie down. She squeezed out of the crowd, into a hallway, and ducked into a small, foam-padded VIP room in the back.

"Hello, darling." It was Davey, ridiculously handsome as ever, muscled and taut from his shoulders to his legs, which disappeared into dark blue boots. "I'm glad you got back alive."

"I am too. You were great to do join our concert, from Tokyo."

"Oh, yes, thanks for the tip. I like to do things like that. Haven't been in Kathmandu in years, it was nice to go back, sort of."

"We have to thank John, he arranged it." Veronica stared at him, trying not to flinch. For an instant she felt giddy and terrified, like the first time they'd kissed in the recording studio. "Where's Tiger?"

"She just left. She's flying to London for a job."

And just then, true to form, he pounced, seizing her face in his hands and moving his lips over her face and neck. She waited for the sensation of his mouth and hands on her skin to arouse her, but he could've been anybody. She put her arms around his neck and held him. He collapsed and leaned quietly against her chest. She stroked his hair and kissed his forehead and eyebrows.

Davey opened his eyes and smiled. "Won't you see me tonight?"

"I can't."

"Why not?"

"Because I just got back, I'm tired, and sad . . . I really miss John."

"Me too. I kind of thought he'd live forever. Certainly thought he'd outlive me. Light me a cigarette."

She did, and handed it to him. She had never seen Davey so calm, so . . . normal. He seemed human, no longer a God. He stood up and pulled a magazine out of his briefcase.

"Look what I found on the quay in Paris." He tossed it into her lap. It was her old *Page* cover. "So how'd you end up like this?"

"Like what?"

"In this scruffy mountain gear. You were such a little glamour bird. I was quite impressed with you. Still can't get over how you left me alone in Paris."

Veronica was stunned. She thought he'd hardly noticed her. "As I recall, you left first."

"I suppose I did. Who was that dharma groupie, that Janey girl? First thing she did was demand money for her meditation center. I kicked her out straight away."

At that, Veronica started to laugh. It all seemed so funny. And Davey started to laugh too. For the longest time, they lay in the little padded VIP room, laughing and smoking and telling stories about John and Nepal and rock 'n' roll and everything else, and Veronica's mangled head and heart were soothed into peace.

# Among the Nomads

**WHEN THE PARTY FOR JOHN WAS OVER, VERONICA KNEW THAT** she couldn't go back to the Park Legend. She couldn't risk running into Dolly Seabrook or Dickie Drake, and a collision with Helena might prove fatal. There was only one thing to do, and that was to walk through the city.

Night was falling hard and fast. The Manhattan sky was streaked with purple-and-black clouds. Veronica wobbled in warped heels through the fumes that rose from the subway's seething underworld. Everyone had a glint of hope and hunger in their eyes. Everyone had somewhere to go. That is, everyone except Veronica Ferris. How strange it was to be back in New York City, a tired wanderer, exiled from normalcy, with only a few dollars, francs, and rupees left in her pocket. To whom might she appeal for mercy? With whom might she flirt for her dinner? What was she now, after all, but a stranger in a strange land?

She had always believed that money, protection, and luck would flow from an invisible, beneficent source that would forever feed and sustain her. But now she understood what Mr. Norbu had warned—that luck was something you could expend, like a savings account. On that night when she was trapped by Romi in that filthy alley, with no one to protect her, no one to hear her, it was luck alone that saved her. So what would happen when her luck ran out, when it was too late to say good-bye to John, or follow Auntie Lhanzom on her journey home, or try to salvage one's double life? And if you had a double life, did that make you a liar, a cheat?

At mid-block Veronica saw an authentic old-fashioned French bistro, now an endangered species of Manhattan restaurant. Its glowing warmth and antique charm summoned the memory of her beloved grandparents, Jack and Lilly, who loved to take the family out for jovial, wine-soaked dinners at French bistros on the Upper East Side. Jack would speak to the waiters in cheerfully bad French, and Lilly would always read a poem over dessert and make everyone play some kind of game.

Veronica envisioned Grandpa Jack, like a ghost in the mist, his coat and his old-fashioned hat floating in the air, his arms aloft to embrace her. She followed his ghost into the bistro, into a sea of happy people with intelligent hands and thoughtful smiles, opening menus and playbills and art catalogs. She took a seat at the long wooden bar and ordered a red wine. Her nostrils filled with the healing scent of potatoes and herbs. She raised the wine glass to her mouth and drank. The primal, curative aroma of warm food, the soothing tones of handsome, graceful dinner guests murmuring and eating, filled her with delight and remorse. These rare, amusing people, with their curiosity and tolerance and humanism, had once seemed so shallow and cruel, poised to cause her harm. Now they were everything she wanted to be a part of. How could she have slandered and relinquished them for an Asian slum? Such shameless, deluded romanticism, always her weakness.

A man took a seat at the end of the bar. She knew him, didn't she? Yes, it was Sandy Graver, the writer-journo she'd blithely exploited for a disco ticket one inebriated wintry night, long ago. She'd only seen him that one time, though she'd often wondered if he had deployed the tabloid matron Beth Armstrong to exact revenge for the way Veronica Ferris had so casually teased and dumped him. He ordered some kind of cocktail, probed the nut bowl, and stared anxiously into his knotted hands. She felt instinctively sorry for him. She wondered if she should say hello. Why, she could commence her penance at once, in this warm, welcoming bar, by saying hello and asking forgiveness of Sandy Graver! She gathered her purse and notebook and slid off her stool to go join him, but when she looked up again, Sandy Graver was gone.

She darted through the dining room, out onto the street, searching for him. Had he seen her and run away? She walked past the Chinese laundry, the punk boutique, the Greek diner, the Pakistani deli, and the Yemenite newsstand. People moved in civilized paths around Manhattan's stone lingams, not unlike the pilgrims at Boudha, completing their circumambulations, together and alone. Her mind began to throb and pulse in rhythm with the honking cars and the dense, pedestrian swarm along the avenue. She spied a man by the newsstand up ahead, thumbing through a magazine. It looked like Sandy Graver, a vision of redemption! She had to speak to him, to apologize—but by the time she had wedged her way through the crowd to get there, the man was gone.

Veronica saw a cluster of Tibetans moving toward the Armenian Church. Were they ghosts, like Jack and Lilly? No, they were alive, they were wearing Tibetan hats and coats and jewelry, and they were laughing. She followed them into the Armenian Church, down the stairs and into a large hall decorated with balloons, streamers, and banners in Tibetan, Hindi, Japanese, French, German, and English, which read "Tibetan Refugee Exile Support Society Mission Council Annual Dance Festival." The room was filled with Tibetans, Sherpas, Nepalis, Indians, European, and Japanese hipsters, and of course, the dharma bums. At center stage five enthralled Asian teenagers performed deejay duties. Exceptionally filthy rap music issued from the speakers while contented elders gleefully hopped about.

She sat in a broken chair in a far corner. No one noticed her, no one stared. She had been swallowed whole, rendered invisible by the night. Where was it, that weird, dangerous charisma that magnetized the Black Eye? Was it gone, along with her natural beauty, the currency that had nearly destroyed her? And if it was gone, would she be cursed, or let free?

The deejay played an irresistibly tacky Bollywood disco number, indigenous to South Asia. Veronica began to cry. She felt utterly ridiculous, thank God no one was watching.

"Stop crying like that. I told you, it hurts your lungta." Mr. Norbu handed her a napkin.

"But—you're in Hong Kong!"

"Am I? Not anymore. I finished my business and I came here for more business."

Veronica wiped her eyes and steadied herself. "You missed John's funeral."

"Yes, and I am sorry that I wasn't there to say good-bye to my old friend." Mr. Norbu sat down and withdrew his pipe from his green velvet jacket. A new diamond shone on his right ring finger. "So how does it feel to be back in your hometown?"

"This isn't my hometown."

"Then make it your hometown. You are a lot safer here than you will ever be in a place like Nepal."

"Please tell me why."

"Because here you have your tribe." Waving his pipe over the dance floor, Mr. Norbu continued, "These people might be your friends, but they aren't your tribe, so they will never rescue you. They could never imagine that you might need to be rescued. I don't understand these westerners who want so badly to be Tibetans. We Tibetans have so many problems!"

Veronica closed her eyes and saw Auntie Lhanzom, Sonam, and Stupa Joe, the pilgrims at Boudha, the children at Sujata's camp. "So what did I do it for?"

"Maybe you did it to finish what you started in your past life. Maybe you wanted to find something of your own. Maybe it was the ripening of luck. It was Auntie Lhanzom's good luck that you found her that day in the alley. She might have died if you had not come down that road. And it was luck that you saved that beggar child from Romi. Maybe he is still alive because of it. Luck is very random. It is also a design." Under the table Mr. Norbu took Veronica's hand and pressed it. "Tonight I will take care of you."

"What about tomorrow?"

"Tomorrow I am flying to Paris. I would ask you to come with me, but maybe you need to spend time with your father and your mother. Don't make them unhappy. We Tibetans feel it is most important to take care of parents, because we will need them in the next life."

"Will you always be a nomad, always preparing for the next life?"

"Of course. It would be a great mistake not to."

"But what about—now, tonight, and tomorrow?"

"We say don't cry till you see the corpse. All this worrying will waste your life force, your precious luck." He pulled her hand up to his heart and smiled at her. She felt as if he were blessing her, in his secret way.

# Bodhicitta on Avenue A

**VERONICA STAYED WITH MR. NORBU UNTIL FIVE IN THE EVE-** ning the following day. They never left his hotel. They made love into the night and he held her in his arms throughout the next morning and afternoon. They ordered room service. He told her more stories of his Khampa childhood and his international clients. She told him of her life among the ex-pats and her father, and her adventures with John Penn. They said good-bye in front of the hotel as he stepped into a taxi and headed to the airport for his flight to Paris.

She started to walk along the sparkling sidewalks, past the magazine shops and Laundromats and Indian restaurants. She looked up at the Chrysler Building and the Empire State Building. Why had her theory that skyscrapers were illuminated lingams ever been remotely contro-versial? It was simply a fact: New York was a city of lingams, as divine as the Boudha Stupa.

She wandered into a dark, unmarked bar and sat down at a small table. She ordered a beer, lit a Lucky Strike. She heard multiple dialects and languages mixed with soothing electronica. How had the whole planet converged on this skinny island? Where did all the wine bottles come from? A trio of Gallic hipsters breezed past. At the next table sat three strenuously anachronistic punk rockers with an elderly woman in red plumage. Four supermodel facsimiles strolled toward the jukebox. What a relief it was not to feel the old, instinctive urge to be superior, to compete. Now she just loved these people for spending money on pink shoes and vinyl pants.

In honor of downtown's deceased mascot, the bar displayed a John Penn portrait gallery of international rock stars, those vaunted macho cowboys, forever thrusting deep into the squalid, sensual night. Hedonists had lineage traditions too, just like Tibetan lamas and Renaissance painters. Veronica studied the punk rockers, the model girls, and the cheerful, tattooed waitresses. Where did they live? When did they sleep? Did they sleep? She felt that avid curiosity and admiration that she felt in Asia, the need to uncover and celebrate these wonderful strangers. Asia would always be a part of her—all those years of eating its foods and nectars, breathing its air, washing her face and hands in the Naga pools, it infused her body and soul. But Mr. Norbu was right, *this* was her tribe, these serene, eccentric people strewn along the bar, gazing into sound waves.

She walked over to the jukebox, slipped in a few coins, and scrolled through the song selections. She saw a photograph that looked oddly familiar. It was her face, from the Willy Westwood photo shoot, below the name "Maya Smith." There were her songs—"Disco Darshan," "Khampa Boy," "Green Cards and Blue Jeans"—produced, packaged, and pirated. Here was her double life immortalized by John Penn. So she'd become a rock star, after all.

And then, in the smoky haze by the jukebox, Veronica envisioned John Penn, and Jack and Lilly, and Auntie Lhanzom, whom she knew she would never see again, and everyone who had ever come and gone through a tavern door. She saw them standing at the bar, holding drinks and laughing. The pull and tug of old grudges, fears, and taunts, all dissolved. Suddenly, what had eluded her in the cathedrals of Europe and the temples of Asia—Bodhicitta, universal love—flowed through her being. She prayed that everyone would find peace, Helena, Winston, Jamie, Davey Name, Tiger Street, Dolly Seabrook, Sonam, Jet Lag Janey, Stupa Joe, Passport Pete, Venice Beach, Jerry Dollar, Meryl, Mr. Norbu, and Auntie Lhanzom. She prayed that John Penn and Jack and Lilly were safe, and that one day she would see them again. She felt the absolution of the shining sidewalks as the city forgave her, at last, for all her vanity and folly. She purified a million lifetimes sitting in that smoky, unorthodox temple on Avenue A.

# The Net of Jewels

**"VERONICA?" HELENA MARCHED INTO THE MAID'S ROOM WHERE** Veronica had collapsed across the bed. "Get off the laundry, you'll wrinkle it. Why didn't you tell us you were coming?"

"John was my friend. Friends go to memorial services."

"Yes, he was a wonderful friend! Oh, it's so awful." Helena grabbed a napkin and blew hysterically. "I can't believe it! He was about to finish my portrait. Oh, God, why?" She sobbed wildly, unaware of her collapsing hair and the tear stains on her silk blouse. "Water, I need water! Wu! Wu, get me a mineral water, please, immediately."

Helena rushed off to her bedroom. Veronica heard Winston's distinctive tread coming through the vestibule, mixed with Wu's voice, hushed and serious, Winston's muffled reply, then Winston's gentle tapping on the bedroom door.

"Helena darling, are you there?"

"Please leave me alone!"

Winston stepped into the hallway and motioned Veronica toward the living room.

"Dear, your mother isn't feeling well. Maybe it's best if you—"

"If I leave."

"No, dear, I won't have you leave us again. Just stay clear until your mother calms down. I'm so glad you received my fax. I thought you'd want to attend Mr. Penn's memorial service."

"Yes I did, thank you, Dad. Where's Jamie?"

"Jamie is in California and he seems to be doing well with his various health projects. Your poor mother is under a great deal of stress at the moment. She and John were planning so many wonderful projects together, and his death was so very sudden." Veronica heard a knock and opened the door. Dolly Seabrook and Dickie Drake stood side by side, bearing flowers. "Veronica dear, isn't it awful." Dolly swept in, bejeweled and tearful. "How's your mother?"

"She's taking a nap."

Dolly peered down the hallway with suspicion. "Anything wrong?"

"She's heartbroken about John."

"Well yes, isn't all of New York?"

"Veronica," said Dickie Drake, who'd grown more plump and florid since Veronica last shared a cocktail with him. "You haven't been around so you don't know what we've all been up to. John and Helena and I were collaborating on a book project, and Helena was posing for his Lady Liberty series. There was going to be a show at the Whitney."

Dolly's eyes kept roving toward the bedroom. "I should really poke my head in there to see if there's anything I can do."

"Just wait here," Veronica said.

"What?"

"I'll tell her you're here."

Dolly flashed her best school principal frown as Veronica went to the bedroom and knocked on the door. It opened very slightly, revealing Wu's nose and left eye. And then Winston appeared, resolutely cheerful. He greeted Dolly and Dickie in the living room and set about preparing their drinks. Soon Helena emerged in a fresh silk blouse, hair and eyes under control, arms outstretched to receive Dolly's embrace.

"Darling, I'm a wreck. It's really just so sad."

"Helena, dearest girl!" Dickie kissed her on both cheeks. "But you must admit it was a lovely service."

"Absolutely marvelous. Dickie, you were just wonderful. We were all counting on you to pull us through." Dickie beamed satisfaction. Helena eased herself into the seat beside Winston. "It's been days since we lost him, but I'm still in a state of cruel, unending shock. It happened so fast, how does one adjust? New York will never be the same."

Dickie stood before Helena and held out a bouquet of lilies. "Helena love, John left you one last glorious gift. Days before his death he finished his very last painting, a portrait of the peerless Helena Ferris, muse and friend. He didn't get around to framing it but I'm sure one of his helpers can do that. I'm writing a dedication to be read aloud at the official installation, here at your residence. When shall it be? The choice is yours!"

Helena pressed a tremulous white hand to her heart, and was, for once, speechless.

"John Penn's final portrait," Dickie continued, "so it will have tremendous cultural impact."

This was Veronica's chance to sneak into the bedroom and restore the sapphire and the topaz necklaces to the bottom of Helena's treasure chest. Veronica raced down the hall, into Helena's dressing room. She unbolted the jewel chest and slid the gems into the bottom.

"Veronica, please sit. I have something I want to discuss with you." Helena blocked the doorway.

Veronica dumbly lowered herself on a chair.

"Losing John has made me realize how—how little time we have for anything. I know you felt very badly about how everything disappeared from Jack and Lilly's after they died. But I did manage to save some things. I was going to keep them until you got older, but now I want you to have them." Helena opened a long wooden chest. Veronica peered inside and saw her notebooks and photographs and some of the Balinese masks and Bhutanese cloth and other things that she had thought were lost forever.

"Mom, I—I thought it was all gone—"

"I should have told you, but I thought you'd lose it all. Sometimes you can be so careless. And this—" Helena then opened her jewelry box. "—there's lots in here that I've been saving for you. They're yours. Again, I held onto them because I thought you'd lose them, the way you go from place to place. I know it's our fault, the way your father and I raised you and Jamie. But I didn't want you selling off things the way your brother Grayson did."

"Oh, Mom!" Veronica hugged her mother. Helena couldn't say any more, but she didn't have to.

"Ladies, where are you?" asked Winston from the hallway. "Since we're all here, I have some important news I wish to convey." Winston put a protective arm around Helena, who was now dabbing tears from her meticulously mascaraed eyes. "Helena and I are moving to London. I'm taking a new position with UNESCO. We have found a splendid townhouse in Maida Vale, which I hope will soon be filled with friends from around the world."

"Oh my goodness! This is news!" cried Dickie. "But what of New York? How can you give up this flat? It's much too special. You must hang on to it somehow!"

"I've thought about that, and I'm giving it to Veronica."

"Veronica?" Dickie sputtered.

"Veronica!" Dolly shrieked.

"Helena and I realize that our dear daughter needs a stable home after all the years we dragged her from place to place. We simply ask that she'll let us stay here when we are in town, and look after her little brother Jamie. And I saw how hard she tried to help those people in Nepal. My chief of staff Aaron Eastman has published the work she did with the lady who endured all those years in a Chinese labor camp. He said it taught him more about the Chinese occupation of Tibet than any document he has ever read. Veronica, this is for you, from Aaron, who sends his best wishes."

Winston handed Veronica a neatly bound, crisp United Nations report with a photograph of Auntie Lhanzom and Veronica on the cover.

"Helena and I have decided to make our daughter a trustee of my family's philanthropic holdings, which I should have done before, because I know she will work hard and give all her heart."

"But, what about Jamie? And Grayson and Bradley?" Dolly scowled; she seemed to be taking the news rather hard.

"My boys will all be fine. I have set up trusts for them as well, separate trusts. You can't ask the children to work these things out, that's not fair to them."

"My goodness, dear Veronica!" Dickie bowed and kissed Veronica's hand. "You're going to be a marvelous Benefit Lady!"

Veronica gazed at her kind, wise, beneficent father, who smiled back at her with the undying love that only a father has for his daughter, and she realized with amazement that whatever she may have done in a past or present life, he loved her and forgave her, and that made her the most blessed woman in the world.

# A Letter Arrives

**ONE MONTH AFTER JOHN'S MEMORIAL SERVICE, VERONICA RE-**
ceived a fax, sent via Winston's office. The letterhead was in Chinese,
the text was written in a strange, cursive hand. It read:

*Hello, Veronica. I am hoping that you are in good health. I am in Hong Kong
and go to Beijing soon for business. I wish to inform you that Auntie Lhanzom has died. She passed away in my house in Lhasa, after visiting the
Jokhang Temple, which was her final wish. As she was dying the lama blessed
her, and she passed very calmly in sleep. We Buddhists feel that a good death
is important so you should feel happy that Auntie Lhanzom has left this life
in peace.*

*Things in Kathmandu are not so good. There is curfew at night. Every-
one is trying to get visa to the West but the embassy is not giving so easily
now. Mr. Sonam was badly hurt in a fight and has gone to India to get some
medical treatment. Stupa Joe and Passport Pete have been keeping their visas
to Nepal after the problems those people made for them, but Bangkok Bill had
to leave because he did not pay the correct visa officer in time. Janey is again
trying to find a sponsor for her meditation center but she is not having success
so she is looking for a job as Dharma Tour Guide.*

*Do not think that your efforts to help Auntie Lhanzom were lost. We
Tibetans feel that it is the motive that determines the karma and you had
a sincere wish in your heart. I send you blessings of Lord Buddha. Soon I*

am coming to New York on business and I am hoping to see you there. Please send my fond regards to your mother and your father. Do not forget me.

Your friend,

Norbu

# Losar, or the New Year

**A YEAR HAD PASSED SINCE HELENA AND WINSTON HAD MOVED** to London. Helena had never been happier, and neither had Winston. Helena embarked on an interview spree, declaring her allegiance to her new city. She won over the British press overnight, and befriended all the royals, the playwrights, and the painters. Winston started collecting classical manuscripts and studying Sanskrit. Grayson ran for office and won. Bradley got married, happily, and Jamie got his macrobiotic cooking certificate.

Veronica sat at her favorite local cafe on Madison Avenue and ordered a double espresso. After a lifetime of nomadic flight, even Veronica Ferris, that orphan of the five continents, had found a home in New York, with its multiple tongues and rich banquets, its greed, courage, and endless distractions. Life had certainly changed. What an experience to have order and solvency, to possess credit cards and functional zippers and gloves that covered the whole of one's hand. When she glanced in the mirror, she liked seeing the way her long, shiny, auburn hair complemented her white complexion, which rarely needed makeup. Today her eyes were almost purple, and gleaming. She adored her new life as a stylish, benevolent hostess and patron of the arts. And she didn't have to relinquish leather skirts or eccentric jackets or fishnet stockings, not at all. The only thing that was nonnegotiable for a Benefit Lady was money, and thanks to Winston, she had plenty.

All her efforts were sensibly directed toward the ballet, arts scholar-

ships, and other worthy cultural and educational endeavors. No diseases, there was too much competition and not enough accountability.
With the ballet, you saw exactly where your money went. Who wants
to spend the evening staring at a hospital? She made exceptions for specific development projects in Asia, such as Sujata's clinic, to which she
donated funds for three new dormitories, salaries for more nurses, and
food and clothing for two hundred children.

Meryl was coming to interview her for a book about John Penn
and his glamorous muses, the Penn Girls. Veronica's mysterious origin
as a Penn Girl yielded considerable benefits, as did her past association
with the Tibetan refugees. When she was written up in the society
columns there was always a reference to her "humanitarian" concerns
and her "artistic" gifts. She always took a magnificent photograph,
which inspired talent scouts to exhume clips of her rock star moment
and to press promises and offers. She demurred without actually saying
no, lest it prove useful in the future. She would forever nurture a secret
dream of being a rock star, and would occasionally pull out her notebook, write a song, and give it to one of her aspiring rock star protégés.
And from time to time, a song got recorded and published, and the roy-
alties were always paid to Ms. Maya Smith.

But she didn't want to be too famous, because then she couldn't sit
in a cafe and study her fellow New Yorkers, her tribe of talented, civilized hedonists, which is what she was doing on this bright January afternoon. She selected a few magazines from the rack and started paging
through them. There was a photograph of a current flirtation, Jean
Carnac, a dashing philosopher with a new book. He was outrageously
handsome in the modern Gallic style, unruly hair, oversexed eyes under
a fine and noble brow. He was supposed to be coming over for dinner
next week with Davey Name. Since Veronica had become a Benefit
Lady with a fabulous apartment and an artistic inner circle, Davey
Name called her whenever he was in New York and regularly attended
her small, delightful dinner parties.

And there was a photo of Tiger Street, the fantabulous cat herself,
who was in a bit of trouble lately. Tiger had made a fatal miscalculation
about the extent to which her power resided in her hair. When she'd
debuted short brown ringlets, the new look sparked international out-

rage and was pronounced a disaster by her former advocates in the press. She was ludicrously obstinate about the debacle and refused to go back to orange blonde, but then word got out that the blonde thing was a hoax and that she was a mousy brunette in real life. Both her modeling career and socialite standing took a nosedive. She started to look frayed and exhausted, but Davey never quite left her. They remained an official couple and that kept her going as a talk show guest and miniseries cast member. Davey, for his part, was frequently caught slipping in and out of nightclubs with other, younger women. Critics kept predicting his professional death, but he kept making albums that people loved and girls kept trying to get into his limo.

Veronica flipped through the latest *Page* to see the latest crop of Beautiful Girls, who were no doubt trying to land an athlete or rock star or movie star boyfriend. *Good luck, all of you.* Then she came across an ad, an expensive one. It was a fundraising appeal, with a photo of Todd and Angie, looking pained and serious, standing behind a fragile young man with an eye patch. The text read: "After half a century, East Timor is still not free. East Timor needs you to pay attention. It's time to take a stand for justice. It's time to take a stand for truth. It's time for you to make a pledge to support . . ." Veronica couldn't read further.

Veronica paid the bill and headed toward the Park Legend. Realizing that she wasn't far from the Modern Antique Showroom, she decided to go take a look, for old time's sake. A large mandala hung in the window. The scent of rose perfume floated from the gallery door. She saw a man leaning over the desk, wearing a green jacket, like Mr. Norbu's, but she knew it wasn't Mr. Norbu. She was waiting for him to come back into her life, and she knew that soon he would, or she would go find him. He always appeared, unexpectedly and as promised. And he always brought jewels and silks from his travels, and sometimes an amulet or a protection cord, blessed by a lama, to impart good luck. One of the several Mr. Jarewallas settled behind the desk and caught Veronica's eye. Yes, she would go in there, but not today.

Veronica turned around and walked back toward the golden-pink glow of the lobby, past the statues of Artemis and Athena, past the luggage trolleys, and the magazine stand with headlines in fifteen languages. Old Park Legend guests were hailing taxis, new guests were opening wallets and signing the register. Day was melting into night, friends would meet and part, luck would be found, or lost. The lobby glistened with pink and orange lights, left over from Christmas. Someone was singing to a waltz that floated from the old cafe. Veronica blinked, and felt her heartbeat pulsing with hope and wonder. *Yes, everything is changing, again . . .*